A STICK IN THE DIRT

VIDIT UPPAL

Leadstart
INKSTATE

ISBN 978-81-94804-41-3
Copyright © Vidit Uppal, 2020

First published in India 2020 by Inkstate Books
An imprint of Leadstart Publishing Pvt Ltd

Sales Office:
Unit No.25/26, Building No.A/1,
Near Wadala RTO,
Wadala (East), Mumbai – 400037 India
Phone: +91 969933000
Email: info@leadstartcorp.com
www.leadstartcorp.com

Disclaimer: The views expressed in this book are those of the Author and do not pertain to be held by the Publisher.

Editor: Vaibhav Pathare
Cover: Swapnil Behere
Layouts: Victor Patali

CONTENTS

Part 1

...any man more right than his neighbors constitutes a
majority of one...

Henry David Thoreau
(Walden & Civil Disobedience)

Chapter 1

Madam Sinha's greatest fear, which generally and frequently manifested itself in the form of sharp insults and bitter rebukes, was that of losing all of her nurses to marriage.

When Vidya stepped inside the hospital ward that morning, she saw her hunched over her desk, preparing the daily report for Dr. Hari. It was one of those rare instances when, unencumbered by anyone else's presence, fully invested in a task she knew well, and with a large glass of tea by her side, one couldn't find a trace of indignation or worry on her face. The window just behind her chair was open. A strong beam of light shone through her tangle of unkempt and rapidly graying hair. The effect was rather amusing.

"Go check the queue," she said, looking upon hearing Vidya's footsteps and then frowned on noticing her feeble smile.

Her fear, though somewhat exaggerated, wasn't completely unjustified. A childless widow herself, she had watched many of her young and well-trained nurses leave to get married and then never return. This seemingly archaic societal norm, which was still quite widespread, continuously and systematically robbed her of her staff, a feeling she always made known to them in her typically aggressive and condescending manner.

"Can't you see the lack of thought in your decision?" she would ask them rhetorically, using more or less the same words each time in a cold and precise tone. "There are young women who would kill to be in your position - holding a steady job in a respectable place with a guaranteed income. But you would rather drape yourself in red, walk around a flame, and be done with everything! Don't....don't tell me it isn't your decision. That only makes you look even more stupid!" Their responses and pleas and justifications never mattered and were thus seldom heard.

Madam Sinha was twenty years old when she arrived at the town of Ketupur as a newly married woman. After two months of idleness, she joined the hospital as a nurse, where she first trained and then worked uninterruptedly for the next few years until the day her husband was electrocuted while working on an old transformer at a factory. The owners, burdened by guilt and fearful of a legal backlash, offered her a sum of ten thousand rupees as compensation, which she accepted and then returned to her parents' house in the village she had grown up. There, however, she encountered a much more powerful enemy - pity. Her friends, family, neighbours....everyone around her seemed to be convinced that this was a tragedy from which there was no return, that at the age of twenty-four she had already lived through the best that life had to offer her. This stifling and suffocating environment forced her to leave her village once again for Ketupur. She still had some of that money saved and used it to rent a small room near the hospital, to which she returned and then continued to work forever since. Her story, she realized as time went by, was the sort that always came across as a great example of will and resourcefulness, even though it had never felt so at the time. Hence, she never missed an opportunity to relay it to her young nurses to further substantiate her point of view.

She was now well over fifty years of age, a bulk of which she had spent within the confines of this hospital. The years of work had created within her a fierce and almost matriarchal sense of obsession with this modest establishment. This was her home. As the head nurse, she occupied the front desk. From this vantage point, she could uninterruptedly monitor and supervise the workings of her team of three to five nurses while simultaneously keeping an eye on the main door, as well as on Dr. Hari's small cordoned off section beside it. She always managed to do all of this with a remarkably constant look of disdain.

Vidya peered through the wooden slot in the main door. There were already quite a few people sitting on the floor of their small courtyard. Some of them were asleep.

"Eight," she called out aloud without looking back. "Three children."

"Beds Five and Twelve to be released today. Before Dr. Hari arrives."

Vidya walked back towards the ward without acknowledging her statement. Everyone who had ever worked with Madam Sinha, including some patients, wasn't sure whether to dislike her caustic demeanor or to admire her work ethic. It was the same for Vidya, who, in an attempt to reconcile both of those feelings, couldn't ever do justice to either.

She approached Bed Six where an old lady, flaying her arms around wildly, was in some obvious discomfort. She helped her to sit up and then gently started to pat her back continuously and in a rhythmic manner until she began to cough out the phlegm. Vidya handed her a spittoon.

"Don't hold it in," she said firmly on seeing the lady's face turn red as she tried to restrain her cough. "Why do you do this every time! No...no...I didn't ask you to say anything. Cough!"

"I...I wasn't trying to hold," she sputtered out after Vidya took away the spittoon from her. Her face gradually attained its normal colour even though she was still struggling to breathe properly. "It just happened too quickly."

"Well one of these days you will simply explode," said Vidya, helping her to lie down once again. "And I suppose I shall have to carry away what's left of you in one of these," she added, holding the spittoon high near her shoulder.

As Vidya carried it towards the basin, the rear door opened and Palak walked inside, smiling on seeing Vidya.

"Beds Five and Twelve," Vidya told her.

She placed the spittoon under the tap and let the water run, not stopping after it had been rinsed completely, but instead watched the water overflow and fall from its sides. Palak was quickly on to her task. Vidya could hear her trying to make the reluctant patients of those two beds gather their belongings and leave. The hospital's system of admitting and relieving patients was based as much as on matters of health as on those of convenience. They had only twenty beds at their disposal, on which they were strictly instructed by Dr. Hari, who in turn had received the same instructions from the local municipality, to not have more than 40 patients at any given moment. Hence, they were often forced to make compromises between patients based not only on a quick subjective assessment of their ailments but also on their gender and size to have the most efficient pairing system. Madam Sinha made this rule even more stringent by constantly trying to not go beyond one patient per bed unless required. Dr. Hari had tried several times to persuade her by explaining that their establishment wasn't exactly a hospital but a slightly revamped daily clinic to which one of the larger hospitals of the nearby city had decided to donate their old beds; they were under no obligation, and neither was it expected of them, to maintain the standards of a full-time hospital. Everything, he said, is a bonus here. Madam Sinha remained unconvinced.

Vidya wiped and returned the spittoon to Bed Six. Meera and Asha had joined Palak by this time and were receiving instructions from Madam Sinha. Vidya, standing apart from them all, glanced over the ward as the rest of the patients began to stir and wake, marking the start of another frantic and busy day. Being the oldest nurse now for the past two years, she was always the first one to arrive at the hospital by around 7 am, by which time Madam Sinha had already relieved the night-duty nurses, made a round of all the twenty beds and started to prepare the daily report. The rest of the nurses arrived within the next hour. This routine, while not officially dictated, was strictly observed each day.

As was the norm, Dr. Hari came at 9 am. They could all hear the sputtering noise of his scooter's engine, which he brought to a halt and parked near the main gate. He entered and smiled at everyone before disappearing behind the curtained section that hid his little desk and chair. He was tall and very thin, his clumsy bone structure further made conspicuous by his ungraceful movements. Madam Sinha barely lifted her head to acknowledge his presence. She nodded towards Vidya who joined her as they began receiving the patients one by one. They noted down their basic details and assigned them a number each. At 9:30 am, Madam Sinha allowed the first patient to see the doctor.

Dr. Hari's day mostly began and ended behind that curtain. From time to time, generally at the behest of Madam Sinha, who coaxed him into seeing the previously admitted patients, he would take a laboured stroll through the ward, his gaze sweeping across all the nurses and only intermittently falling on the patients. The two of them, standing next to each other, were the most contradictory of all pairs - Dr. Hari's lanky and uninterested demeanor was quite a sight against Madam Sinha's robust and determined presence. It felt as if he was a child who had just been reprimanded and didn't believe that he deserved it. He would glance at the four nurses from time to time, smiling awkwardly as if this was all a big joke that they were sharing at Madam Sinha's expense. He wasn't much younger than her but always managed to assume that air of juvenile condescension.

After the morning rush, very few patients continued to trickle in. Using the opportunity, Madam Sinha forced Dr. Hari out of his corner and proceeded to give him an update on each admitted patient, walking from one bed to another. Despite his nonchalant look, he never undertook these sessions as lightly as everyone assumed he did. Trudging alongside Madam Sinha, he performed his role rather diligently, to the extent that it was required of him. But his outward demeanor never changed. Vidya watched him as he appeared to listen quite attentively to Madam Sinha, rocking back and forth on his feet, visibly annoyed with her fastidiousness. He wanted to move along quickly. Vidya quite deliberately avoided looking in his direction. Palak, however, obliged his glances with a smile but stopped immediately when she noticed Vidya frowning at her.

Around 1 pm, Vidya and Palak slipped out of the back door and into a small room that further opened into the alley behind the building, which all the nurses used each day to go in and out of the hospital. The room had a square table in the center along with a few chairs on each side. There was a small granite slab in one corner with a basin in its middle. On its one side lay a pot of drinking water with a few steel glasses, while on the other side four plastic boxes were kept stacked together. The nurses took turns to have their lunches in groups of two, while Madam Sinha and Dr. Hari ate at their respective desks. Vidya and Palak were always the first ones to eat.

"Why do you enable him?" began Vidya immediately as they sat down and opened their plastic boxes. The smell of oil and vegetables rose through the air.

"It is so harmless," she replied, adopting a very casual tone that only further irked Vidya. "He is such an old fool."

The afternoons were always the quietest and the easiest. Most of the patients stayed asleep and the number of visitors too dwindled significantly. Even Madam Sinha, despite her wish to the contrary, could be found dozing on her desk from time to time, her head awkwardly bobbing back and forth. A lull would descend within the hospital, ushering in a period of laziness and inactivity. It was also the hottest time of the day. The warm and stale air recirculated by the old ceiling fans felt heavy and suffocating. Vidya would stroll through the ward from one side to another as if stuck in an endless loop. The other nurses huddled together in a corner, keeping a lazy eye on their respective patients; sometimes Vidya would join them.

At exactly 5 pm, Dr. Hari would emerge from behind his green curtain, ready to leave for the day. Before exiting through the front door, he would give a polite and mildly apologetic nod to the patients he had not yet examined, and steal a glance towards Madam Sinha, who never failed to lock her eyes on him at that moment. She always felt annoyed when he left at his usual hour even when patients were waiting for him. Despite the fact that she usually considered him a hindrance to the proper functioning of the hospital, she couldn't deny the absolute necessity of his presence. He was a required but unwanted blemish in the order of things she had created and managed. Now, after his departure, accompanied by the onset of the evening that somewhat cut through the heat, she brushed off the afternoon's drowsiness and once again became her boisterously active best.

"Please try to come before 9 am tomorrow," she said to the remaining disgruntled patients and walked past them into the ward before any of them could react. "Any problem?" she demanded in general. Asha, Meera, and Palak, who still stood huddled together in one corner immediately looked at Vidya, who knew that Madam Sinha's question was simply an announcement that she was present, aware and in-charge. She took her around the twenty beds while the others updated each patient's chart with her input so that the same could be referred to by the night-duty nurses. There were two of them who came between 7 and 8 pm each day and relieved Madam Sinha and her staff until the next morning. Meera and Asha would leave during that hour while Madam Sinha and Vidya would stay until everything had been handed over. Palak, as a general habit, would wait for Vidya so that they could go home together. Madam Sinha was the last to leave.

It was quite dark when the two of them stepped outside. But they had to walk only a short distance before they reached the market, which was brightly lit and bustling with hordes of people moving from corner to corner. They negotiated their way through the crowd, walking past the street vendors that had encroached a sizable portion of the road, selling everything from vegetables to fruits to clothing to utensils, etc. Their calls and pleas traveled through the air, cutting across each other, yet somehow still understandable to those who were paying attention. Palak's head turned each time a particularly enticing offer reached her ear. She slowed down and meandered from one stall to another, staring at the varied products with a glimmer in her eyes. Vidya walked beside her, letting Palak set the pace, firmly shaking her head at all the offers thrown at her.

The small room that Vidya and Palak had rented together was just at the end of this road, but it took them more than half an hour to traverse their way to it. Mrs. Shankar, their old landlady, smiled at them as she opened the door.

"Come in! The food is almost ready. Quickly wash and come down!"

A small staircase took them to the above floor. Vidya unlocked the door and put aside the keys. Two narrow single beds with a small table in between greeted them. There were separate sets of steel cupboards on either side of the beds and a writing desk at the front, just adjacent to the attached washroom. Vidya was home.

Chapter 2

The next day, when Vidya entered the ward, the woman in Bed Six immediately raised her arm and waved rapidly, straining her neck to lift herself. Vidya instinctively picked up the spittoon and rushed towards her. She waited until the woman was in a stable enough position before proceeding to firmly pat her back. Her eyes turned towards Madam Sinha, who was sitting behind her desk, making the report. Once the woman was done, Vidya put aside the spittoon for a moment and stared at her.

"Why were you waiting for me?"

"I am scared of that old lady," she replied, gasping for breath.

"I am as bad as her."

The lady started to cough once again. Vidya shook her head and cleared away the spittoon, before walking back towards Madam Sinha.

"Everyone stays today," she said.

Outside, more people were waiting than yesterday, so much so that there wasn't enough space for everyone to sit within the courtyard. Vidya's gaze quickly darted over them and settled at the small stretch of road just outside their porch. She waited for a while, anticipating the arrival of a small van that could come into view at any moment.

Twice a month, on Tuesdays, the hospital received their ration of basic medicines, which they could use and distribute for free among their patients, and of which they always ran out at least three to four days before the next batch was scheduled to arrive.

"The quantity of medicines hasn't increased for the past seven years!" Madam Sinha would beseech Dr. Hari frequently. "The number of patients is always increasing and they can't afford to buy medicines. You know that!"

Dr. Hari knew it well enough. He had often spoken about it to his superior at the city hospital, who had advised him to write an official letter to the local minister. He did so but never received a reply or even any sort of acknowledgment. But that wasn't enough for Madam Sinha, who refused to consider his failed efforts as a form of consolation. And so he continued to listen to her requests and admonishments, as one listens to a sermon, nodding and shaking his head at the familiar places.

Vidya was aware that Madam Sinha was too preoccupied with her report, and so she kept standing by the door for the next few minutes until the familiar sound of a horn rang through and a van came to a stop outside their gate. Vidya smiled and stepped outside, shaking her head at the hopeful glances of the patients waiting to be allowed in. Two men climbed out of the van and opened the rear door. Vidya recognized one among them who was responsible for the delivery. He was short and thin, with a face that was too small for the large spectacles he wore. His clothes too, as always, weren't in proportion to the size of his body. The other guy was the driver who kept on changing frequently.

"You are late today," she said while walking towards them and opening the gate so that they could carry the cartons of medicine inside. There were five cartons in total and the driver began to take them one by one. One of the patients held the door for him.

"You know it!" he replied. He took out a list of items that were being delivered and gave it to Vidya for verification. "Neither the van nor the traffic is in my control."

"You can save time by talking less," she said, going over the list. "That is in your control."

"Not really," he laughed and took back the list. "How is our Madam?"

"Same as ever," she smiled.

"There are many people today," he remarked. "Should I be worried about some disease?"

"Maybe. If you stay long enough."

"It's done," said the driver and went back to his van.

"Alright then," he said. "I will come again in two weeks."

Vidya closed the main gate and walked back inside. The moment she entered, Madam Sinha turned towards her and asked, "Have you checked the quantity?"

"I always do."

Palak had arrived by then and the two of them opened the cartons and began refilling the medicine cabinet. The day was going to be busier than usual. The charts of all the patients would be checked, and those who required the medicines the most would be the first ones to get them. Some had not had their last dose for over a week because of the shortage, and even now it would be impossible to continue with their regular dosage without completely denying some other patients. It was a horrible game of rationing that had to be played. Years of practice had made Madam Sinha quite adept at it.

While they were sorting the medicines, Vidya noticed Palak taking a leaf of one of the tablets and putting it inside her pocket.

"She isn't going to get better," she said, shaking her head, referring to the woman in Bed Six. "Don't waste it on her."

"Please!" replied Palak, limiting her plea to just one word. There was nothing else she could have said.

Vidya was about to add something when the telephone at Madam Sinha's desk rang and distracted her. She wouldn't have given it any more attention had Madam Sinha not instantly looked in her direction after picking the receiver.

"Vidya!" she yelled across the ward in a voice that was louder than required. "It is your mother."

Vidya remained where she was for a moment, trying to remember what day it was. It was extremely unusual of her mother to call her at the hospital. Vidya had explicitly forbidden her from doing so frequently as she knew that Madam Sinha didn't approve of it.

"It's Tuesday," said Palak.

She frowned and quickly walked towards Madam Sinha who held the receiver in her outstretched hand.

"Hello," she began. "It isn't Sunday."

"I know Vidya," she replied, surprising her with the lightness in her voice. "When are you coming home?"

"Not before another two months. You know that already. And you shouldn't call me here. I have told you...."

"Vidya!" she interjected, raising her broken voice by as much as she could. "Listen to me. Saurabh is back. He has been sent back."

Madam Sinha was constantly looking at her. Vidya stared back, not knowing how to react to what her mother had just told her. A mixture of incomprehensible emotions rose within her. There was anger in there....and surprise...and pain and confusion. Her throat involuntarily made some noise, as if letting out the excess pressure that had been building inside. Her mother waited patiently, understanding the unexpectedness of the news.

"He was expelled. He came back yesterday. We didn't know about it either. Parashar Aunty and Uncle hid it from everyone."

"How is he?" she asked, finding her voice.

"I am not sure."

Madam Sinha deliberately cleared her throat loudly. Vidya frowned and turned away from her, lowering her voice at the same time.

"So what do you want?"

"I just wanted to let you know. Am I not allowed to do that?"

"I don't think I can come sooner."

"I am not asking or suggesting anything. You do whatever you want to. You always have."

"I can't talk for long. I will call you tomorrow."

In one swift motion, Vidya put down the receiver and walked away, not giving Madam Sinha the chance to inquire about the phone call. Without saying a word, she once again began to help Palak to sort and store the medicines.

"Is everything okay?" she whispered, with evident concern in her voice.

"Yes. I will explain later."

The day progressed as it always did, slowly and efficiently, ticking through the same boxes as any other day. Vidya trudged through her tasks, her absentmindedness and stronger than usual irritability betraying her feelings of discomfort and confusion. They could all sense it; all except Dr. Hari. But by some unspoken agreement, either a product of fear or empathy, none including Madam Sinha tried to question her. Vidya, aloof and distant, her mind racing through a medley of familiar and uncomfortable thoughts, spent the entire day in virtual silence and isolation. She even refused to have lunch for fear of having to spend some time alone with Palak. It was only late in the evening, after the night-duty nurses had arrived, that Madam Sinha approached her.

"What did your mother have to say?"

"She wants me to come back soon," replied Vidya.

"Why?"

"My father is not well."

"I see," she said slowly and then paused for a while. "When do you want to leave?"

"I am not sure yet."

"Anything else?"

"No."

Madam Sinha nodded and walked away. Vidya joined Palak who was waiting for her at the doorstep.

Later that night, Palak lay awake in her bed, her head tilted towards Vidya who she knew was awake, even though she could only sense her silhouette in the dark.

"Vidya?" she ventured.

"I have never told you about Parashar Uncle and Aunty," she said. "Or about their son Saurabh."

"I don't think so."

"I haven't..of course. They were...are..my neighbours back home. They are very close to my parents."

Vidya paused for a bit, gathering her thoughts while Palak patiently waited for her to continue, not wishing to interrupt her in any manner.

"I used to take care of their son," she said. "Saurabh. He was much younger."

Vidya was finding it difficult to articulate her thoughts in the manner she desired. The more she mulled over things she knew to be certain, the more they appeared absurd, and thus not worthy of mention; while those feelings that lay deep within her, couldn't be said aloud because she wasn't sure what they were or how they made her feel.

Palak waited patiently for Vidya to say more. She could sense her uneasiness and reluctance, and though she felt quite inclined to press her further, she remained quiet and waited. Her friend's current demeanor was unlike anything she had ever witnessed before. She was used to seeing her be strong and firm willed, often rude and irritable, sometimes distant and lost. But this was different.

"He was unwell," she said finally, "for a long time. That's what everyone thought. He probably still is."

"What's wrong with him?"

"I don't know."

"So..so will you have to go back?"

"Maybe. Though what good would it do?"

In the morning, Vidya woke up earlier than usual, despite having not slept well enough. Last night's deliberations lay somewhere forgotten in the back of her mind. She felt tired and lethargic, quite unwilling to leave the bed and get ready for another long day at the hospital. But the more she kept lying idly on the bed, the more those recessed thoughts began to claw their way back to the front.

She got up and looked at the time. It was still only 5:30 in the morning, but she knew she couldn't wait any longer. She quickly dressed and left the house without waking anyone else. The roads were deserted, and it was much colder than usual. A fruit vendor had just begun to set up his cart. Vidya hurried past him, her arms huddled across her chest, trying to save herself from the cold as much as she could.

Upon entering the hospital, she saw Madam Sinha hunched over the patient in Bed Two. She had only just started her morning round after the night-duty nurses had left. Vidya came closer and stood next to her. Madam Sinha didn't show any surprise on seeing her this early. She removed her spectacles and looked at Vidya with either concern or disappointment in her eyes. Vidya wasn't sure.

"When do you have to leave?"

"I'll go tomorrow," she replied. "The morning bus."

"For how long?"

"I don't know. But not too long."

Madam Sinha continued to stare at her for a while, not saying a word or reacting in any manner to Vidya's response. Her eyes seemed to lose focus and Vidya felt as if she was looking straight through her. She put on her glasses and turned back to the report she had in hand.

"You can collect your remaining salary in the evening. Teach Palak everything."

An hour later, Palak arrived and Vidya finally told her about her decision and her conversation with Madam Sinha.

"But why did you lie?"

"I had lied yesterday. It was automatic."

Now that Vidya knew she was going home tomorrow, she remained distracted and disturbed for the rest of the day. She worked and attended to her duties in a very perfunctory manner, to the extent that if anyone had asked her as to what she was doing at any given moment, she wouldn't have been able to answer them. Her thoughts constantly drifted to her parents, the Parashars and Saurabh.

At various instances during the day, she took out time to explain Palak about the duties she would have to undertake from tomorrow onwards. The other nurses too found out about her imminent departure and thus a general murmur spread around the ward and hovered over everyone, creating a rather solemn and serious mood. Vidya involuntarily kept glancing at the clock at regular intervals.

Madam Sinha didn't tell Dr. Hari that Vidya was leaving. She didn't consider it important or necessary to do so. Vidya's sudden departure would affect the proper functioning of the hospital. But that was her domain and not Dr. Hari's, and thus she would do what was necessary without having to involve him at all.

The lady in Bed Six raised her arm and Vidya approached her with the spittoon in her hand. She stopped beside her bed and frowned.

"You don't have to cough," she remarked on not seeing the strain and the redness that always characterized her face before a coughing fit.

"But what if I have to tomorrow?" she asked.

"Palak will be here. You can trouble her. Or any of the other nurses."

"What if I cough a lot?"

"You always cough a lot."

As the evening drew nearer, Vidya grew more and more restless, and as a direct consequence of that, a lot more irritable. She now marched almost frantically from one corner of the ward to another, with a constantly annoyed look on her face. The next day's journey was on her mind, and much more than that was the uncertainty as to what awaited her back home.

It never occurred to her to inform her mother that she was coming home. She completely forgot that she had ended the call quickly and on a very ambiguous note. She hadn't made any commitments or promises. Madam Sinha's presence and her prying gaze were one of the reasons for that. Now, after she had decided to go, it felt like such an obvious choice. It would have seemed incredible to her had her mother too not naturally reached the same conclusion. Thus her subconscious mind reasoned that her mother knew she was coming.

Just before she was about to leave that evening, Madam Sinha called her aside and handed her an envelope that contained the money she was due.

"Did you tell Palak everything?" she asked. She was looking rather calmly at Vidya, her expressions betraying nothing.

"She'll be able to manage."

Vidya expected Madam Sinha to react to the contrary, to say that she didn't believe her and that she had put her in an extremely difficult situation, that she hadn't even once thought about the difficulties she would face trying to run the hospital in her absence. But Madam Sinha made no such remark and simply nodded. This unexpected sense of restraint on her part surprised Vidya.

"And you don't know when you will be back?" she asked after a pause.

Vidya shook her head in silence.

"Alright."

Back home, she finally started to pack and get ready for a long and uncomfortable journey. Palak, whose offer to help had been firmly declined, simply sat on one side and observed her friend.

"How long will it take you to reach there?" she asked.

"Half a day by bus."

Palak could sense that Vidya didn't wish to talk anymore. So she reserved her questions and comments and patiently waited for her to finish her packing and lie down. But Vidya was taking her time. She stood next to an empty bag with her hands on her hips. Heaps of clothes lay on both sides of her. She would pick something and place it in the bag, fiddle with the position in which she had kept it, before taking it out and placing something else inside. Palak couldn't decide whether Vidya was confused or lost. More than an hour later, Vidya put aside the packed bag in a corner and lied down.

"Should I switch off the lights?" asked Palak. Vidya nodded.

"It will be better than you think. I am sure of it."

Vidya gave her friend a wry smile. "Let's sleep."

Palak slept soon enough, but Vidya lay awake for a long time, as she had imagined she would. A deep sense of foreboding, which had slowly started to develop after her mother's phone call, had by now completely taken hold of her. For the first time, ever since having decided to go home, she was alone and not preoccupied with any activity that would divert her mind. Her full attention was on what lay ahead; on what awaited her back home when, after many years, she would see all those faces in the context she had first left them.

The next morning, she left before Palak could wake up.

CHAPTER 3

One of Vidya's earliest and most vivid memories of the Parashars is that of Shashi tending to the flowers in her garden with a narrow water pipe while Vinod sits nearby on a plastic chair and goes through the pages of the local newspaper, or perhaps it is a book. The memory is in the form of a slow-moving image, discernible but cloudy, gliding simultaneously into the future and the past. Vidya is present in it as well. She is right behind Shashi, following her around the garden excitedly, pointing out the small patches that she missed watering, which Shashi would then dutifully cover. It is a cool Sunday morning. The two of them are struggling to control their laughter. Vidya is trying to remember the names of the various flowers that Shashi is quite diligently making her repeat.

"But where are these flowers?" she asks.

"All over the world! A few are here in Konkur as well."

"I want to see them!"

"I'll take you," says Shashi and places the pipe on the ground, the water running through the grass. Vidya picks it up and begins to imitate Shashi's manner of watering the flowers.

Her parents aren't a part of this memory, though she was sure they would have been somewhere nearby at the time. Perhaps they were there in the garden itself, sitting alongside Vinod or even standing next to Shashi. If that were the case, then her memory chose to exclude them.

There are other memories too; earlier ones that aren't as vivid. The garden's presence is constant; the garden and Shashi Parashar. There are times when there is no grass and only mud on the ground, surrounded by thick bushes; there are no flowers either. Vidya's fingers are in that mud and Shashi's chastising yet loving hands running across her dirty face and hair. Her mother's yells are somewhere in the background - an aberration, a constant disturbing flicker across this otherwise idyllic image. Those early years have left behind some other fleeting elements too - her father's laugh, Vinod's indifferent expression, the wooden swing - all forming a small and somewhat essential part of those recessed memories. But the bedrock always remained the same - the garden, Shashi and her mother's voice.

Konkur was an isolated and insignificant town, situated in one of the lesser hilly regions of Northern India, its existence a reality only for its inhabitants and a few of its closest neighbours. The town was an amalgamation of small unplanned developments that had sprouted from place to place as befit the contours of the surrounding hillocks. They were built in a way to least disturb their natural surroundings, mostly because of economic rather than environmental concerns. The houses were far away from each other, present mostly in groups of two or three, many standing alone, surrounded by thick forests all around. The particular geography meant that there was no real sense of community among its sparse population, all of whom were used to lives of enforced peace and solitude, comfortable within their own small cliques, brought together only by their work or by social occasions of some importance. But this wasn't to say that the people of Konkur were inhospitable or unsocial. While they didn't actively seek company, they welcomed it without hesitation. The town's economic heart was the bus terminus that connected it to the nearby villages and cities; its only link with the surrounding world. Around the terminus had sprung a commercial center - a few markets, offices, a school, a hospital, etc.

Vidya's parents, like most of the people of Konkur, had spent their entire lives here. Their fathers had lived on opposite ends of the Market Center and had known each other quite well. To them, the marriage of their young children appeared as the most obvious thing to do. Mahesh was twelve and Lata seven when their impending marriage was already a foregone conclusion.

Mahesh's family-owned and operated a garage at the Market Center, where each successive generation had worked and earned their living. Mahesh had grown up knowing nothing else but how to work in the garage, with the knowledge that he would be running it one day. When Lata turned sixteen, their marriage was formally conducted, and she moved from one part of the town to another - to the house where Vidya would grow up in. Uneducated, barely literate, she, like her husband, had been well trained to perform one specific task. Her mother had taught her how to properly play the role of a wife, instilling in her steadfast ascetic values and a deep belief in God, which she carried with her while making this transition. By the time Vidya was born, Mahesh's parents had died, and he had inherited both the house and the garage.

The Parashars were outsiders. Neither Vinod nor Shashi had any connection with Konkur. They had moved to the house opposite Vidya's when she was only three years old. Theirs were the only two homes in the area, which was at a distance of a kilometer from the Market Center. The narrow road that passed in between their houses ran straight and through, well ensconced between the dense rising trees on either side. After some distance, it widened and merged with similar roads coming from different directions and converging at the heart of the Market Center. This was the very road that Vidya would take each to go to school. For years, once she was deemed old and responsible enough, she would walk alone at a leisurely pace, enjoying the calm and tranquility that the surroundings offered her. At the time, she would have never attributed these feelings of joy to them. She was a child for whom such happiness could seldom be attributed to abstract sources. She liked the trees, the small rocks, the sound of the birds, the roughness of the tarmac beneath her feet, the brown leaves - she liked all of it - but they meant nothing to her together. These individual elements that combined to form this beautiful envelope of positivity were not, according to her, the reason behind her happiness each morning as she made that short journey. She was happy simply because it was that hour of the day when she was always happy. Years later she was joined by Saurabh, who at first walked with his fingers grasped tightly across Vidya's wrist, quite terrified of the menacing trees that seemed to hide the blue sky, before slowly and gradually becoming comfortable with them.

This narrow road also led to the small pond, whose existence depended on the annual rain. Buried deep on one side of the forest, it remained largely unknown and hence seldom frequented. The lack of human interference meant that the pond had not benefited from any sort of upkeep that it might have received had it occupied more of a central location in the town. And so its charm was in its wilderness, and the promise of seclusion it provided.

Vidya was first taken to the pond by her father when she had barely turned three. She had no recollection of that time, except for an intangible feeling of familiarity, which had developed on having listened to her father recount the event on several occasions.

"You were so lazy as a child," he told her. "Just refused to walk! When I told you that we were going to go and see a pond, you looked so confused and unimpressed. So we walked all the way there...well, I carried you. It isn't that easy to find. At first, we almost missed it because it was so green with leaves and algae. There was no proper clearing around it either; it just appeared, enveloped by thick trees and bushes. You were unhappy that it wasn't blue like we had told you. But you were definitely curious. You asked me whether you could walk on it. I said yes!"

"Why did you say yes?"

"I don't know," he shrugged and smiled. "It was impulsive. Still, you were lazy enough not to try. The wooden swing got your attention. It looked so old and not at all safe. It was near one of the edges of the pond. I fixed it for you."

During those early years, before Saurabh and his obsession with the graveyard, the swing was her constant companion. Accompanied by her mother and Shashi, she would make frequent excursions to the pond, often several times a week. Of these visits, her memory offered much more vivid scenes.

"Don't go too near the water Vidya," said Lata, as she always did, even though the water had never held Vidya's interest. They were standing next to a tree near the pond. Vidya carefully observed as her mother helped Shashi sit down on the grass with her back propped against the thick bark.

"You really shouldn't have come," Lata said to her. "This isn't the time to bother with things like these."

"Oh you are always so worried," Shashi laughed through her apparent discomfort. "I enjoy this."

Vidya, convinced that the extremely delicate act of sitting down had been successfully accomplished, ran away and jumped onto the swing, scampering through the sand to gather some speed.

"Push me!" she demanded.

"Just a second Vidya," replied Lata, who was still standing beside Shashi.

"Push me!"

Her mother's halfhearted pushes were enough to give her the momentum she desired. Vidya's legs rose and then fell, further propelling her higher. She liked to focus her eyes below her, watch the ground give way to the water and then come back again. The rope that clasped the wooden plank on either side chaffed against the branch of the tree and produced a recurring noise, with which Vidya was so familiar that it was as important as the swinging itself. After Vidya was contentedly set in her rhythm, Lata went back and sat with Shashi.

"What will be the baby's name Aunty?" she suddenly asked.

"Oh I am not sure yet," smiled Shashi, her eyes following Vidya. "Your Uncle likes the name Shreya if it's a girl; for a boy, maybe Rajesh. I don't know."

"I want a girl," she proclaimed loudly.

"Why?"

"Because I am a girl."

"And if it's a boy," she laughed. "Will you not play with him?"

"Maybe. But I want a girl."

"And what do you want?" Lata asked Shashi.

Shashi shrugged her shoulders. "I can't say. It seems somewhat unfair to want one or the other."

"Push me!" yelled Vidya as she began to slow down, and her mother exasperatingly got up and gave her another good shove.

This was how she always spent her time by the pond. There was no other possible activity; nothing else to do. During the rains, when the moss cleared for a bit and the water was cold and fresh, they would sometimes sit near the edge of the pond with their feet lapping gently on its surface. Vidya would throw little stones and pebbles across it, trying to hit the frogs that hopped at a rapid pace.

But that day, when Vidya was swinging freely from the tree and when Lata's eyes kept darting between her carefree daughter and her pregnant friend, wasn't the time of the year for rains. The dirty water was off-limits; the ground was dry and strewn with dull leaves and twigs. The grass grew intermittently and without any consistency, forming patterns around the most trodden paths. Sunlight scattered through the surrounding trees, warming the air around them and making them sweat a bit.

"Aunty!" she exclaimed suddenly and pushed her feet against the earth, slowing down and bringing the swing to a stop. "Let me push you!"

Shashi burst with laughter, shaking her head at the absurdity of the proposal as well as Vidya's enthusiastic manner of suggesting it. Lata too smirked with disapproval.

"Don't be stupid Vidya," she said. "Parashar Aunty cannot get on the swing."

"But I'll help her," she pleaded.

"She cannot! It isn't safe for her."

"Your mother is right Vidya," said Shashi in a softer tone, seeing the disappointed look on her face. "And I won't even enjoy it like this."

"But the swing isn't for you! It's for the baby. When I push you, I push the baby."

Lata clicked her tongue with impatience and looked sternly at her daughter.

"That's enough Vidya! Don't cause any more trouble. Get back on the swing. I'll push you."

"Oh it does seem quite harmless though," intervened Shashi. Vidya's spirits rose. "Maybe just a few shoves."

"You don't always have to humour her," argued Lata. "You know it isn't right. Why take the chance?"

"It's alright! Come one," said Shashi, holding out her hand towards Vidya. "Help me. You can lift me!"

Vidya's face was alight with a sense of triumph. She slowly led her towards the swing and held it firmly while Shashi gingerly sat down on the plank. Immediately, it sagged significantly, emanating a horrible creaking noise. For a moment, Vidya was afraid that it would break and then her mother would scowl her endlessly. But it didn't.

The image of this scene is imprinted fairly well in her memory - Shashi is on the plank with her hands gripping tightly onto the ropes; Vidya starts to push her gently and soon the swing is on the ascent; Shashi is tense at first but then the swing comes down and goes up again, and now her grip loosens and a huge smile comes across her face; Vidya is smiling too, and after a few shoves, they are both laughing with apparent glee, while her mother stands beside them, clearly unimpressed and dissatisfied.

"You are both such children," she says but they pay no attention.

CHAPTER 4

For the people of Konkur, where entire generations of citizens had lived and died surrounded mostly by those they had known since birth, the arrival of the Parashars was a significant event. The sudden presence of these strangers, who held no previous ties with their town, stirred within them feelings of curiosity and inquisitiveness.

"The new neighbours are here," said Lata to Mahesh as he returned home one evening. Vidya and she were sitting together in the living room, working on one of Vidya's pencil drawings. "They arrived in the afternoon."

"He is here to replace Sharma Uncle," said Mahesh. "He is retiring from the Municipal Corporation. I found out at the garage today."

"Is that so!" remarked Lata, lifting her head. "Isn't he too young?"

Mahesh shrugged and sat down. "Sharma Uncle worked his entire life in that office. He too must have started young. And I didn't see him. How young is he?"

"Oh very young! They have been married only for a year. No children. I invited them inside for tea. He left soon after though. He seems quite serious."

"They said he has a college degree. That too from the city."

"Well, I liked his wife. She was great to talk to. You know she is a trained nurse. She'll try to get work here at the hospital. At her age!"

"They are both quite something."

That was the preliminary consensus among the people. There was something about the Parashars that intrigued and impressed them at the same time. In Vinod, they saw a quiet and unassuming personality, unassertive and kind, not prone to making big statements or gestures. Sometimes they felt as if he was too reserved and shy, almost unresponsive on certain occasions, though this only seemed to further amuse them. With Shashi, they found everything to be much simpler. She was fun and always at ease, seemingly equipped with bundles of energy that she could summon and disperse at will. It was a period of immense infatuation.

The Sehgals' were perhaps the most affected. The Parashars were their first neighbours in over five years. They weren't ideal matches in terms of their backgrounds and their personalities; in fact, they were quite different from each other. Vidya often thought that had the Parashars not been living right across the road from them, her parents might not have made the efforts they did initially to develop and sustain their friendship and that their relations were simply a matter of convenience influenced primarily by their proximity. However, as a child, she too shared her parents' affection for the Parashars, especially for Shashi.

Almost every other evening, Vinod and Shashi would walk across the road and be welcomed by the Sehgals. These gatherings, lasting not more than an hour or two before dinner, were mostly unplanned and frequently initiated by Mahesh and Lata. Immediately on entering, Shashi, Vidya, and Lata would congregate in one corner, leaving the two men to themselves. It was on one of these evenings, a year after they had moved to Konkur, that Shashi told Lata about Saurabh's impending birth.

"Oh my God!" she squealed, instantly hugging Shashi who burst into laughter. Mahesh looked over in astonishment while Vidya impatiently tugged on Shashi's clothes, wishing to understand exactly what it was that had made her mother scream in this manner.

"What happened?" asked Mahesh and then looked at Vinod who simply shook his head. "It's best you ask them."

"They are going to have a baby!" shouted Lata from across the room. She was still holding Shashi in her arms, unable to let go.

Mahesh grinned and clasped his hand on Vinod's shoulder. "You have to drink now. I won't listen to anything!"

"What does it mean?" asked Vidya, still furiously tugging at Shashi with such intensity that she was almost jumping up and down.

"It means you are going to have a little brother or sister," smiled Shashi, placing her hand on Vidya's head.

"When?"

"Oh...in about a year."

"That's too long!" she complained.

"It's just wonderful!" beamed Lata and led Shashi towards a chair. "Sit down now! Come on! I'll make you some tea."

"I am not yet completely useless!" laughed Shashi. "I don't have to be seated while you make tea for us. I can help you."

"There is no need!" replied Lata in a gentle but firm manner. "You just keep sitting. Vidya! Don't bother Aunty too much now. Be still!"

"But it's too long!"

"Enough Vidya! How long has it been?"

"Around 8 weeks."

"So we should expect the new arrival by either December or January," she beamed.

"It should be January," proclaimed Mahesh. "Then the baby would be part of the new decade. That would be appropriate!"

"Oh I don't want that at all," replied Shashi immediately. "It may seem appropriate now, but I know that in the end, I would just want it all to be over as quickly as possible."

"Still," pressed Mahesh, and looked towards Vinod for some support but didn't get any. "Wouldn't it be nice!"

"Anyway!" said Lata firmly, glaring at her husband, "this is just wonderful news. I am sure it's going to be a healthy baby! Destined for greatness!"

Later, when Vinod and Shashi had left, and the three of them sat together to have dinner, Lata turned towards Mahesh.

"What were you thinking?" she began in a loud and dramatic manner, almost scaring Vidya. With great swift movements, she put food on all of their plates, her arms working at such a furious pace that some of the food splashed off the plates and onto the table. "How could you say all that to Shashi! Giving birth to a child is not something to be taken or spoken about lightly. Such blasphemy! You wish to make a game out of that poor woman's misery! You want her to suffer for some additional weeks for your fanciful reasons! It should be in January.....I cannot believe she didn't say much; what a heart she has! She probably didn't want to offend you much. Oh, dear...how aghast she must have been on hearing your proposition and how hard it must have been for her to control herself! And Vinod too! Such patience! That man has such patience...and tact. If only you could learn something. But no! You would rather have fun at the expense of a pregnant woman and her unborn child. God have mercy! Such horrible blasphemy!!"

Vidya was almost too scared to eat while Mahesh listened to his wife calmly, nodding occasionally with a look of self-reproach, waiting for the storm to pass. Lata, however, didn't let the matter go by easily and returned to it from time to time in the months that ensued. She didn't cease to remind and reprimand Mahesh of his cardinal mistake until the very end, by which time Shashi's discomfort had compounded because of intermittent instances of painful contractions and false labours. Her barrage of outbursts, though successively reducing in severity and bitterness, finally came to an abrupt end when Vidya's father's wish came true and Saurabh was born during the first week of January 1990.

The birth was protracted and difficult. For more than two weeks, Shashi remained in bed at the hospital amid many of her patients. Though their presence had served as a welcome distraction during the first few days, later the pain and discomfort rendered everything tiresome and annoying. Kamili, one of Shashi's friends at the hospital, who was also a full-time nurse, voluntarily embraced the role of a midwife and stayed beside Shashi at most hours of the day. Lata and Vidya were frequent visitors, hovering around Shashi's bed for as long as they could before Kamili would ask them to leave. Vinod, whose office was nearby, too would visit several times during the day.

The atmosphere of revelry that had followed Shashi's pregnancy and, on the day of Saurabh's birth, escalated to such staggering heights by building on its layers of enthusiasm, was brought crumbling down by the stiff and determined look on Kamili's face, who stood between the hospital ward and the other women of Konkur. Among them, muttering and cursing softly, stood Lata at the front with Vidya right beside her. She was arguing with Kamili, demanding to be allowed to see her best friend. Her appeals, though earnest in nature, were somewhat subdued, as if subconsciously she knew that Kamili was right in refusing them admittance.

"Just for a few minutes!" she pleaded softly.

"I want to see the baby!" added Vidya, much louder than her mother.

Kamili ignored Vidya and looked at Lata with that air of condescension that comes easily with experience. "Shashi and the boy need to rest right now. It was a long and tough delivery. The boy's forehead is too warm. I cannot allow anyone inside. Even the father has only seen been inside once for just a minute. Go home for now. Everyone! Go on!" she dismissed them all with a slight tilt of her head and went back inside. Vidya clutched at her mother's waist and walked back home with her, with mingled feelings of concern and disappointment.

A week after giving birth, Shashi was finally allowed to go home, and she was accompanied by Kamili who continued to play the role of her personal guard. The throng of women returned day after day, the numbers reducing with every successive visit; but each time, the infallible Kamili stood outside the doors and kept them all at bay. Even Vinod had limited access to his own house and spent most of the day at the Sehgals' after coming back from office.

The vigil lasted for almost three weeks before Kamili finally let her guard down and allowed inside the swarm of curious women. When they entered, Shashi was lying in bed with Saurabh by her side. Her face was pale with big shadows around her eyes. The physical toll that the birth had taken on her was clearly visible. Yet she was beaming with pleasure and happiness on seeing all of them come in. They gazed lovingly at the newborn baby and his proud mother, whose emaciated look was no match to her feelings of contentment.

Vidya remained quietly on one side, feeling uncomfortable and restless among this group of women who kept fawning over Saurabh, gasping and gushing at his slightest of movements. She too had wished to hold Saurabh in her arms but Shashi's look had frightened her. She climbed on the bed and lay beside her.

"My dear Vidya," smiled Shashi, stretching out her arms and enveloping them around Vidya.

"Vidya! Get off the bed," remarked Lata.

"Let her be," said Shashi, still holding her in an embrace. "Do you wish to hold him?" she asked her and Vidya nodded with a smile.

Shashi placed Saurabh in Vidya's arms, carefully placing her hand at the base of his head. Vidya stared at his tiny frame. His eyes were closed and his lips pressed tightly together. He was trying to move and stretch his arms and legs as if attempting to free himself of Vidya's clutches. Vidya looked up at Shashi and then at his mother, both of whom were looking at her expectantly. Saurabh started to struggle even more, till the point that it was uncomfortable for Vidya to keep holding on to him. She stretched her arms outward and let her mother take him before he was eagerly snatched away by one of the other women. In this manner, he was passed around the room slowly until everyone had had the chance to hold him.

"Such a handsome little thing he is!"

"The ears! Just like your Shashi!"

"He has a good colour too!"

"Oh, he is going to be such a star!"

"Of course! With the parents he has!"

Vidya sat among them all and quietly observed their apparent excitement. Soon she waved her arms and demanded to be given Saurabh once again. However, just as before, the experience was completely underwhelming. She could feel everyone's gaze on her, as if they expected her to say something, to share their enthusiasm. But she held him away just as he started to fidget and cry. Kamili took Saurabh and placed him in Shashi's lap, where he calmed down within a few seconds. Vidya climbed down from the bed and slipped away to one corner of the room. She stood with her back to the wall, looking over as the rest of them hovered over the mother and her new-born baby. She sat down on the floor, her eyes trying to search for Shashi among the crowd that engulfed her, waiting for the revelry to end.

As an infant, Saurabh was obsessed with ants; an obsession born out of intrigue and curiosity. He would stare at them endlessly, sometimes crawl and scamper after them, following their urine marked trail that ensured they all traversed a fixed path in the most peculiar and half-hazard manner. When they would disappear within the cracks in the walls, he would claw at them with frustration and anger, hurting his fingers. Many times, this would be followed by a torrent of tears, forcing Vidya to act as a reluctant pacifier. His fixation with ants wasn't simply limited to their movements. At times he would try to prod or pick some of them up with his small fingers, trying to capture a few, only to accidentally kill or maim them. The ones he did manage to capture, he would place in his mouth and then subsequently make weird expressions as he tried his best to swallow them. Vidya never bothered to intervene during such instances.

"Oh God! Why don't you stop him Vidya?" asked Lata, once when she managed to witness such an event. She immediately rushed towards Saurabh, picked him up and took him to the washbasin to rinse his mouth clean.

"It doesn't matter," she replied. "He does it often."

"Don't be stupid. Shashi would be furious," she said. "Don't mention this to her. And watch over him."

Until Saurabh's birth, Vidya had been the only child in her neighbourhood. Among the four adults she had grown up with, she had effortlessly and unconsciously commanded their love and attention. She was habitual of always being talked to and about, ruling the lives of those around her in a way only children can. And now, all of a sudden, she found herself upstaged by a toddler who was too young for her to compete against. This was a development she hadn't foreseen. She was growing older and taller, looking lesser and lesser as a child, without outgrowing a child's need for constant attention at the same rate; a need that was not being met in the manner it always had been before. All of her excitement and enthusiasm surrounding Saurabh's birth dissipated rather quickly as she soon realized the ramifications of being the elder and relatively independent child.

During Saurabh's infancy, Vidya and her mother would spend most of their evenings at the Parashars', huddled around Shashi and Saurabh. They didn't go to the pond anymore or spend time in the garden. It was just this bedroom, with Shashi and Lata on the bed, and Saurabh between them. Vidya would hustle from one corner to another, bored and irritated, her appeals for activity firmly refused.

"Why can't we go?!" she asked. "We can take him too. He can just lie in one corner."

"Don't say things like that!" retorted his mother. "It isn't good for the baby. We'll go some other day."

"Here Vidya," said Shashi with a smile. "Why don't you hold him?"

Vidya took him in her arms and, as was his habit, Saurabh began to move restlessly, uttering small cries and eliciting a look of disgust on Vidya's face.

"You are hurting him!" frowned Lata. "You need to hold him gently. Be nice Vidya. He is just a baby."

"He is your little brother Vidya," said Shashi, her tone betraying her disappointment. "Won't you take care of him always?"

As guilty as Vidya felt on hearing Shashi's words, she couldn't suppress what came to her naturally. Her early association with Saurabh was tumultuous and uncomfortable. She felt as if his birth had left her languishing in the obscure recesses of the minds of all those who knew and adored her. Her dislike for him was palpable, further heightened by the fact that she spent an inordinate amount of time with him, a fact that angered her mother and troubled Shashi.

When Saurabh was old enough to let Shashi return to the hospital, she would drop him off at the Sehgals' for the day until she returned home in the evening. Vidya would come back from school and be welcomed by Saurabh and her mother. She would sit by and try to not engage herself much in his activities, while simultaneously keeping a watchful eye on him. He wasn't exactly a nuisance. On the other hand, he could be frustratingly comical at times. The most mundane of objects and beings would catch his fancy, a trait that was easily observable in his bizarre infatuations.

The only other activity, to which Vidya was a daily witness, and which perhaps rivaled and sometimes exceeded Saurabh's fixation with ants, was that of him digging small holes in the ground using sticks. Vidya couldn't recall how and when Saurabh had developed this particular habit. But whenever they were outside, Saurabh would look around for a small wooden stick and then sit down on the ground with his legs ensconcing a patch of earth that he liked. The procedure he followed was simple but thorough. He would dedicatedly scrape on the earth with his stick for long periods with unwavering interest and focus, which would only be interrupted when Vidya offered him some food or water. It was quite a slow process, during which time Vidya would simply sit beside him, as bemused as she was indifferent. Then, once he had dug a hole deep enough for his liking, he would fill it back up with the very earth he had extracted, until it was whole again, and then he would plunge the stick on top of it as his final act. The first time he did this, Vidya couldn't help but laugh so loudly that he looked at her in a shocked and bewildered manner before repeating the entire process on another patch of earth.

And then Saurabh began to talk; not just the few inaudible and unintelligible words he could muster as an infant, but long strips of phrases that though were not inaudible, still somewhat remained unintelligible. Despite this observable fact, there seemed to be no dearth of adoration for every syllable that spewed forth from his lips. He was the delight of the crowd and continued to be paraded around like a trophy that everyone loved to gush over. He reveled in it as well, aided by the inherent capacity for attention that all children have and coupled with, perhaps, his mother's genetic influence. At that age, he was a star, constantly displaying his little teeth when he laughed without restraint, indulging in one non sequitur to another - either through his behaviour or through his words; and everyone simply loved it.

Initially, all of this baffled Vidya, until much later when she realized that she too had probably been shown the same degree of tolerance when she was his age, unlike after when a single misspoken word from her lips or even an inappropriate gesture was immediately censured and followed by corrective advice. There seemed to be some imaginary line beyond which one wasn't allowed to do what came naturally and easily, a line that Vidya had crossed but Saurabh was yet to. Thus her initial dislike and confusion surrounding him continued for a long time, slowly diminishing in its intensity, and receding into smaller and smaller pockets that occupied her mind. Saurabh, along with his idiosyncrasies, was now a constant presence in her life. Inevitably, she found herself associating with his daily habits and activities, making them into her own. Apart from her classmates at school, whom she only met for a certain controlled period during the day and who all were around her age, she had only known and observed people much elder to her. Saurabh was the only child she knew well; the only person whose incremental growth from infancy to beyond she would be able to witness.

CHAPTER 5

Once Saurabh was old enough to go to school, Vidya would arrive at his doorstep each morning, and the two of them would then walk together on the narrow street towards the Market Center. Saurabh, his small hand firmly holding on to Vidya's, would stare intently at the surrounding trees that gave way to the dense forests on either side, looming large on the road and almost enveloping it in their shade. In the morning, it was always very quiet, with a bit of chill hanging in the air and a mild breeze blowing the fallen leaves gently in random directions. The path was seldom occupied and often the two of them had the road to themselves the entire way. Sometimes they would come across a lone cyclist, a few unknown pedestrians crossing their town, fruit vendors pushing along their carts....and all of them would be met with Vidya's hostile gaze. There lay within her such a deep sense of entitlement, akin to an absolute feeling of ownership, that someone else's presence on this path always felt like an encroachment, a violation of her rights.

Somewhere in the middle of this short journey, the heavy cluster of trees on their right opened up just a little to reveal a small iron gate. For many years, while walking along the path by herself or with

Shashi and her mother, Vidya had barely given it a momentary glance. Her focus had always been about a hundred meters ahead and left of this gate, where a small opening among the trees marked the entrance that led towards the pond. But Saurabh, noticing the anomaly in the largely unbroken scenery around them, was intrigued by this gate's presence and insisted that they venture inside. The gate was bolted with an old and rusted padlock, which appeared as if it would give away at the slightest of force. Even so, the lock's purpose seemed merely ceremonial as the gate itself was only five feet tall, made with criss-crossing iron bars that enabled the two of them to jump over it with ease.

Their feet landed on rough gravel. The land didn't stretch out too far in front of them. It was rectangular, interspersed with small white headstones, and framed on its corners by a withering gray stone wall that had huge gaps in between at intermittent distances. The forest, which enclosed this hidden compound from all sides, almost seemed to have taken a detour to accommodate this graveyard. However, years of neglect and disuse had led to spurts of random growths within the area, as if it was once again being slowly reclaimed by the surrounding forest.

Vidya and Saurabh placed their bags on the ground and walked further inside slowly. Saurabh was quicker than her, making his way to the nearest headstone, while Vidya's eyes explored the area around them, unsure as to what exactly they were witnessing. Saurabh stood and stared at the engravings on the headstone, which had withered and faded over the years. The lines and patterns meant nothing to him and were nothing like he had ever seen before. Vidya came closer. She finally understood.

"What is this?" he asked.

"It's a person," she replied. "This is where he was kept after his death. That's his name."

"I don't understand it."

"It's a different language."

Saurabh approached the headstone and touched it gingerly, tracing his fingers over the unfamiliar patterns.

"Can he hear us?"

"I don't know. Maybe."

He continued to stand beside it, clearing away some dirt with his hands. "Hello!" he shouted suddenly, startling Vidya.

There was no response. Saurabh walked away from it while Vidya stayed, staring blankly at the headstone as if still expecting a reply. Her stupor was broken when she heard Saurabh's quick steps approaching her. She turned towards him, noticing his big beaming smile as he proudly brandished a long stick in his hand.

"They are many," he exclaimed enthusiastically.

"I suppose we should go back," said Vidya, looking uneasily around her. "We are getting late."

"No! Just a little more time."

They didn't go to school that day. Their bags lay where they had left them and they roamed around the area, exploring every inch of the graveyard, before finally settling in front of the first headstone they had come across. That's where they stayed for the next few hours - talking, sleeping, digging holes, eating their lunches - until they were bored and decided to go home.

Lata was surprised to see them this early and equally astonished when she heard about where they had been. She knew about the existence of the graveyard; she had heard her parents speak about it when she was young. It had been there even before their time - an unused and desolate piece of land - dating back to a period of which nobody in Konkur knew about. As a young girl, Lata had been forbidden to go inside or near it. It was considered to be a bad omen.

"So that's what you did instead of going to school!" she screamed at Vidya. "Saurabh is too young. But you should have had more sense. Wait till I tell Shashi what you two did today!"

Shashi, on the other hand, hadn't known about the graveyard and was thus quite interested to hear about it.

"At least you have found some other place to dig your little holes. My poor garden can breathe once again," she smiled and then looked at Lata, who was struggling to see the lighter side.

"Isn't it disrespectful?" she said, feeling perturbed and uneasy at the prospect of the two children spending their time at such a place. "It's a graveyard!"

"They are just children," she replied. "There is no harm. It is fun for them."

"If other people found out..."

"Oh, it doesn't matter. Don't worry. I'll deal with them."

"It's just wrong!"

Despite Lata's concerns, the graveyard became a permanent feature in their lives. Each day, during the evenings, the two of them would rush towards it and return home only just before it got dark. The initial hesitancy and awkwardness that Vidya had felt the first time quickly dissipated. Both of them were soon completely at ease with the place. The dead didn't worry them at all and they managed to include them in the silly games they came up with. The graveyard replaced the pond and became their new playground. For Vidya, it offered the same degree of seclusion and anonymity that the pond had offered; the same sense of exclusivity and control. But the pond had been hers and the graveyard belonged to them both. It was to be the place for shared memories, for mutual feelings of independence and happiness.

Saurabh had just turned eight years old when, as they would on any other day, the two of them walked towards the graveyard in the evening. The sun was out and the air still. It was too warm for that month of the year, and thus they were both sweating a bit by the time they reached. The iron gate with the padlock greeted them; they still hadn't considered forcing it open. Once they had jumped over it, they sat down at some distance from the nearest headstone. Vidya immediately leaned back against the trunk of a tree and watched as Saurabh began almost instantly, looking for the perfect stick to start digging yet again.

Often Vidya would carry her schoolwork with her, utilizing the time when Saurabh was busy by himself. But on that day, the unexpected and excessive warmth of the sun made her incredibly lazy. She was quite satisfied to just see Saurabh do what he always did without engaging herself in any manner. She had already decided to firmly say no to his inevitable requests to either climb some trees or play some other games. She watched him contentedly from a distance as he continued at his general pace, the heat not affecting his enthusiasm one bit. He was already in possession of a short and sturdy wooden stick, with which he had begun to scrape a piece of the earth. It was a sight Vidya was extremely used to - the rise and fall of his arm, the repetitive noise of the scraping. It was all so mechanical and methodical, so rigidly familiar that soon Vidya's eyes lost focus and began to water. She fell asleep.

It was the total absence of noise that woke her up. At first, this was the only aberration that she noticed as she gradually regained her awareness about her surroundings; it was then that the more obvious aberration quickly caught her attention - Saurabh was not there. The stick lay abandoned in the half-dug hole in front of her. Vidya was neither alarmed nor did she feel any panic - not because she was sure that nothing had gone wrong, but because she had never known anything otherwise. Even so, if not worried, she certainly felt a little confused and uneasy. How long had she been asleep? And where was Saurabh? She got up slowly, brushing the sand from her clothes, and scanned the surrounding area from one corner to another.

She spotted him near a particular section of the bushes that grew in the far-right direction from where they had been sitting. Saurabh was on his knees, his head thrust inside those thick bushes. Vidya yelled across but he didn't respond. She decided to walk over.

"What are you doing?" she asked, stifling a yawn.

"It's stuck."

"What's stuck?"

He didn't answer and kept plunging further inside until both his head and shoulders disappeared from view. Vidya, slowly feeling the drowsiness leaving her body, bent down and tried to peer inside but the bush was too thick. She couldn't see what it was that had so captivated Saurabh, and she had no intention of getting inside the bushes herself.

"Stop it Saurabh! You will get scratches all over you."

But Saurabh was immune to her words at that moment. He continued to wrestle with his arms inside the bushes. Vidya tried to hold him by his waist and pull him out but he instinctively went rigid and held firmly, digging his knees and toes into the dirt. She couldn't move him at all.

"No, no, don't!" he yelled and extended the last word to such a feverish pitch that Vidya let him go immediately. Surprised, annoyed and unsure as to what to do next, she just sat down beside him, listening to the rustling of the leaves and twigs, waiting in anticipation.

"I'll tell your mother," she remarked feebly, lacking any conviction.

A few minutes later, Saurabh relented and emerged from within. He had dust all over his clothes and face, including his hair, which was disheveled and littered with leaves. Small and thin red lines were visible across his face and arms; he was badly scratched. Vidya knew that her mother was going to be furious when she saw them. But at that moment, his scratches and her mother's impending rebukes were somewhere at the back of her mind. Her full attention and focus were towards his hands that lay empty.

"What happened?" she asked.

He shook his head dejectedly and looked at her in a contemplative manner, as if thinking about his next course of action.

"It's still stuck."

Before Vidya could say something further, he plunged inside once more, this time at a slightly different angle. As before, all she could do was sit, wait and listen to the rustling of the bushes; her mind oscillating between feelings of curiosity and concern. She now thought of his scratches. They were too many and too noticeable to be attributed to a casual fall or cut. They would require a proper explanation and, as of that moment, Saurabh hadn't provided her with one.

A sudden noise broke through the bushes and startled Vidya; it was akin to a high-pitched whine, faint but audible. It was the first time that Vidya got some indication of what Saurabh was after. She was surprised that whatever little animal was stuck in the bushes, evading his grip, had not uttered a single sound as of that moment. The whine hadn't even been loud or continuous enough for her to ascertain the type of animal. Perhaps it was a little dog, she thought. Maybe it was hurt or unwell. Saurabh, on the other hand, continued to struggle against the brambles, which were re-paying him rather unjustly for his steadfastness. It reminded Vidya of his tirades against ants when he was just a toddler.

Finally, Saurabh came out, his prize held safely in his hands; it was a kitten. It was so small that it fit almost completely within his two palms, where it lay curled up in a frightened manner. Its hairless body was light pink with little spots of white. Its eyes were closed with fear. Saurabh smiled at Vidya victoriously and started to walk back towards the place where his half-dug hole lay waiting for him. Vidya didn't share his feelings of enthusiasm and quickly caught up with him.

"Was it alone?"

"Yes."

"How did you know it was there?"

"It ran into the bushes. You were sleeping."

Vidya stared at the frail little creature. It was unlike any kitten she had ever seen. She felt sure that it was diseased.

"Let it go, Saurabh. It doesn't look well."

"Not yet!"

"What if its mother comes along?"

"Then it can go."

"What are you going to do with it, anyway?"

"It's going to watch me dig the hole!"

That's exactly what Saurabh made the little kitten do. As Vidya once again, albeit reluctantly, nestled against the bark of the same tree, Saurabh sat beside his unfinished hole and set the kitten down nearby. It was too petrified and hurt to move. He picked up his stick and started to scrape at the earth, his arm falling dangerously close to the kitten. Just as before, despite the best of her intentions, the drone of the scraping, the mechanical motion of his arm, and the heat of the sun, made Vidya fall asleep.

This time it wasn't the absence of a sound that woke her up, but rather a continuous noise of a different kind. She awoke slowly, still not having completely registered the nature of the new but somewhat familiar noise, half expecting Saurabh to not be present again. She opened her eyes and saw him sitting exactly where he had been before.

The noise was familiar because she had heard it less than half an hour ago. As she rose from her slumber, she recognized it for what it was - a whine; the kitten's whine. The kitten who now wasn't sitting near Saurabh but rather lay sprawled within the hole he had dug. Her body, instead of being petrified as before, was excessively animated, being held hostage by Saurabh's left arm that gripped its legs. His right arm fell up and down as before; but the stick, instead of digging through the earth, was now scraping the kitten's midriff.

For a few moments, almost infinitesimally brief, during which time Vidya's bewilderment prevented her from reacting immediately, she saw the stick plunge into the kitten, piercing its skin and causing it to bleed. Saurabh's face was red and swollen, his eyes wide open and focused. Vidya quickly regained her composure and pushed at his right arm, involuntarily screaming his name out loud. Saurabh lost his balance and fell backwards, dropping the stick. Freed from his clutches, the kitten sprang from the hole and ran away. Its injury didn't seem to impede its movement, aided perhaps by the pain and terror it had just experienced. Vidya's eyes followed the kitten's path as it disappeared into the bushes once again.

Saurabh got up and touched Vidya's shoulder, instantly making her recoil from both fear and disgust. She looked at him warily from afar. He was a horrible sight to behold. In addition to the disheveled hair, the dirty clothes and the red scratch marks, his body was now trembling perceptibly and he looked a little pale. It was this very look that gave Vidya the courage to grab him by both of his arms.

"Why did you do that?" she asked loudly.

He said nothing and continued to tremble while taking deep breaths.

Vidya didn't know what to do. Saurabh looked confused and a little afraid so she didn't press him any further. His breathing became normal again after which he began to cry, and so Vidya held him until he settled down. She had seen him cry many times before, but at that moment, she felt extremely uncomfortable.

"Let's go back," she said, helping him up. "It's okay."

On the way home, Vidya cleared away as much dirt from him as she could with her hands and attempted to brush his hair into submission, trying to make him look as presentable as possible. She wasn't making much progress though and the red scratches were easily visible. Saurabh didn't say a word the entire time, and she didn't force him to. While they were still some distance away from their houses, Vidya stopped, bent down, and spoke to him.

"Listen Saurabh. You will not say anything to Parashar Aunty. Do you understand? She won't like it and will get upset. So please don't tell her. Don't tell anyone at all!"

He nodded gently and Vidya was afraid that he might start to cry once more. She gave him a quick hug, and they started to walk again.

Shashi was in her garden when they reached. She smiled at them as they came nearer, a smile that disappeared the moment she saw Saurabh.

"He got inside some bushes," began Vidya immediately. "There were a lot of thorns. He didn't know. I am sorry I didn't stop him."

"Oh I am sure he didn't let you stop him," she said and squatted on the ground to look at her son more closely. She shook her head with a wry smile. "What have you done Saurabh!"

Vidya was looking intently at him, afraid that he might say something, or start to cry once again. He remained quiet and calm, silently listening to his mother's admonishments.

"Go inside now," she said. "You need to take a bath right now."

"It's okay Vidya!" she added on seeing Vidya's face while Saurabh walked away inside. "It isn't your fault. Don't worry! I'll get him cleaned nicely!"

"I'm sorry," she said again, not looking at Shashi, who came forward and hugged her tightly.

"You are such a sweet child. It is all fine. Go home now! Your mother would be waiting."

The next day, when Vidya stood outside the Parashars' house, Saurabh greeted her with a cheerful smile, which remained on his face the entire time till they parted ways inside the school's gate. Later, in the evening, when they walked towards the graveyard, he was still rather upbeat, talking about the things he generally liked to talk about - his classes, his friends, his teachers, etc. - without once referring to the incident or betraying any emotion that might be linked to it. They sat at the same spot as always. Vidya took out her books to complete her homework while Saurabh searched all over the ground for the perfect stick. It was as hot as it had been the day before. Soon Saurabh settled down and Vidya too commenced her work, fighting the urge to fall asleep, her eyes lifting to scan the area at the slightest of noises.

CHAPTER 6

There was only one school in Konkur and it was run by the local government. It didn't have more than a few hundred students, who, apart from those that belonged to the town, came from the surrounding villages. The school comprised of a cluster of small brick huts placed side by side around the perimeter of the school with the small open yard in between. Here, each morning, all the students and teachers would assemble to start the day with a short assembly followed by the national anthem. Afterwards, they would all depart for their respective classes. The five-year difference between Saurabh and Vidya ensured that they were part of very different circles and thus didn't spend any time together during school hours.

Vidya was mostly an indifferent student. The value she placed in her education was too sporadic, too inconsistent to matter. Her periods of attention rose and fell rapidly, depending on what caught her interest and for how long. Her performances too reflected this carefree attitude, which her mother had long ago stopped to question or complain about. All of this was also a result of her being fixated on the idea that she was going to grow up to be a nurse like Shashi. She was sure of it. No other profession attracted her, and neither was she aware of many of them. She would learn all that she required to know through Shashi and thus school was just a formality that she had to go through before she was old enough to take her own decisions. In most classes, she either sat gazing blankly at her surroundings or make small pencil drawings in her notebooks, and even the strictest of teachers eventually relented in front of her obstinacy.

It was in one such class of hers, as she sat scribbling on a piece of paper, that a sudden murmur traveled at great speed throughout the class.

"Vidya!" told her companion excitedly, tugging on her sleeve, with the expression of a person who greatly believed in the importance and worth of what they were about to say. "Listen! Saurabh broke someone's nose!"

For a few days ensuing the incident in the graveyard, Vidya had thought a lot about what had happened and how it had all transpired, especially as to what could have prompted Saurabh to hurt that little kitten in such a deliberate manner. Exactly what had fascinated him about the kitten in the first place? She played the entire scene over and over in her mind - Saurabh's disappearance, the struggle inside the bushes, the red scratches over his body, the small and pink kitten that she was sure was diseased, her falling asleep, Saurabh's right arm brandishing the stick that repeatedly fell over the animal, the little spots of blood - wondering about and questioning every detail. From time to time, these thoughts would enter her mind at unexpected moments, akin to an embarrassing memory that haunts one relentlessly. They planted a seed of perpetual doubt and curiosity, which made her keenly observe Saurabh's actions and mannerisms for a while. It was purely an involuntary act, a subconscious attempt to find some answers, though she wasn't even sure what she was looking for. She wished she hadn't fallen asleep.

She never asked Saurabh about it again, who too never mentioned it. But their daily visits to the graveyard made it impossible for her to erase the incident from her memory. On several occasions, she felt the urge to talk about it but then she remembered that look of sorrow and fear on Saurabh's face when he had started to cry. She couldn't do it. The incident was to forever remain between the two of them, or, as Vidya sometimes believed, solely with her as it seemed that Saurabh had completely erased it from his memory. Gradually, she stopped dwelling on it so regularly and managed to content herself with the explanation that it had just been an aberration and that it would thus always remain a mystery.

And so, on that day in school, more than a year after the graveyard incident, the thoughts that Vidya had wrestled with for so long before letting them dissolve in the watery depths of memory, resurfaced. The fears and the dilemmas returned, this time with an acuter sense of urgency.

"Why?" she asked her friend. "And whose?"

"I don't know! I am just telling you what I was told."

Vidya rued the fact that once again she couldn't be a witness to the actual moment that made Saurabh do what he did. She wished to know everything she could but had to rely on the verbal accounts of other students, which naturally tended to swing wildly between inaccuracy and exaggeration. The entire school was buzzing with the same news, and despite the multiple sources and their varied versions, a common thread ran through them all - a minor altercation between Saurabh and his friend had spiraled suddenly and violently out of control, with Saurabh breaking the other boy's nose in addition to the other minor injuries he had caused. Saurabh himself was unhurt as the other boy had been taken by surprise and wasn't able to retaliate in time.

That day, Vidya went home alone after school. Saurabh, soon after his fight, had been escorted to the nearby hospital where Shashi worked. Vidya was glad of the solitude and walked back slowly. She wondered what she would have said to Saurabh had he been beside her right then. What would she have asked? Would he have been as afraid and confused as he had been the last time? Would he have given her a good reason for why he fought? Was this even related to the kitten or was it simply an isolated event that her mind was falsely associating with the former to find a pattern that didn't exist?

On reaching home, she had lunch with her mother but didn't tell her anything. Later, she retired to her room where she lay on the bed with one eye outside her bedroom window. The view of the incoming road stretched far from where she lay. She waited for their return, falling in and out of sleep.

A few hours later, a firm clasp on her shoulder made her open her eyes. Her mother hovered over her, calling out her name over and over again. Despite her sluggishness, she could sense the anger in Lata's tone and in the expressions she wore on her face. She rubbed her eyes and sat up, instinctively looking out of the window before turning towards her mother.

"...Vidya!" she exclaimed. "Why didn't you tell me about Saurabh? I felt so foolish talking to Shashi. They have just returned."

"I forgot."

"You forgot! That's no excuse. How could you forget something like this?"

"I don't know. It slipped my mind."

"Go back to sleep!" she said, frowning. "Should do you some good. And you are not going out this evening. Stay at home."

"Why?!"

"Just listen to what I am saying. Not today."

"That's not fair!" she retorted but Lata simply shook her head and left the room.

Even though she had retaliated against what she felt were unjust impositions, Vidya was content to stay inside and not go through the awkward situation of meeting Saurabh that evening. She sat on the bed with her back resting on the wall, looking through the window towards Saurabh's room. The light was on but she couldn't discern whether he was in the room or not. Conflicting thoughts arose in her mind and struggled against each other. She knew that she was over-thinking and over-analyzing Saurabh's brush with violence, linking it to an earlier event that had transpired more than a year ago, and an event that she didn't understand well enough. Yet she couldn't just dismiss the apparent similarities between the two. There was a strong sense of fear and dread that she was finding difficult to shake off, even though a part of her knew she had no concrete reason to feel the way she did.

Sometime later she felt thirsty and went to the kitchen where she found her parents huddled together near the counter. She hadn't known that her father had returned from work. She had been in her room for quite a few hours.

"Vidya," called Mahesh. "Did you speak with Saurabh in school? What happened?"

She shook her head. "I wasn't there. I don't know."

"But did you speak with him later?"

"No."

"It's alright," he turned towards Shashi. "He is a young boy. Sometimes, these things happen."

"But he has always been such a harmless child. How embarrassed Shashi must have felt!"

Vidya slowly sipped her glass of water, listening to their conversation.

"I think we should go over there," she added.

"But why?" "Just like that...to show...support."

"You are overreacting. Boys fight."

"When was the last time one of our children broke some other child's nose?"

"So...he was a little too strong for the other child. It will all settle down in a day or two."

"You don't have to go if you don't want to! They are our neighbours and friends!"

"Alright," he resigned. "We'll go in a while. All three of us."

"Oh Vidya doesn't have to," she said immediately.

Mahesh looked at his wife and then at Vidya. "Don't you want to?"

Vidya wore a blank expression on her face, seemingly caught off guard by the question. She was struggling to come up with an answer.

"It's no need," Lata intervened.

"He won't harm her," he said to Lata with a little smile, to which she responded with a strong glare.

Vidya frowned but didn't say anything, returning to her room once again. She lay on her bed and intermittently stole glances outside her window, unable to concentrate on any other activity. As much as she had been bothered by her mother's reaction, a part of her had been glad of the intervention - a realization that did nothing to raise her spirits, instead plunging her further into that swarm of fear and confusion that occupied her thoughts, which she now began to also associate with guilt.

That night, they all sat at the dinner table, with Mahesh and Lata having decided to go to the Parashars' after they had had their food. Vidya sat beside them quietly, listening to their conversation, slowly gulping down morsels of food that tasted bitter the moment she put them in her mouth.

"Be quick Vidya!" said Lata. "We have to go."

When they left, Vidya watched their progress from her bedroom window. Shashi opened the door and hugged Lata before letting them in. For a moment, Vidya felt that her eyes drifted beyond her parents and then eventually lingered in her direction. She receded from the window and drew the curtains.

Having nothing to occupy herself with, she sat down and started thinking of all the things that her parents and the Parashars would be saying to each other. *How badly was the other boy hurt? Did he say why he did it? Has he said anything at all? What did the principal say? He can come back to school, right?* These were some questions that she wished her parents would ask.

But would Shashi ask why she wasn't there? Were they both extremely shocked and upset? Would they call Saurabh and talk to him as well? What would he say to them? Would he even remember what he had done? Would he tell them about the kitten?

Slowly, but with increasing potency, she grew impatient and frustrated with wrestling all of these ideas in her head. She got up, wore her slippers, and quickly walked out of the house, trampling over her garden and then that of Shashi's. She tapped on Saurabh's window, gingerly at first and then with greater speed and force to ensure that it would be audible even if he were asleep. It was quite dark outside, a single street light faintly illuminating the area around their two homes. She began to shiver a bit because of the cold. She tapped on the window once again.

Saurabh appeared and opened the window soon after. He hadn't been sleeping. By looking into his eyes, Vidya could discern that he had cried a bit. Even so, he didn't seem that surprised to see her.

"Hello," he said nonchalantly.

"Why did you do it Saurabh?" she began immediately, surprised at the tinge of anger in her voice. "What's wrong?"

As she had feared, he didn't reply, bowing his head and refusing to meet Vidya's eyes. She didn't know whether it was regret, guilt or embarrassment that attributed to his silence. Maybe he was bored with having to answer this question multiple times already. Maybe he didn't have an answer at all. In any case, she wished to know something.

"Why Saurabh?" she pressed, placing her hands around his shoulders. "Tell me."

"We fought."

"But why?"

"I don't remember."

"Did he say anything or do anything to you before you started fighting?"

"I don't remember."

Vidya wanted to continue and press him further but she could see that he was on the verge of tears. She felt awkward and cold standing by his windowpane, watching him struggle with something she couldn't understand yet, torn between her curiosity and her inclination to help him.

"Come out," she said. "Take my hand."

Saurabh slowly placed his feet across the window sill and, holding firmly onto Vidya, jumped into the garden.

"Sit down now," she said, her arms embracing his body. "It's all okay. I won't ask anything now."

They both sat down on the grass that was wet and cold with dew. Vidya took Saurabh's hands and kept holding them. He was still not looking up, still on the verge of tears.

"Do you want a stick?" she asked him gently.

He sniffed and shook his head slowly.

"Let's dig!" she said. "With just our hands."

Vidya started pulling on the grass between them, slowly at first but then with more vigour. Saurabh remained idle for a while, but then lifted his head to intently watch what Vidya was doing. Bits of grass and earth were flying around them.

He got up and climbed back inside his room, making Vidya think that she had somehow upset him even further. But he came back out a minute later with two sticks in his hand. He handed one to Vidya.

"You are spoiling it," he said. "It is much better with this."

Vidya smiled and took the stick gladly. They both sat down and started digging at a moderate pace.

"Show me how you do it," she said and he obliged.

"Vidya......," broke through Lata's voice. She turned around and saw that all four of them were standing at the doorway, visibly surprised to see the two of them in the garden.

Except for Lata, the three of them looked calm and relaxed, as if they had just finished the most pleasant of conversations. Vidya's eyes naturally found Shashi, who was smiling at her gently.

"What are you doing out here so late?" asked Lata, walking towards them. "You will both catch a cold. Come on now. Let's go. Bye Saurabh."

CHAPTER 7

Saurabh had very faint memories of the years when he was one of the most beloved children of Konkur. These memories were fleeting at best, vague enough that they had acquired a dreamlike nature, brought to his knowledge only by the stories he was recounted. He was told that his arrival had been celebrated with great joy and excitement; that he was doted upon, praised endlessly simply because of the apparent virtue of his birth and of the status his parents had held at the time. It had been a monumental occasion for this little obscure town, a reason to come together and celebrate the beginning of a promising future. But Saurabh never got to experience those moments, nor the ones that followed for a few years after them. The deficiency of memory, an inevitable by-product of growing out of infancy, rendered the best years of his life at Konkur redundant.

However, those very memories were strongly imprinted in Vidya's mind. She had always been there, and thus had witnessed, mostly with jealously and sometimes with pride, the level of affection he had always received. She had seen all of it. And so it was to her that the contrast was the greatest, the most noticeable and the most baffling.

Saurabh's great unraveling had begun in virtual secrecy at the graveyard, with only Vidya as the witness to a seemingly unprovoked and sudden violent reaction. It had been followed, more than a year and a half later, by that incident in school that brought him in the limelight. Ever since then, the episodes had become more and more frequent, with varying levels of severity, all of them taking place at the school itself. His fall from grace was quick and rapid, and the way he was then treated by those who had once loved him unconditionally also followed in the same direction. It was this that annoyed Vidya more than anything else.

Her frustration was two-fold; partly at Saurabh, whose behaviour she continued to find inexplicable, and partly at the adults around them, whose premature judgments against Saurabh were nowhere near in congruence with the ambiguities that brew within her. Soon, the veneer of perfection that had been readily attributed to him completely eroded, replaced by hostile presumptions, which Vidya felt were hastily made. He was no longer the perfect child, destined for greatness; all of these illusions had washed away within the space of a year. The people of Konkur didn't take too kindly this betrayal of their faith. Tacitly, but with extreme conviction, Saurabh was branded as an incorrigible young boy who was to be avoided at all times. They feared and loathed him, while somehow managing to pity his parents whom they all still immensely respected, even though the nature of this respect had changed from admiration to empathy, with perhaps just a hint of sadistic glee.

Saurabh was 11 years old when the storm hit Konkur and blew for almost two days. It was sudden and strong, a continuation of the heavy rains that had been falling the entire week before. Manohar, the local fruit vendor, who would push his fruit-laden cart from house to house, despite the long stretches of emptiness in between, was outside the Parashars' home when it began to pour, accompanied by huge gusts of wind. The terrifying speed of the raging winds carried and sprayed water in all directions with such force that it felt as if one was getting slapped in the face by the rain. It was almost impossible to keep one's eyes open. Manohar was struggling to keep his fruits from falling all over, and so Vinod quickly grabbed a sheet from inside the house and helped him to cover his cart. Vidya saw them wheel it inside and leave it in the Parashars' garden, tied to a small tree. Manohar quickly thanked Vinod and rushed away, his slippers splashing with water, his left arm placed above his head, trying in vain to avoid getting drenched.

That had been the beginning of the storm. The two days that followed, they all stayed inside their homes, making sure that all doors and windows were properly closed and sealed. The water still came through, finding its way in through the endless cracks that weren't visible to anyone. They put towels around their main doors, which had to be replaced and wrung properly every few hours. There were small cups, buckets, and bowls spread around the house at those locations where the roof was leaking. Vidya's bed, which was near to her window, wasn't spared either, and she had to thus sleep on the floor in her parents' bedroom. All offices, schools, and markets were closed. Konkur had been brought to a standstill.

On the third day, when the rain had slowed down to a drizzle, and the wind was blowing much more gently, Vidya and Saurabh stood outside their homes, ready to leave for school in the morning. The smell of the damp earth rose through the air. All of their surroundings - the green leaves, the gray road, the brown earth, the blue sky - were more vivid and clear, as though deliberated painted over. Vidya felt as if all of her senses had been heightened by some magic trick. A light cool breeze blew across, a harmless remnant of the gale that had passed over, and it brought an involuntary smile to her face. The sun was still early on its ascent in the sky, its rays scattering through the trees and forming interesting patterns on the ground. The insects and birds too seemed busier than usual, their calls and creaks creating a pleasant mixture of sounds. The only jarring element in this otherwise idyllic morning was the shattered remains of Manohar's cart, which lay strewn about in the Parashars' garden. The rope they had used to tie it to a tree still hung from it, with a small piece of wood attached to it. They walked past them and towards the Market Center, encountering pieces of fruit that had been blown away from the cart, most of them reduced to their pulps. Saurabh couldn't resist giving a good kick to all those that lay within his range.

When they returned home in the afternoon, the mess in the garden had been cleared and the little piece of rope no longer dangled from the tree. Vidya overheard her parents talking that Manohar had come over in the afternoon to clean everything and salvage what he could of his belongings. Even though he had refused profusely, Vinod had reimbursed him for his loss.

"There was no need for him to do that," remarked Lata. "It wasn't his fault."

"You know how he is," said Mahesh.

This seemingly banal incident was soon forgotten by everyone, until about a week and a half later, when Mahesh came home after work with one of his coworkers. This man had come over a couple of times before as well but wasn't a frequent visitor. Upon seeing him enter the house, Vidya quickly retired to her room. She knew that he was one of her father's occasional drinking companions and she had no inclination to engage in any sort of conversation with him. He had always treated Vidya as if she was the same five-year-old girl with whom he had spoken for the first time, employing a casually condescending tone that always irritated her. Even Lata disliked his presence but did her utmost to tolerate him as best as she would any unwelcome guest.

He had a tall and stocky built, which he rather conspicuously lowered on entering the house, smiling ingratiatingly at Lata, who greeted him meekly in return. Mahesh, aware of Lata's feelings towards his friend, quickly offered him a seat and proceeded to the kitchen with the bottle of whiskey they had bought on their way over.

"Not more than an hour I promise," he whispered to Lata who shook her head. "He invited himself."

He quickly made their drinks and took the two glasses back to the living room, one of which his friend gladly accepted.

As much as Vidya tried to not let their conversation disrupt her, the thin walls between them ensured that all of their words were easily audible. She managed to neglect as much as possible and thus only caught snippets of their conversation that ranged from work to politics to their other friends, and which, inevitably, included the weather. When they had had a couple of drinks, their voices, in particular, that of Mahesh's friend, became perceptibly louder. Soon their conversation, turning and twisting aimlessly in accordance with the fertility of their thoughts, led to the storm and the destruction of the fruit cart, at which point Vidya started to keenly listen involuntarily. Even Lata, who had so far restricted her involvement to mainly serving them food and glancing at the clock, sat down beside them with interest.

"Those two days were so unusual!" he said, well inebriated by now. "So bizarre!"

"Yes..it was," replied Mahesh.

"And how about that poor Manohar's cart! Such a bad loss for him."

"It wasn't a loss," said Mahesh.

"Why?"

"Vinod paid for it," said Lata. "All of it! The cart and the fruits."

"Did he?!"

"Yes! I felt so bad for him and Shashi. There was no need to. I don't understand why he did it. Just bad luck."

"It was in their garden, right? Outside their window?"

"Yes. Tied to the tree in the garden; next to Saurabh's room."

"Oh well, maybe then it isn't so strange that Vinod paid for it," he said and grinned sheepishly, his face turning red. He suddenly became very serious. "I feel sorry for them. They have so many responsibilities, they work so hard, and in addition, they have to deal with him. It must be so hard."

Vidya's parents nodded slightly and looked at each other, shuffling uncomfortably in their seats, unsure of how to respond to his remarks.

"Let me get you another drink," said Vinod and got up to take Neeraj's glass. On his way to the kitchen, he passed Vidya's room just as she emerged from within. She avoided her father and walked directly towards where her mother and her father's friend were sitting.

"Oh hello Vidya," he greeted her rather jovially.

Vidya had heard everything he had said and had been immediately incensed by his not so subtle allusive remark. She had waited for her parents' response before giving in to her urge to go out and face him.

She didn't reply to his greeting instantly, trying to find the right words. Lata was looking at her firmly but Vidya's anger was helping her to maintain her courage.

"It is not fair," she blurted finally, much more meekly than she had imagined. "How could have Saurabh broken that cart? He is just eleven. And there was that storm. It was impossible to even leave the house."

Vidya tried to fix her gaze towards him, without glancing towards her mother who she knew would be enraged by her behaviour.

"It...I...I didn't mean that" he said, visibly taken aback, clearly not having expected Vidya to approach him in this manner. "It was...just like that...a joke."

Vidya stood there uncomfortably, unsure as to what to say or do further. Her impulsiveness had brought her this far and now seemingly abandoned her at this important juncture. Her feet jostled together, her fingers entwined and her eyes darted from one corner of the room to another. The anger still simmered somewhere beneath the surface but had currently been superseded by the awkwardness of the situation she found herself in.

"It isn't fair," she said once again, her voice barely rising above a whisper. "Always."

"Go back to your room Vidya," said Mahesh from behind, as he walked past her, holding the drink in his hand. He hadn't even looked towards her, but the curtness of the voice had been enough for Vidya to know that he was extremely displeased. Lata, on the other hand, didn't say a word, seemingly in disbelief of what had just transpired. She just glared at Vidya until she went back inside.

"Sorry," she heard her father say.

"Oh, it's no problem at all!" Neeraj replied, once again in that enthusiastic tone of his. "They are all our kids."

Vidya sat on her bed, dejected, angry and close to tears as she continued to replay in her mind all that she had said. For a brief moment, she felt that perhaps she had overreacted, that his remark hadn't been an allusion to Saurabh's behaviour but simply a harmless joke. He hadn't exactly spoken against Saurabh, had he? It had been more of a general statement, an attempt at humour, the type of which is natural when one is in a social setting where conversations tend to drift from one subject to another, without dwelling for too long on anything in particular. Moreover, hadn't his statement been a sort of acknowledgment for the Parashars, empathizing with the difficulties they faced regularly because of Saurabh, all while continuing to handle their professional responsibilities. And who could deny the hardships that accompanied being the parents of Saurabh? As much as Vidya wanted to, she couldn't. So perhaps he had been right in saying what he did.

But right beneath the surface of these conflicting thoughts, was the feeling of self-assurance that severely doubted the intentions behind those seemingly innocuous statements. And the more she thought about them, the more she was able to overcome her momentary self-doubt. Yes, she was sure of it. After all, these slightly veiled verbal attacks on Saurabh weren't a rarity anymore. This was how Konkur had subconsciously decided to respond to Saurabh's problems. They, having forgotten how much they had loved the same child when he was born, had turned him into a social pariah, an easy target of uninspired jokes. Parents strictly instructed their children to avoid being around him at all possible times; all of his minor incidences were retold with a generous influx of exaggerations, sometimes to the point that the incident itself became beyond recognition. Employed all too frequently and erroneously, these verbal attacks and allusions were becoming proverbial in nature. Saurabh was, directly or indirectly, seriously or in jest, blamed for everything that went wrong in Konkur. Broken windows, trampled grass, fallen trees, dead animals, and broken fruit carts. There was nothing that he wasn't capable of.

The bus rolled along noisily, shaking violently at every bump or depression on the uneven road. Vidya glanced at her watch and sighed deeply, shifting uncomfortably in her seat, continuously trying without success to find a more convenient position to sit in. She had been traveling for over ten hours and there were still a few more left. It was rather hot inside the bus, a condition that was only worsened by the thick throng of people that were jammed inside it. Her head rolled lazily towards the window on her left and her eyes gazed absentmindedly at the familiar fields outside that rushed past her. Do they still do it, she thought. After all these years, after Saurabh had been first confined and then turned away, maybe they still couldn't resist it. Perhaps even now they blamed him for a frigid winter, or the paltry rain; a low yield crop season or the parasites that feasted on the vegetation. She wouldn't have been surprised if they did so.

CHAPTER 8

After Saurabh's famous altercation with his friend, he had returned to school following a two-week suspension period and apologized to his friend whose nose he had broken. Since then, till the year of the storm, there had been many other incidents - minor fights in the school playground, broken chairs, verbal fights with his friends, and sometimes even his teachers. Once he had taken one of his classmates' stationary case and slammed it fiercely on his desk, instantly breaking the case and sending its contents flying in every direction. These incidents occurred almost in a cyclical manner, at least once or twice a month, as if they were part of an inexhaustible source of energy within him that brimmed over from time to time. During this period, he had been further suspended on six to seven occasions, always for a week or two, and each time Vinod and Shashi found themselves making reassurances to the school that they themselves were finding hard to believe in.

Vidya and Saurabh still walked to school and back together every day; and then in the evening, the graveyard continued to retain its importance in their lives. By now Saurabh had outgrown his fascination with sticks, an obsession that hadn't been replaced by anything else.

Still, they frequented that graveyard, aimlessly wandering amid the trees and the headstones, spending less amount of time as they used to, both of them too old to play the games they once did. Vidya did not notice any substantial change in Saurabh's mannerisms over these years. He had always been on the quieter side, which made it even more difficult to gauge any difference. If anything, she felt that Saurabh had become quieter and more solitary in the way he spoke and carried himself. Even when he was with Vidya, he wasn't as forthcoming as he was before. However, of all the relationships that had changed and developed over time in their families, greatly affected by Saurabh's troubling incidents, it was theirs that still most closely resembled the past.

The day after Mahesh's friend had visited their house, Vidya had to face a tirade of rebukes from her parents; especially from Lata. She had fought back bitterly, more out of instinct than belief, unsuccessfully holding back her tears, which embarrassed and thus, as a result, angered her further. Mahesh, who usually refrained from using a harsh tone against his daughter, letting Lata handle that domain of parenting on her own, was too annoyed to let go of the matter.

"Do you realize how embarrassing that was, Vidya? And how disrespectful of you?"

"He shouldn't have said it," she replied, her voice meek and broken. There were tears at the edge of her eyes. She wasn't used to her father being angry at her.

"So what! How does it matter? He just said it!"

"But it was wrong."

"Maybe it was! In that particular situation, maybe. But there was nothing wrong with what he said in general. And..even if he was wrong, you shouldn't have done what you did. He was a guest! And so much elder to you! It was extremely embarrassing!"

Vidya, stubbornly, did not apologize, but just lowered her head and let her anger and tears flow across her face. Mahesh walked away, greatly disappointed with his daughter's behaviour, leaving Lata behind. She sat down beside Vidya and placed her hand on her head. Her mood had softened by now.

"It's been so long Vidya. Everyone knows how he is. What are you trying to do? What's the point?"

Vidya looked at her mother in silence, detecting, for the first time in her voice, a touch of empathy. She shrugged and shook her head. "I don't know."

A few months later, Saurabh hurled an inkpot at his teacher, splitting open her forehead.

Shashi was at the hospital when Saurabh's teacher was helped inside by two of her colleagues. One of them held a handkerchief to her forehead, ebbing the flow of blood that had stained through the cloth and trickled down her face. Her wound was cleaned, examined and then closed using five stitches. During this time, Shashi was already on her way to the school, where she found Vinod waiting for her. The school's peon had immediately been sent for both of them. They were asked to take Saurabh home, but not before they had to sit for an hour in the Principal's office, where they were told in no uncertain terms that Saurabh had been suspended indefinitely and that the school would decide on a future course of action of which they would be intimated within a few days.

Inevitably, the news of Saurabh's latest incident spread almost instantly among the other students of the school, and from there, to virtually every household in Konkur. By the time Vidya had reached home, once again walking back by herself, Lata had already been to the Parashars' and back and was now impatiently waiting for her daughter's return.

"Do you know what happened?" she asked her. "Saurabh is not saying anything."

Vidya shook her head. "I just heard he threw an inkpot at the teacher. That's all."

"I know that!"

And so like before, the events repeated themselves. Vidya and Saurabh didn't meet that evening, staying within their rooms while their parents were hunched over in discussions separately. Mahesh was visibly shocked when Lata told him what happened and asked Vidya about it, who once again assured him of his ignorance. It was almost akin to a performance, a game in which they all played their parts. The only difference was that this time they decided not to visit the Parashars that day itself.

"He has crossed a line," said Mahesh. "Something is seriously wrong with him."

"I just feel so sorry for those two," said Lata. "They don't deserve this."

"I don't think they are going to spare him this time. Vinod's and Shashi's influence has already gotten him this far. I think he might be expelled."

"Oh God! Don't say that! What will they do?"

For the next few days, Vidya went to school and back alone, always peeking through Saurabh's window on her way past it. Sometimes the curtains would be drawn; sometimes she would find him asleep; occasionally he was awake and sitting on his bed quietly with Shashi beside him who had taken leave from the hospital; other times he wasn't even in the room, but never was he aware of her presence as she went by his window. It wasn't as if she wasn't used to it. Saurabh's multiple suspensions had made her quite habitual of this practice. But this time she couldn't forget her father's words, wondering if this was going to become a permanent feature of her day from then on.

She hadn't met Saurabh since that day and neither had he ventured out of the house. She had thought about going over and accompanying him to the graveyard as usual, to retain at least a semblance of normality for them both. But she couldn't will herself to do it. She just wasn't sure of what she would say.

The day before the school's Principal was to meet with Saurabh's parents in order to let them know of her final judgment, Shashi was sitting with Lata at the latter's house, sipping a cup of tea. Vidya was with them.

"You'll take care of him tomorrow, won't you Vidya?" asked Shashi. "You'll be with him? The two of you haven't met the last few days."

The Principal had set the meeting for the evening after school hours so that there would be no hindrances or disruptions. And the Parashars had no inclination of leaving Saurabh alone at home during that time.

"Of course," she replied, catching her mother's eye who frowned slightly. Vidya felt as if Shashi's last statement had been a reprimand in some way, and it made her even more determined to be with Saurabh the next day.

"Don't worry about it," said Lata to Shashi. "I am sure it will be fine."

Shashi smiled at her friend's unconvincing attempt at reassurance. "Let's see. I don't know."

Later, when Shashi had left, Lata went to Vidya's room and sat down beside her.

"You don't have to do it. I can make some excuse. I mean...if you feel..."

"I am not afraid of him," she replied instinctively, more to herself than to her mother.

"Well...," she paused, lowering her voice. "You should be. We all know how he is."

"Do we?" she asked, loud enough to startle her mother. "Do we really? How is he?"

"Why do you have to be so difficult!" Lata retorted. "I am only saying it for your safety."

"I am safe," she replied and then turned away, fixing her gaze towards the wall. "There is nothing to fear."

Lata sighed and stood up to leave. When she was near the door, she turned back and said to Vidya.

"You are not always right Vidya. You need to realize that."

The next evening, Vidya stood beside Saurabh as Shashi walked past them both and gave them a little pat on their heads accompanied by quick fleeting kisses. She then climbed aboard the rickshaw that was waiting to take her to the school. Vinod was going to join her directly from the office. Lata was also standing outside, silently watching from a distance.

"What will you two be doing today then?" she asked in a slightly cheerful manner.

"I thought we could go to the pond," replied Vidya. "It has been a long time."

"That's nice," she replied with a smile as the rickshaw began to pull away. "That seems quite harmless."

"Good luck," yelled Lata and then looked at both of them. "And you two be safe. Stay away from the water."

Vidya nodded and turned towards Saurabh. He seemed just the same as ever, unaffected by all the events surrounding him of which he was the centerpiece.

"Shall we go?"

"What pond?"

"I'll show you."

The thought of going to the pond instead of the graveyard had come to her that very morning. She didn't know why but she felt that a change of scenery would benefit them in some way. It might offer a bit of distraction, might ease some awkwardness between them by offering something different to do and talk about. It had been a while since she was with him alone, and although she wouldn't have liked to admit it, she was nervous about spending this day with Saurabh. Perhaps as nervous as her mother was, albeit for different reasons.

They both set off down the road, walking in the same familiar direction as they always used to. The air was somewhat cold, blowing with a strong enough force to make the small overhanging branches of their surrounding trees tremble. Vidya wasn't sure if she remembered the way to the pond, relying instead on muscle memory. There was a particular section of the forest, which they had to enter directly from the road, and it was this section that Vidya's eyes were earnestly looking for. Soon they crossed the graveyard and Vidya noticed Saurabh's head-turning in that direction.

"I think you will like the pond. It should be a nice change."

"Maybe."

They walked a little further along the road, and now Vidya's eyes were pierced towards her left, aware that soon they would be reaching the Market Center. A few minutes later, she finally found the location she was searching for, even though she had no perceptible memory of what it looked like. Even so, there was something about the arrangement of the surrounding trees and the colour of the barks that convinced her that this was the place. She confidently turned left and walked off the road, onto the dirt path. Saurabh followed her in, somewhat reluctantly.

Their surrounding quickly became much more interesting and intimidating at the same time. Saurabh looked around with amazement at the dense envelope of trees around him, the leaves glowing with a yellowish hue because of the sunlight. The sights and sounds of the forest fascinated him, in particular, the soft crunching noises his shoes made on every other step. He was now starting to enjoy this little excursion to the pond while constantly keeping an eye on Vidya, who was busy rediscovering the correct path. They were barely talking to each other throughout the way, each fully consumed in their own activity.

"How much further is it?" asked Saurabh, with perceptible enthusiasm.

"Not too far."

While Saurabh was evidently feeling quite at ease in the forest, Vidya's mind frequently switched to the Parashars, who were most probably sitting with the Principal at that moment, trying to save Saurabh's future. At the same time, she was struggling to find her way to the pond, unsure of the steps she had taken until then. She was afraid they were going to be lost inside. But within a few moments, rather unexpectedly, their path started to clear; the distances between the trees widened, and the sunlight managed to break through at frequent intervals. A smile of relief and contentment broke across Vidya's face. Her steps quickened, and she gestured at Saurabh to follow her quickly.

In a short while, they were standing in the clearing, facing the pond whose dirty green water dimly reflected the sunlight. Vidya's eyes automatically rushed towards the old tree at the far end where the swing used to be. The tree stood there alone, without its companion.

"Do you want to touch the water?" she asked Saurabh.

"Can we? Isn't it too dirty?"

"That doesn't matter."

Vidya approached the edge of the pond and sat down. She remembered the time when she used to come here frequently with her mother and Shashi all those years ago. It seemed like a different time. She wondered what happened to the swing, whether the storm had blown it away or whether it had been stolen, though she couldn't think why anyone would steal it. She took off her shoes and gently touched the surface of the pond with her toes. The water was cold. She placed both of her feet inside.

"Come."

Saurabh joined her and soon he too had his shoes on the side and his feet in the water. He smiled at Vidya who was looking far ahead, her eyes unfocused. The area they were sitting on had softer earth than it appeared. There were small stones that pinched them slightly but the pain wasn't strong enough to incite a reaction from either of them. It was a comfortable space to sit and relax. The stillness and tranquility of their surroundings reminded Saurabh of the graveyard, with the dirty green lake replacing the dirty white headstones.

"Do you know why Parashar Uncle and Aunty have gone to school today?" began Vidya.

Saurabh turned towards her after she asked the question. She was still looking straight ahead.

"Yes. They are all deciding if I can go to school again or not."

"Do you want to be able to go to school again?"

"I do."

She pressed her chin against her shoulder and looked at him with clear distress in her eyes.

"They why do you do it?"

She didn't want to ask him this question, certain that he had been asked this before by his parents and his teachers. But it just sprang spontaneously from within her, and now she was waiting for his reply, somewhat afraid of what it would be. Saurabh's arms and legs fidgeted restlessly beside him. His smile had disappeared and was replaced by a palpable sense of discomfort.

"I don't know," he answered in a whisper. "I really don't know."

"What do you mean Saurabh?" she asked, her voice rising ever so slightly. "How can that be? Why did you hit your teacher?"

"She said something."

"What?"

"I don't remember."

Vidya shook her head vigorously and a sound of frustration escaped her lips. She opened her mouth to speak and then stopped, unsure of what exactly she wished to say to him. Saurabh looked at her expectantly, his fingers digging deep into the soil. They were sitting fairly close to each other, and this proximity increased the awkwardness of the moment.

"Do you know how everyone is saying things about you?"

He nodded.

Vidya, feeling increasingly exasperated, was struggling to maintain a calm exterior. Saurabh's head hung low and away from her. A period of tense silence ensued. It was slowly turning dark now, the evening approaching at a leisurely pace. With the coolness of the water around their feet and the mild draft of the flowing wind, it was a good time to be outdoors.

"I don't understand," said Saurabh finally, staring fixedly at his feet that mechanically went in and out of the water. "I get angry and then I don't remember why....sometimes I do...but....," he stopped, his voice beginning to break. "I don't know."

Vidya, on the verge of tears, placed a hand on his head and sighed. She felt marginally better after hearing what he had said.

"You have to do better Saurabh," she said firmly. "You must control it somehow. We can't let them win."

"Okay."

Vidya sighed once again and wiped her eyes. She leaned back and stretched on the damp and cool ground, her face pointing directly upwards towards the sky. She closed her eyes. Saurabh looked at her and did the same.

"They will be back soon. Do you want to go home?"

"No."

"What do you want to do?"

"Can we go to the graveyard?"

"Okay."

They both got up, brushed the dirt off their clothes and started to walk back. They found it much easier to retrace their steps and were soon on the main road. Saurabh was walking ahead of Vidya now, a small but noticeable skip in his step. They quickly neared the graveyard's locked iron gate and, like always, jumped over to enter inside.

CHAPTER 9

The meeting with the school's principal had lasted barely over an hour. Shashi and Vinod had already reached back home when Saurabh and Vidya were still sitting near the pond. They were quickly joined by Lata, who had been keeping an eye out for their return since the time they had left. Their glum and downcast faces were a good enough indication. Saurabh had been expelled. Shashi had not expected the school to be so resolute, especially after their earnest pleas. And thus she had been struck rather hard by their decision, somehow managing to escape the school's premises without breaking down. However, she couldn't control her tears when, back home, she was sitting alone with Lata.

Vidya and Saurabh returned after a few hours. She accompanied him to his house, expecting his parents to be home by then. She was anxious to know what had transpired and was a bit surprised when her mother opened the door. Lata gave them a weak smile and moved sideways to let Saurabh in so that he could join Vinod and Shashi who were sitting in the living room. She then immediately took Vidya by her hand.

"We should go," she said to the Parashars, pulling Vidya outside.

"We'll meet in the evening when Vidya's father is back."

The two walked out and across the road to their house. Vidya, frowning, went directly inside her room before her mother could say anything. Shashi's red and tear-stained face was imprinted vividly in her mind.

The next day Vidya left for and returned from school alone, an experience that wasn't new for her but of which she was now sure she would have to permanently become habitual. She didn't see Saurabh that evening or even for the next few days. Even his parents hardly ventured outside except for work. There were even days when Shashi stayed at home, not finding the energy to go to the hospital. A stillness seemed to descend on the Parashars' house, too heavy at that moment to be easily cast off.

Lata and Mahesh would visit them a few times, leaving Vidya behind on each occasion due to Lata's insistence.

"There's no need," she said, trying to shake her head and wave her hand nonchalantly, but unable to honestly convey that emotion. "And I believe it is best to leave Saurabh alone for a while. This isn't easy for them. They probably think the same, or they would have called you."

While Vidya easily saw through her mother's weak excuses, she found herself lacking the will to argue against her. The school's decision had left her bitter and disheartened at the same time, a feeling that was quite visibly reflected in the sour expression she permanently wore on her face. Once again, she felt anger towards everyone in general rather than anyone in particular. The time she had spent with Saurabh at the pond had also increased her frustration. She had felt helpless at his responses to her questions, a fact that also attributed to her disinclination to meet him. How often could she go through the same conversations repeatedly? She felt that she needed some time on her own as well and relied on keenly listening to her parents' conversations to keep herself updated.

"They have been speaking with some teachers," said her father. "Home schooling is probably the only option they have now."

"Of course," sighed Lata. "There is no other way. That child is not meant to be among people."

"It could change."

"I don't think so. Shashi told me that she might have to leave the hospital for good."

"Well, that is unfortunate."

"Yes! But what can she do? I was afraid she would ask us to take care of him. Thank God she didn't. Can you imagine the risk?"

A few days later, after it had been almost a week since she had last met Saurabh, Vidya saw Shashi sitting in her garden as she returned from school. She was cutting bits of grass with what was an extremely large pair of garden scissors. Shashi's presence at that time of the day confirmed what her parents had been discussing. She had left the hospital. Saurabh was not with her at that moment.

"Hello Vidya," she greeted her, with a meek smile that betrayed her embarrassment.

"Hello."

"It's a nice day today, isn't it?" she added. Her each word and movement felt rather conspicuous as if she was feeling extremely conscious of herself. "You and Saurabh should be out today in the evening. It's been so long. He is very bored being inside the house all the time. Aren't you?"

"A little," she replied. "I'll come and take him later."

"That's great."

Vidya nodded at her and walked away. It was only later when she sat in her room by herself that she regretted having given such curt responses. She couldn't fathom why she had behaved in such an aloof and distant manner. She had always liked Shashi, had always related more to her than to her mother. Perhaps it was the surprise of seeing her there and at that time that had reminded Vidya of all that recently passed.

In the evening, when Vidya was about to leave the house to meet

Saurabh, Lata found out Shashi's request to her daughter. Undoubtedly, she was greatly displeased and struggled to hide those emotions from Vidya.

"You should have told me earlier! How can she just ask you like that!... Anyway, you don't have to go. I will take care of it."

"It's okay. I want to."

Shaking her head at Vidya's reply, Lata glanced haphazardly around the house, feeling caught between her desire to not endanger her daughter in even the slightest way possible and to not offend her friend.

"Nothing is going to happen," said Vidya, impatiently, standing near the door. "We'll just go to the graveyard as usual."

The awkwardness she felt on seeing Saurabh after such a long time soon went away as their minds automatically responded to each other, subconsciously drawing on years of familiarity. Saurabh's demeanor showed no indication of the recent events, no sign of remorse, irritation or anger, which, while Vidya found somewhat perplexing, helped her to be more at ease. She had already decided that she wasn't going to question Saurabh anymore regarding his incidents. She had learned her lesson at the pond. She now knew that he had no answer to the questions that burned within her. As strange and inexplicable it seemed to her, she began to believe that he was as much of a bystander as she was. And so these periods in the evening with Saurabh became a regular fixture once again, despite Lata's constant disapproval. However, they commenced much later in the day than before and were for a much shorter duration since Saurabh was now being homeschooled.

Indeed, Saurabh had resumed his studies in a matter of weeks. Two of the school's teachers had agreed to come to the Parashars' house in the afternoon to give lessons, while Shashi and Vinod had decided to distribute the rest of the subjects among themselves to the extent to which they could manage it.

One of those teachers was Harish Irani, the oldest teacher of the school, who had once taken Vidya's science class. He was short and heavy, with a belly that spoke of years of comfort and of a sedentary lifestyle. He had a compassionate and empathetic face, one that came with years of dealing with confused and reluctant students. He was the first of the two teachers to arrive for Saurabh's lessons each day, and Vidya could often see him approaching the house from her bedroom window. His clothes always seemed to be the same - a pair of gray pants with a white shirt, sometimes accompanied by a blue home-stitched woolen sweater. He didn't wear any spectacles, even though it always felt as if he was leaning forwards while reading.

Vidya had always liked Harish and was thus glad that he was teaching Saurabh. She believed that he could have a positive effect on him, though she wasn't sure as to how that would happen. It wasn't as if Saurabh was an overly energetic or distracted child who could benefit from Harish's calm and sage-like demeanor. If anything, Saurabh was always in a somber mood, quiet and reclusive, traits that had become more and more prominent over the years, especially since the beginning of his violent outbursts; whether those incidents had influenced his behaviour in any way was something Vidya could only speculate about, though her instincts led her to believe that it was true. Despite all of this, she was still of the opinion that Harish's presence was going to be a positive factor, even if it would only be due to the lack of negative stimuli he would expose Saurabh to.

"Do you like him?" she asked Saurabh once.

"He is fine," he replied with a gentle smile that then quickly disappeared. "He gives a lot of work."

"And how about your other teacher?" she asked.

"I don't like her. She is weird."

Vidya was in her final two years at school and she still steadfastly wanted to work in a hospital like Shashi used to. She knew her parents didn't have the resources to send her to a proper medical school, and she also didn't want to go to one. She knew how Shashi had directly started working as a nurse at the hospital and was thus hoping that she could do the same. Earlier she had always thought that she would be working under Shashi at the local hospital, learning from her the entire time. While she knew that wasn't going to be possible for the time being, she still couldn't think of anything else she would want to do after finishing school. Somewhere in the back of her mind also lay the fear that her parents might start insisting on getting her married if she was unable to find a proper job; and as much as she was confident in her resoluteness to fight against any such coercion, she knew that a steady job would further help to support her argument.

An ally she had always relied on in this regard was Shashi, who she knew would support and encourage her to take her own decisions, sometimes even against her mother's liking. She had had a strong influence on Vidya, a fact that Lata could neither deny nor stop feeling slightly jealous about. It was from Shashi that she got her fierce sense of independence and the courage to do and say as she pleased. The only difference being that Shashi managed to accompany all of that with an amiable and pleasant personality, or at least she used to be able to do so.

But now, over the last few years, Vidya was aware of the distance that had developed between them. They weren't as close as they used to be, a feeling that had started becoming much more discernible once Shashi started staying at home to be with Saurabh. All her life, she had never known what it felt like to wake up in the morning without a definite purpose for the day and then spend it mostly indoors. This change had been a radical one, and the experience of living through it even more so. The impact it had on her demeanor was visible to all, especially Vidya. While Shashi, Lata, and Vidya saw much more of each other every day now, there wasn't the same liveliness and bustle of activity that Vidya had always associated with her. She seemed more and more weighed down by her current situation, unable to find her usual cheer in the face of this unforeseen adversity.

"Of course she must feel so horrible," Lata said to Mahesh. "Imagine being virtually imprisoned at home because of your own son."

"It is hard, yes."

"As a mother, I can't imagine what that must feel like. The shame of it! The dishonour!"

"You are making it sound much worse. I am sure it is a temporary situation."

"Especially for someone like Shashi!" she continued," not paying much attention to his response. "So full of life; so popular! She really must feel horrible. She probably thinks she has failed as a mother!"

Lata's histrionics aside, Vidya could easily see the evidence in Shashi of all that her mother had claimed. As more time went by, the more the marks of guilt, shame and despair etched itself across her face, heavily bearing down on her countenance. Vidya felt as if she was the only one who could empathize with her, the only person who could see the anger and anguish emanating from Shashi and relate to them with her own. Sometimes she longed to speak to her about it, to know exactly what was in her mind and whether it corresponded with her thoughts. But she was afraid to do so, unsure of what she would say, and unable to bear the thought of further hurting Shashi by her unfounded presumptions.

And so this was the new bond she shared with Saurabh's mother - once her best friend; a bond of mutual discontentment held taut by the one person they both loved the most. Each day she would walk back from school and find her sitting alone in the garden, mindlessly tending to her flowers, a mug of water and a pair of garden scissors in each hand. Her arms would work mechanically - a little snip here, a splash of water over there - going about their task in a perfunctory manner. She would raise her eyes at Vidya as she passed her by, breaking into a smile followed by an enthusiastic greeting. Vidya would respond similarly, but not as convincingly as she did. And then they would both quickly avert their gazes and be off on their own, unable to sustain the farce for a prolonged stretch of time; it was too difficult. Vidya would remember her mother's words, her assertion that Shashi probably blamed herself for Saurabh; and it was this strand of thought that made her believe that the look of sadness and despair on Shashi's face was, in fact, a look of guilt and torment. It was quite possible that it wasn't. But the more Vidya dwelt on the matter, the more she believed it, and all her powers of reasoning and logic contrived to confirm it. Yes, it was true, she thought. Why wouldn't Shashi blame herself? It was perfectly natural. As a result, it wasn't long before she reached another conclusion, which again seemed, on deep and constant reflection, inevitably true - she blamed herself as well. They had been, and still were, Saurabh's two most constant companions, and they both had failed. And so their mutual bond of discontentment was also a mutual bond of guilt, which was driving them further apart.

More than a year after Saurabh's expulsion, Vidya found her mother anxiously waiting for her when she reached home in the evening after school. There were tears in Lata's eyes and a stricken look of absolute aghast that instantly alarmed Vidya. Her first thought was of Shashi, whom she hadn't seen in the garden as usual, and following that her mind shifted to Saurabh. Things had been extremely quiet with him for a long time now and she wouldn't have been surprised if there had been a bit of an outburst. She looked expectantly at her mother, who was still gathering herself. Lata motioned Vidya to sit down and then proceeded to wipe her tears before speaking in between light sniffles.

"Vidya, please listen to me....and you have to agree," she began, in as firm a voice as she could manage after the strain of crying. "You just have to!"

"What is it?"

"Just promise you will agree!"

"I cannot do that," she replied indignantly and noticed a look on her mother's face that was a mixture of despair and irritation.

"God Vidya!......why are you always so difficult!....just listen then. You are not to meet Saurabh again. Never.....at least not for a long time."

"What happened?"

"He hurt Shashi! His own mother," she almost yelled and then burst into tears once again. She shook her head on seeing the questioning look on Vidya's face. Don't ask because I don't know the details. Shashi was here just a while before you came. She was hysterical, and I didn't ask much. All I know is that it happened yesterday and that she has a sprained ankle. But you see, don't you! There is no trusting that boy. I just cannot allow you. It's too dangerous."

"You are overreacting," she mumbled softly without any real conviction.

"I am not!!" yelled Lata and stood up so suddenly that she almost lost her balance. Her hair was frazzled from the number of times she had run her hands across them in frustration, complementing the look of anger on her face. "Why can't you listen! For once, I beg you!! I have not said anything all these years, have never stopped you from being with him even after everyone knew what he was capable of. And now we know he has no limits. His own mother! What are you, or any of us, in front of her?"

What was she indeed? thought Vidya. She looked down at her hands, which were entwined with one another, twisting and turning with force as her thoughts swarm in multiple directions. She was too overwhelmed to continue to argue with her mother. She hated the fact that she couldn't think of anything to counter Lata's opinion. As difficult as it was for her, she understood that Lata might just be right and that it would indeed be wise for her to not see Saurabh for some period. But then this had happened before. How could this ever end? When would they ever know whether it was safe or not? Wouldn't they worsen the situation by isolating him? Wasn't this an act of cowardice? Akin to an open declaration that they were giving up hope.

But at the same time, he had crossed a line that she hadn't believed he could. For the first time, even if for the briefest of moments, after which she felt guilty enough to berate herself, she feared for her safety and felt tempted to agree to her mother's conditions. Soon she was back though, her naturally argumentative self taking over the reins once again. There was much to think about. She hung her head limply and responded without looking at her mother.

"I'll think about it," she said and got up to go to her room, "I am not sure."

"Let your father come," Lata scorned. "We'll discuss it then."

The wait for her father proved to be unnecessary; Vidya wasn't given much time to think over the situation either. Shashi and Vinod visited them in the evening, and the four adults sat together to have a discussion of which Vidya was allowed to be a part. There wasn't much to discuss though. The Parashars had arrived at a conclusion already. An indefinite curfew had been imposed upon Saurabh. He was not to leave the house under any circumstances, barring an emergency, until which time they were going to decide the best way to proceed regarding his education.

"Maybe a boarding school," mentioned Vinod, but didn't say anything further.

"I am sorry Vidya," said Shashi. She was in tears throughout. "I don't think you should meet him for some time. How can I let something happen to you? It's unimaginable."

Vidya sat among them silently, neither venturing any opinion nor letting her expressions reveal them. Their discussion laboured for some more time as they all tried rather unsuccessfully to end the conversation on a spirited note. After the Parashars left, Vidya refused to eat and once again retired to her room. She sat on the edge of her bed and stared outside her window. It was fairly dark except for a patch of the Parashars' garden where the yellow light from the street lamp shone brightly; the light reached halfway to the top of Saurabh's window. But as much as Vidya strained her eyes, there was nothing visible for his room's lights were turned off, a black wall of impermeability settling between them.

CHAPTER 10

Vidya waited until she felt sure that her parents were sound asleep before she slowly opened her bedroom window. The sliding edges produced a little noise, but she wasn't too worried about it. She leapt across the window and landed on the grass outside. The grass felt damp and slippery under her feet. She closed the window, leaving it just a little ajar before walking across the road and on to the Parashars' garden. The window to Saurabh's room was unlatched; she was late. She rushed back again and started walking hurriedly down the main road, guided by the street lamps that shone the way at intermittent locations. It was a dark and cloudy night, with neither the moon nor the stars visible. She clung her hands close to her body, shivering just a little because of the cold drafts of wind that blew across the street.

At no moment did she feel scared or apprehensive about what she was doing. But that was only because she had undertaken this onerous venture before. That time, she had first resolved upon and then abandoned this idea, endlessly switching between these two states, constantly weighing the ramifications of getting caught. Her fears were not for herself. She wasn't worried as to what her parents would say or do to her if they found out about this. Her concern was for Saurabh; she didn't want him to go through any more unpleasant experiences. And so it took her a while to consider taking this risk.

On the first night, she had knocked carefully on Saurabh's window, her eyes constantly surveying in all directions, her ears primed for the slightest of noises. Saurabh took some time to respond, during which period Vidya had to anxiously stand outside his window. She fidgeted nervously the entire time and gasped with audible relief once she saw him approach the window in a dazed state. He had been asleep.

"Huh?" he said, rubbing his eyes and looking strangely at Vidya, as though he was meeting her for the first time.

"Let's go," she responded, surprised to feel a lump in her throat. "Quickly."

"Where?"

"The graveyard."

It had been more than two months since Saurabh's curfew, and the facts surrounding his incident with Shashi were still unclear. Only Shashi, Vinod, Saurabh and his teacher Harish knew about it, and they were all keeping silent. But Vidya was not particularly interested to find out more. She, like almost everyone else who knew about the matter, could make a fairly good assumption of what would have transpired. The details were unimportant. As was always the case, it took her some time to digest what Saurabh was capable of; a small period of reflection that inevitably brought back a rush of memories from all of his previous incidents, including the one only she had been a witness to. And as ever, her natural inclination to take Saurabh's side and not, what she liked to consider the narrow and prejudiced views of her parents, clashed against the undeniable evidence that presented itself after each successive incident. It was becoming increasingly difficult to ignore and disregard what her mother had been consistently warning her about.

But she knew she couldn't continue to fight and argue with her parents regarding this, less so with Shashi. And to achieve what? Be allowed to see him again? Get his curfew lifted? Those were shallow aims that offered temporary relief. The bigger and much more difficult goal was to make Saurabh one of them again; a constant and welcome part of their lives rather than just an object of dispiriting discussions. How was she to achieve that? By what means and to what end? She didn't have the answers to these questions. To her, the only viable solution that made sense was to not earnestly go about resolving the situation but to strongly rebel against it. That's what came naturally to her and so that's what she did, a decision that resulted in her standing outside Saurabh's window in the middle of the night.

That first night, a bewildered Saurabh had obediently followed Shashi to the graveyard. She had been extremely nervous, much more than Saurabh who had the look of someone confused about but somewhat indifferent to what he had been asked to do. They sat at their usual place for around an hour, neither of them talking much, unsure of what they were supposed to be doing or saying at that moment. It was a strange and uncomfortable feeling, further heightened by the long period of enforced absence. Still, for Vidya, there was a sense of accomplishment, a small triumph in the face of what she perceived as oppression. During that hour, she learned that the rumour, as propagated by her mother, of Saurabh being sent away to a boarding school was true. It was going to happen. But Saurabh himself was naturally not aware of the details. On their way back, they both silently separated to each other's homes, with the tacit understanding that these nightly ventures were to be undertaken regularly.

Lata, as expected, continued to indiscreetly talk about all that Shashi confided in her regarding Saurabh, and thus soon Vidya found out that he had been granted admission to a boarding school in one of the bigger towns of their neighbouring state, a town that was more than 600 kilometers away from Konkur.

"Why did they have to go so far?" she asked Mahesh.

"Vinod knew somebody. Someone from his days in college. It was easier."

"I don't know how this will help. I mean, him in the presence of all those boys away from their families. Surely he is going to get into more trouble."

"They know what they are doing."

"Hmm. What choice do they have, anyway! I mean, what choice has he left them? Oh, I feel so sorry for Shashi! I could never bear it!"

Now, that night, as Vidya made her way to the graveyard, a few months after their first nightly visit and the day before Saurabh was going to leave Konkur, it was this conversation that played repeatedly in her mind, in particular, her mother's dramatic exclamations at the end. She found Saurabh waiting for her inside and sat down next to him.

"Sorry I am late. They wouldn't sleep."

"It's okay."

"How long have you been here?"

"Ten minutes."

"When do you leave tomorrow?"

"At six in the morning."

"With your father?"

"Yes."

"It will be a long journey."

"Yes. Very long."

Vidya looked around at the silhouettes of the surrounding trees, their presence noticeable in the dark only because she knew they were there.

"I am going to leave too," she said. "Soon."

"Where?"

"I don't know. I'll get work as a nurse but not here. Not in this town."

"Why?"

Vidya looked at Saurabh and thought once again of the reasons she had been going over in her mind for a while now. Her final school year was going to end in a few months. While she didn't want to study further, she was determined to not sit idly at home and thus risk giving her parents any reason to consider getting her married. The idea of independent life, away from her parents and this town, greatly appealed to her, even if she was completely unaware as to what that would comprise of. Nevertheless, she knew that it was only by working that she could hope to achieve that. Her intention, of getting a job as a nurse, had remained steadfast from the very beginning, and she was still completely consumed by it. She had never considered or even thought to consider any other path. It almost felt as if this was a decision that had already been taken for her long ago, and now the only thing left to do was to carry through with it.

The thought of working at the local hospital at the Market Center, as appealing as it had been for a long time, now wasn't acceptable to her. Despite Saurabh's imminent departure, she wasn't sure whether Shashi would rejoin the hospital; and even if she did, she was no longer fascinated by the notion of working under her. Shashi's time at home with Saurabh had robbed her of all that Vidya had once found irresistible about her personality - her liveliness, her charm, and her vitality. Now she was a mere reflection of herself, a sad remnant of an enviable past, a broken and distraught woman who had been overwhelmed by all she had been forced to go through, especially since she had never imagined living her life the way she had been for a long time now. The relationship that Vidya had with her, that had formed such an integral part of her childhood, no longer existed. Shashi had been everything to her, but now she had been reduced to being an ineffective and impotent bystander, just like all the rest of them.

But this wasn't the only reason; neither was it the most pertinent one. Vidya was well aware of that. No matter in which direction her thoughts took her, there seemed to be a babble of stimuli coming at her from all sides, and she was trying desperately to mold and channel them in a way that would justify the decision she wanted to make.

She was just tired and frustrated and angry, but always found it exceedingly difficult to place the origin of it all, and thus was prone to direct her wrath at everyone in general but no one in particular. Of course, she was incensed by the way Saurabh was being treated by everyone and of course, that was the situation that troubled her the most. Perhaps everything was simply an offshoot of that. But for some reason, she wasn't convinced of it. Many times she felt close to the reason but it would always slip away, like an itch that was within reach but just impossible to place exactly.

And so amid this wave of anger and confusion, only one thought revealed itself clearly to her. She had started to hate Konkur, despise it in its entirety. She hated the people, the school, her classmates, her parents, Vinod, and now even Shashi. There was nothing left here for her. Only the town's picturesque surroundings still offered some sense of pleasure to her - the pond, the graveyard, the walk to school and back; these elements retained, yet, their majestic nature, especially since she could relate Saurabh with them. But now that he too was going away, she knew she would lose this connection as well, and thus could no longer see any reason to remain here.

"I don't like this place anymore," she replied to him.

"Will they let you go?"

Vidya shrugged. "I don't know. They won't agree. But I will go anyway."

A little smile escaped Vidya's lips as she remembered how her mother, when she had been speaking about Saurabh's departure, had exclaimed at how difficult Shashi would find sending her child away. And now she would have to face it herself, she thought, and this realization's ironic nature amused her to a certain extent.

"I don't like this place either," said Saurabh. None of it. I just like it here."

He raised his arms and made a large sweep in front of him, capturing as much of the graveyard as he could within that tiny arc.

"I don't know when we will come back here again," said Vidya. "I don't think anyone will. We were always the only two people here."

"There are so many others," he said, pointing at the grave markers. Vidya followed the direction of his outstretched hand. The white headstones were visible in the dark, and her eyes sought out those patterns etched on the markers that were so familiar by now and yet meant nothing to them. "So many people. They are not afraid of me, are they?"

Vidya raised her eyebrows and glanced questioningly at him. He had a calm and placid expression on his face, nowhere in conjunction with the allusive nature of the question he had asked. Was that a reproach, thought Vidya? Was it directed towards her? Was that the first time Saurabh had ever expressed his feelings at being treated the way he had been for so long? Or was it simply rhetorical? In any case, she felt compelled to place her hand on his shoulder and say something.

"I am not afraid of you."

"I know," he said as if amused by the suggestion that she would be afraid of him. "You are here."

"Yes. Do you want to go back now? You have to leave early."

"Just a little more time."

The two continued to just sit where they were, looking around at nothing in the darkness. Vidya could feel her other senses heightening to compensate for the lack of sight. She was still shivering a bit because of the cold, and now she could even sense the rustle of her clothes as the wind lapped gently across her body. The hum of the insects felt vaguely rhythmic to her, interspersed as they were by the movement of leaves and branches. She dug her hands in the earth tightly and leaned back, staring into the sky above. She could feel the onset of tears and she tried to overcome them by tilting her head as far back as she could. They rolled through anyway, sliding down her cheeks before getting absorbed by her clothes. She resisted the urge to wipe them away with her palm.

"Let's go," tapped Saurabh on her shoulder and she looked away from him and got up. She felt a little disoriented but then soon gathered herself. They walked back slowly the way they had come and climbed back in through their respective windows. Vidya lay onto her bed and closed her eyes, trying to fall asleep.

The bus driver honked violently to wake up his passengers as he slowly brought the vehicle to a halt. Vidya woke and glanced out of her window, the familiar sights of the Market Center coming into her view. She grabbed her bag and got down from the bus, her entire body aching from the long and tiring journey. A thick throng of rickshaw and auto drivers rushed at the travelers, offering their services with vehement enthusiasm.

"10 rupees per person Madam," said one directly to Vidya, pointing towards his rickshaw and automatically taking a step forward to grab her luggage. "Where do you have to go?"

"No no," said Vidya, shaking her head vigorously. "I'll walk."

Part 2

The mass of men lead lives of quiet desperation

Henry David Thoreau
(Walden & Civil Disobedience)

CHAPTER 11

Vinod sat in dazed silence, his knees joined together, his shoulders tucked inward in an uncomfortable position, a small plastic smile dangling on his lips. His eyes roamed slowly around his surroundings without registering anything in particular. It was essential that they continue to move in this manner, lest they fell immobile and revealed the exceedingly heightened level of boredom and annoyance that he was struggling to fight against.

His mother and his father's sister flanked him on both sides, sitting in such perfectly synchronized and dignified postures that Vinod suspected they had practiced them beforehand. Their smiles were very similar too, appearing much more genuine than Vinod's, showing just the right number of teeth. Occasionally, when facing Vinod, their smiles were accompanied by raised eyebrows and bulging eyes, urging him to follow their example.

The plastic chair on which he sat creaked noisily every time he moved even a little, which only further added to his discomfort. The house they were in was fairly similar to their own. The walls were a light shade of yellow, covered mostly by wooden shelves and some old portraits of people he assumed were deceased family members.

They all looked as if they were in a state of slow decay, even though they had been thoroughly cleaned and dusted that very morning. A small fan hung directly above them and rotated with loud mechanical grunts, which helped to somewhat mask the creaking of his chair.

In front of him sat the girl and her parents, bending slightly forward with their ears pricked to not miss a single word, their expressions betraying a feeling of obsequiousness that went much beyond hospitality. The father was tall and lean, with a rectangular face that was well framed by his round spectacles and covered with a head of neatly receding hair. Altogether, he looked the most presentable of the three, and also the most comfortable. The girl and her mother wore ill-fitting clothes with such jarringly bright colours that any onlooker couldn't have noticed anything else about them. Between the two families lay a small table on which was placed a tray of teacups. Vinod had refused one initially but had been served anyway. His meandering eyes took all of this in - the medley of colours, the furniture, the noises, the people, the contrived smiles and appearances.

"What's your name?" his mother asked her in an affectedly gentle manner.

"Shashi."

The casual and genuine confidence in her voice made Vinod take notice of Shashi for the first time. She looked fairly young to him, not more than twenty, but then it was hard to judge exactly as she was completely dwarfed by what she was wearing. Even so, she looked as tall as her father. Vinod could see that she had noticed him gazing at her, which, much to his surprise, only resulted in her returning the favour rather unabashedly.

"What do you do?"

"I have finished my studies. I am going to be a nurse."

The moment went away and Vinod once again found refuge in his somber mood. He stared past the three people sitting in front of him, no longer even trying to pretend that he was interested. Behind the three, there was a small window that had a view of the street. He thought he would much rather have been outside, or at home, or at the office, anywhere but here. He didn't pay any attention to the ongoing conversation and instead picked up his cup of tea and started to drink for the sheer want of doing something. He felt determined to say yes solely to not undergo this experience once again, but he was quite aware of the fact that his behaviour until that point wasn't necessarily going to elicit a yes from the other side as well.

Vinod's father had died when he was barely twelve years old. If at that time, anyone had asked Vinod how he had felt, he would have found it almost impossible to express true grief and would have simply shrugged his shoulders. His father's death had not been a surprise to anyone, least of all to his own family. He had been a pathological drunkard, whose misadventures with alcohol grew periodically worse as the years rolled by. He wasn't a violent man, nor was he abusive or belligerent - traits that are easily and stereotypically attributed to alcoholics - and thus Vinod and his mother were never really endangered by his inebriated presence. No, the problem had always been financial. They were a family of extremely limited means, a bulk of which were drowned each evening at the local wine shop. And if Vinod's mother ever tried to make this point across to him, his response was always the same.

"I can't help it," he would say in a tone of indifference. "It's in my genes, you know. My father.....my grandfather.....all drank till the point they died."

But before he drank himself to death, he brought them nearly to the point of ruin. Alcohol had made him lazy and incompetent. He was thrown out from all of his workplaces and soon just didn't have the energy or the skills to find more jobs. The frequent cessations of income, while forcing the family to adopt several austere measures around the house, did not affect his intake of alcohol. He just began to drink cheaper whiskey from more and more unreliable sources, while Vinod's mother took up odd jobs around the town to somehow keep him in school for as long as she could.

She loved her son dearly and was immensely thankful that he

had somehow managed to not get affected by his father's unhealthy presence. He always did well enough in school, and ever since his mother discovered this about him, his studies became a matter of extreme importance to her, something she wouldn't allow to be sacrificed because of her drunk husband.

Within a year of being permanently unemployed, Vinod's father's health started to deteriorate rather quickly. He aged rapidly, becoming more and more feeble as time passed, to the extent that he needed a wooden stick to walk around before he had even reached the age of forty. His skin had become pale, his cheeks were drawn out with wrinkles, his eyes sunk so deep within their sockets that his entire face started to resemble that of a skeleton. He was prone to recurring bouts of indigestion, which would then frequently lead to diarrhea. Everyone knew what the cause and the cure was, but they also knew that there was no point in talking to him about it. His death was inevitable and they, including him, had all realized that a long time ago.

When one morning they found him dead in his bed, his mouth fully open, his eyes gazing lifelessly at the ceiling as he lay in a pool of his vomit, Vinod's mother quickly said a prayer of thanks and hugged her son with an apparent sense of relief. Vinod shared that feeling with her as they stood there embracing each other in front of his father's dead body. They were finally going to get a chance to live without a heavy anchor tied to their feet, constantly weighing them down. They felt free, free to rebuild their lives in the manner they wanted to.

And so they tried. Her late husband's sister, the only member of his family he had managed to not estrange, helped her to get a permanent job with a local tailor who found her sewing skills on the machine to be satisfactory. The work was hard and monotonous. It consisted of sitting for hours in the same spot, straining her eyes on a piece of cloth as one of her hands repeatedly struck the wheel of the sewing machine, whirring it into action. As tedious as the job was, she was quite happy and content with it, especially as she found it a much better alternative to working as a maid in various households. There was more money in it, as well as more dignity. However, the nature of the work was such that it didn't allow her much time to spend with her son. Each day, she left early in the morning, almost the same time as Vinod would go to school, and then came back by late evening, at which point she would cook dinner for them both. She barely had energy left over to do anything but fall asleep. So effectively dinner was the only time that they had with each other. Even during the weekends, when Vinod was mostly at home, she was at the shop, following the same rigorous schedule. As gentle, kind and empathetic the tailor was, he never allowed any compromise with his work. There was simply no respite for her. She had to work more than twelve hours a day, seven days a week, and yet she did so conscientiously, rarely falling prey to the appeals of exhaustion her body made from time to time. She knew how fortunate she was to have the opportunity to work and thus earn enough to sustain her family, while simultaneously managing to afford her son an education.

Vinod saw his mother's tireless efforts, the level of pain and discomfort she was ready to bear for him. He worked harder than before, with a greater focus on his studies. He wasn't the smartest kid or the top scorer, and neither was there any particular subject or class that he preferred more over the other ones. But he developed a love for reading, and re-reading, without getting attached to any particular genre. He devoured through his school books with a great sense of pleasure and found in himself a natural affinity for learning. His penchant for studies was limited to the process of it, which, as a natural but unintentional consequence, helped him with his results as well. Thus, he sailed through his years in school without much difficulty, and with a sense of happiness and contentment that he thought could never possibly go away. He was convinced, with such overwhelming surety, that he would never be happier than he was during those years in school and thus resolved to somehow continue to live the life of a student for as long as he could.

Oblivious to each other's thoughts, Vinod and his mother held much-contrasting beliefs about his future and continued to play through their fantasies in their heads. For her, his average academic prowess was far greater than she had ever hoped for or seen before in their family through generations, and thus she read much more in it than was actually there. She felt extremely proud of him, confident that he would manage to get a good job, live a good and decent life as an honourable man while providing well for his family - something his father had failed miserably at.

"I think you should work in a bank," she would say to him often, smiling and day-dreaming about his future. "A good comfortable job with fixed hours. There would be good enough money, and I know any bank would take you! I am sure of it!"

She would easily lose herself in such thoughts, projecting events several years in the future, and then nodding satisfactorily to herself when they all seemed to align in her mind just the way she wanted. And how could Vinod blame her for such whimsical notions? She, who worked so hard each day of her life, just so her son had the realistic opportunity to harbour such dreams, even if they weren't his own....she, who was beginning to feel the pain, in her back and her limbs, of sitting in the same position each day, and who was sure that she would gradually lose her eyesight to the sewing machine. How could he say anything to her? Each time his mother spoke to him about all the things that could be, he just smiled plainly and without much feeling, quietly nodding along, choosing to vest himself in his fantasies, much in contrast with his mother's, avoiding, as long as he could, the imminent clash of them both.

"And what do you do?" asked the father, looking questioningly at Vinod, who was conspicuously lost in his thoughts, and required a poorly concealed nudge from his mother to make him focus once again.

"Ah...I am sorry?"

"Where do you work?"

"At the Municipal Corporation. In the public health department. I look after the accounts and finances."

"That's really nice," he said, smiling gracefully, and shifted his gaze towards his wife and daughter, as if checking to see whether they agreed with him. The two didn't catch his gaze. The mother looked suitably impressed, while the daughter appeared rather indifferent to the entire matter.

Vinod took a sip of tea. It had gone really cold. He had been holding the cup for a while now, without drinking from it. He set it down on the table and leaned back on his chair. He felt like sleeping.

The clash inevitably came once Vinod finished school and brought up the question, for the first time, of going to college to continue his studies. She was more bemused than surprised, unable to comprehend why her son wanted to study further when he could easily build a nice life for himself here and settle down. And to which college? There were none in this town. The only college she knew of was hundreds of kilometers away. That would mean that he would have to leave town. But what good would that do? What was it for? And what did he wish to accomplish from that?

Vinod, of course, had no response to these questions that could possibly satisfy his mother. He wished to go because there was much more he wished to learn; many more books to read; many more subjects to think about. But more than all that, he just didn't want it to end. He wanted his present life to go on, to be able to follow the routine he had been following for the past several years. It didn't matter to him if he went to college or if they extended school for a few more years - it was all the same to him. But he couldn't say that to his mother. Thus he decided to take the help of someone whose opinion he felt his mother might appreciate - the school's Principal.

Vinod requested him to come to their house one evening after her mother was back from work. They all sat together near the small kitchen, a cup of tea in their hands. Vinod's mother was feeling rather despondent, the Principal's presence revealing her son's rather determined outlook. She smiled at him but didn't initiate any conversation to begin with. He had the look of a stereotypical academic - grey trousers and a white shirt on top of which he wore a light grey woolen sweater, which well hid his widening girth. He had a round irregular face with a big broad nose on which rested his thick spectacles. Vinod looked at him pleadingly.

"It isn't like the old days Mrs. Parashar. With just a school degree, what do you think he can become? An assistant maybe....a clerk. But not much," he said to her in a thin and feeble voice that didn't correspond to his exterior personality.

"How many people in our town have gone to college?" she asked indignantly. "They are all doing fine."

"It isn't the same now. The times have changed," he repeated himself, for want of any other argument. "He wants to study. That is a remarkable thing in itself. Let him go."

"And then what? What will he study?"

"Practical things...accounts...bookkeeping...doing taxes...you know he is good with numbers. This way he would find a much better job with good pay. A government job perhaps. I assure you."

"How expensive will it be?"

He looked towards Vinod with trepidation. "Not a lot. It will be a government college. But more expensive than the school of course. Plus the hostel and his food... it won't be that easy. That's for sure."

Vinod looked down to not catch his mother's eye. This was the one question he had struggled to come up with an answer for.

"I suppose I will just have to work harder."

His Principal left soon after making his pitch and the two of them sat down to have dinner. Vinod's mother was still reluctant, but it felt to him that she was now on the verge of acquiescence. He ate his meal in silence, waiting for her to say something. He had to wait a while.

"So you really want to go?" she began. There were tears in her eyes. "For how long."

"Two years. Three maybe."

"On one condition."

This was how it was done. Vinod beamed with happiness, hardly able to concentrate to hear what her mother's condition was. His inadequately focused mind heard something about him coming back immediately after college and then doing what she told him to. He agreed to everything - readily and wholeheartedly. The stipulations didn't seem to matter to him at all then. They were trivial in comparison to what now lay ahead of him for the next few years. All he knew or could think of at the time was that he now had three more years to study and place himself in an environment he was most comfortable in.

They all stood up and folded their hands together, as dictated the norms of mutual courtesy. Shashi's parents accompanied the three of them outside till their gate. Once at a safe distance away from their house, on their way to the nearby bus-stand, Vinod's mother turned angrily towards him.

"What was that Vinod! You had promised you would behave well," she said with her eyes piercing into him. She then turned towards her sister-in-law. "We better forget about this one."

That very evening, only a few hours after they had reached home after the long bus ride, Vinod's mother received a call from Shashi's father, affirming their willingness to go ahead with this marriage proposal. Much surprised and stunned by the call, she immediately put the question to Vinod, not expecting a positive reply from his side, especially after his performance earlier that day. Once again she was taken aback when Vinod barely took a few moments to digest the offer and nodded without any apparent hesitation.

In the days that followed, her sense of excitement and glee were marred by a cloud of confusion regarding the extremely surprising chain of events. She questioned Vinod a few times who, as usual, gave her rather terse and non-committal responses. She couldn't question Shashi's parents, at least not so soon, and thus simply tried to let the feeling of revelry and joy push away her doubts and concerns. She began to invest herself in what she faithfully believed as the most important duty of her life.

The two families were of extremely modest means and thus they agreed to have just one or two simple ceremonies to mark the occasion. Even so, she undertook them with great zeal and vigour, receiving limited help from her son who was dutiful enough to do anything that was asked of him but refused to show even a little hint of enthusiasm. But she didn't let that affect her greatly. She strongly believed in the cohesive powers of time, habit and families, and was sure that her son too would eventually be held sway by them.

The ceremonies came and went, a whirlwind of colours and music, bright, loud and gaudy enough to further make Vinod disassociate himself from the process. Without making any effort to hide his evident displeasure and lack of interest, he was still respectful enough of his mother's wishes in order to not let his demeanor seem like a mark of disapproval, but simply a reflection of tension and nervousness - two traits that he felt would be more forgivable. He barely spoke with Shashi or the rest of her family during the interim period, despite his mother urging him several times to do so. He started to spend more and more time at the office, as their home was hijacked by a throng of relatives he neither knew well nor wished to know any better. The amount of money his mother seemed willing and capable of spending shocked him deeply. Their whole lives they had lived under an immense financial strain, and it was only after his father's death that the tight grip of austerity around their necks had slackened its hold a bit. But once more, he decided not to question her and simply played along.

The day of the wedding itself was long, arduous and painful. For hours he found himself sitting on an overly decorated chair next to Shashi, a caricature of a man, a dressed-up mannequin waiting for the approach of strangers who would smile and shake his hands vigorously before getting their photos clicked with them both. There were dances and songs, always to the accompaniment of inappropriately loud music. Time went by unendurably slowly as the procession of people started to dwindle bit by bit, until the only thing keeping them from finishing the ceremony was the arrival of the auspicious hour, which clearly had no regard for the people who were waiting for it. Vinod was tired, sleepy, uncomfortable, and in a very bad mood.

Shashi was beside him during this entire ordeal. Up till a certain moment, he had been rather oblivious to the pain she too would have been suffering under. He had hardly said a word to her the whole night, apart from the few cursory greetings at the very beginning. But as they neared the end, the overwhelming fatigue made him overcome any sense of propriety he had been feeling until then.

'"This is too hard," he said impulsively to her.

"It's hard for you?" she replied almost immediately with a short laugh. "Look at what I am wearing!"

It was at that moment that Vinod focused on his bride-to-be for the very first time that evening and had to admit that his own woes seemed significantly less important if her clothes were taken into context. She was covered in a shimmering and heavy red-coloured dress, the outlines of which were accentuated by broad golden borders on which were stuck many tiny mirrors. It reminded him of the day he had seen her for the first time at her parents' house, drowning beneath her clothes.

"Why did you say 'Yes'?"

"Sorry?"

"Why did you agree to this marriage?"

Shashi looked at him intently for a few moments, unsure whether he was asking her seriously or in jest. She took some time to respond.

"The day you were supposed to come," she began tentatively at first and then grew in confidence, "my mother and I prepared extensively. She made me cook all the items we served in the evening while she cleaned the entire house. The *entire* house. She had a piece of dirty cloth in her hand the whole day, going from one corner to the next, wiping all photo frames, the wall clock, climbing a ladder to clean the fans, removing the smallest of cobwebs from the walls, dusting the chairs and the tables. She even scrubbed clean the kitchen and the washroom. I had already decided I was going to say 'Yes' even before you came. I just didn't want her to go through all of this once again."

Vinod nodded and turned away from her, once again staring blankly ahead of him. They were well past midnight now but the end still didn't seem that imminent. He shifted in his chair and tried to make himself more comfortable for the hundredth time. Unsuccessful, he closed his eyes for a moment and tried to block out all the sound and music that reverberated around them.

CHAPTER 12

The first few weeks of Vinod's three-year period away from home were a constant source of bewildering experiences.

The room he was allotted in the hostel had to be shared with three other students, all of whom were from the same city. They could barely understand his particular dialect of Hindi and thus he had to get by using expressions and sign language. He had a single bed and one small cupboard to himself, which was just about sufficient to house all the things his mother had supplied him with. For days he didn't dare to unpack, operating out of the bags he had brought along with him, unsure of how he was to go about arranging his affairs.

The extent of freedom he now had at his disposal was both terrifying and exhilarating. He wasn't used to making decisions for himself, especially those that were concerned with food, money or even studies. He soon discovered the difference between the teachers at school and the professors in college, and initially, he wasn't so sure whether he enjoyed this particular distinction. He was lost within a sea of other students like him, many of whom were much smarter than the smartest ones at his school. The pace of learning was fast, almost bordering on frantic, and, for the first time, he found himself struggling to keep abreast with many of the other students. It all seemed so chaotic and direction-less to him. His penchant for learning, which had always come so naturally to him, suddenly seemed insufficient.

Apart from academics, he was finding it equally hard to manage his finances. He was shocked at how easily he seemed to be spending money without really meaning to do so. Whether it be for books or stationery or food, he was quickly going through a sum of money he had thought would last him twice as long. It was with great trepidation and a sense of shame that he called his mother to ask for more. If there was anything that was troubling him as much as these two concerns, it was that of finding a place for himself among the horde of students. He wasn't comfortable making friends easily; he never had been and had never felt the need to do so while in school.

At a time when he was feeling more alienated and lost than ever before, questioning his decision to enroll himself in a college, drowning in guilt over the financial strain he was inflicting on his mother, he latched himself even more strongly to the one passion he had always cared about and which hadn't, yet, failed him. He read. He read profusely. The quantity and the diverse range of books available at the university's library were beyond his imagination. He had never seen these many books under the same roof. It took him around a week simply to explore all the different sections that were maintained inside. By the end of that week, there was one clear thought in his mind - he knew that an opportunity like this was never going to present itself to him ever again and he had to take full advantage of it during his time here. Initially, most of the books that he read were related to his subjects, a mixture of mathematics and statistics - practical studies as suggested by his school's principal. It seemed inevitable that he was going to chance upon a myriad of other topics and be exposed to many worlds, all varying greatly from one another, and especially from the ones he was supposed to be reading about. But he just didn't know from where to start, and so, for some time, he continued to focus solely on his course books.

Vinod's first brush with literature, apart from the small abridged stories he had read at school, was the result of a combination of two factors - his almost constant presence at the university's library and a seventy-year-old retired man who worked as its librarian.

"Don't you have friends?" he asked Vinod once when he placed his usual set of books in front of him to get them issued. "And don't you read anything else."

Vinod was taken aback for a moment and blinked silently at the old man. "I have some friends," he managed eventually.

"Here. Try this," he placed a thin book in front of him. "And then tell me. It's good to have a change sometimes."

Vinod glanced at the book titled "The Boatman of the Padma" and then looked questioningly towards the old man. "Is it a story?"

"You can tell me that later."

"My English isn't that good."

"It will improve."

The book became Vinod's constant companion from then onwards until the time he finished it, during which period he continued to read a few pages from it every day as and when he got the time. The words in it, as much as he recognized them independently, were placed together in combinations he wasn't used to seeing. He laboured and struggled through it, never managing to flow through the pages as he did with his other books. There was no linearity of thought and action, to which he was accustomed, neither was there a predictable direction towards which it seemed to be progressing. The book, despite its short length, weighed heavily on his mind and continuously distracted him. There were moments that engaged him completely, enthralled and captivated him in a manner he had never expected words to do so. But they were also accompanied by periods of acute dullness when he found his eyes automatically skimming over lines without registering the content. This made him stop and then begin again from the point after which he had stopped comprehending, an activity that was prone to being repeated. A few times, he even considered returning the book without reading it, but some part within him didn't feel inclined to disappoint the librarian, though he wasn't sure why.

It took him almost a month to complete it. He went to the library in search of the old man who, as expected, was sitting calmly at his usual seat behind the small desk at one end of the room. He saw him immediately and smiled. Vinod walked up to him and placed the book on his desk.

"I read it."

The librarian picked up the book, ran his palm over the cover before gently rustling through the pages. "And? What did you think?"

"I don't know," he said, his tone betraying a sense of frustration. "I liked some parts. It was confusing. It was difficult. I don't think I understood all of it."

"That's good. You are being honest."

The old man got up from his chair and disappeared behind one of the sections of the library. Vinod waited for him. He wasn't surprised when the old man returned with a different book in his hand.

"Now try this one. It is a little tougher. You'll manage I think."

Vinod took the book and inspected the cover - *The Red Badge of Courage*. He then looked at the old man who was smiling once again.

"Why are you doing this?"

"I like it," he said and then casually shrugged his shoulders. "It's a hobby of mine. I do it with other students as well."

In this way began the only meaningful relationship Vinod was to develop during his three years in college. With the help of the old librarian, he discovered one book after another across many genres; from fiction to philosophy to science to poetry, the old man was relentless in his pursuit to make Vinod read everything he himself enjoyed or had enjoyed reading at some point. In the beginning, Vinod continued to oscillate between feelings of exhilaration and bewilderment, rapture and ennui, unsure of this new taste that he was almost being forced to develop. He trusted the old man completely, never questioning his judgment or showing signs of disinclination. He was like a blind horse whose reigns were held by a maverick steward as they traveled across mystical paths with ever-changing landscapes. The steward ensured that his horse grew more and more comfortable with the terrain until the time when he could confidently let go, without fearing that the horse might turn around, and the two could finally travel together as companions.

The change that slowly but inevitably took place within Vinod happened gradually and incrementally, such that he couldn't easily notice it at the time. It was only after he had spent almost two years away from home that he looked back at the self who had joined this college and was stunned by the difference between them. He was no longer the demure, unassuming and hardworking young boy who had come from a small town and had been overwhelmed by the life of the city. Now if he had met that boy, he would have looked at him with surprise and contempt, aghast at the lack of maturity and knowledge. He believed his present self to be at the peak of conscious thought, an individual with firm beliefs and opinions, strengthened and backed by his friends from the world of literature. He was an ever-changing product of what he read, a dynamic personification of ideas borrowed from Thoreau, Wilde, Tolstoy, Orwell, etc. At the same time, he too was aware of the dynamic nature of his firm beliefs and the fact that while he may be filled with a superfluous feeling of disdain towards anyone whose thoughts were not in harmony with his, he too, with each passing moment, although with diminishing vitriol, was derisive of his own past. The only other person who had been a part of his transition was, of course, the librarian. The two were now partners in crime, aiding and abetting each other's interests and mannerisms, constantly reinforcing their now commonly held beliefs.

Vinod wasn't surprised when his performance in class started to decline steadily, though he was a bit taken aback at the lack of concern this seemed to elicit out of him. By his final year, he was barely attending classes, focusing just enough to ensure that he didn't fail.

He knew this would greatly disappoint his mother and further give her ammunition to question his decision to continue with his studies. He managed to scrape through his final exams, after which he had no choice but to leave the college and reluctantly go back home.

Any concern Vinod had regarding his mother's reaction to finding about his academic performance was put to rest the first day he reached home. She had been prepared for his return and quickly made him aware of the two objectives she had in mind for him - work and marriage. For her, his three-year sojourn in the city had purely been a superficial matter, undertaken only to satisfy her son's whim and thus had no bearing on the future she had planned.

But this wasn't the Vinod who had left her three years ago, who would have unquestioningly obeyed her mother's wishes. This Vinod, while quite open to the suggestion of getting a job, scorned at the prospect of marriage. He visibly showed disgust at his mother's proposition, arguing against the lack of rationality in her thought process.

"But why should I?" he asked. "What's the point?"

"What do you mean?" she asked, annoyed and confused. "You have studied all you want. You are 21 years old. There is nothing else to wait for."

The two of them had many conversations of such nature, during which neither seemed to be listening to the other but simply reiterating their own point of view. There appeared to be nothing they could say to reconcile or arrive at a certain common understanding. It wasn't just a difference in opinion that hindered this process of reconciliation but something far more entrenched and rigid - a difference in the manner of thinking, not in beliefs but in the method they used to arrive at them. There was never going to be a solution and they both knew it, a fact that greatly frustrated Vinod because he could foresee the end and was aware that it wasn't going to be favourable for him. As much as he wished to continue to argue against her, he couldn't because of the advantage she would always hold over him by virtue of the nature of their relationship. She was his mother; the woman who had endured his alcoholic father, had brought him up in almost abject poverty, had worked so hard and sacrificed so much to educate him, and had then, against her wishes, let him go away to the city for three years. It was this combination of love, guilt, and respect that made him relent. Less than a year after his return, he found himself sitting in Shashi's house, drinking a cup of lukewarm tea and pretending, rather unconvincingly, to be interested in the young woman who sat in front of him.

On the day of their marriage, when Shashi confided in Vinod her reason to accept his family's proposal, he began to finally see her as a companion in this mutually distressful situation rather than one of the main causes of it. Her revelation made him think about what her situation might have been. He imagined her parents coaxing her to get married against her wishes and without her consent, which was somewhat applicable in his case as well. He didn't know whether this was true or not and he didn't ask her. But he found himself empathizing with her to a certain degree. It was she who would have to leave her house and her town and then begin to live with strangers. The situation was indeed much more unfair to her.

But Vinod didn't know what to do with this realization. He didn't know how to speak with her or around her. His only example of seeing a married couple be together for a sustained period was that of his parents, which wasn't of any help at all. What was she thinking? What was she like? Were they both suffering equally in isolation? Should he ask her about that? Could he? And would that make things better? Her demeanor was not suggestive of anything concrete. She seemed comfortable around her mother and some neighbours, even more so than him. She could even converse confidently with him, without letting any sign of awkwardness slip through. But was that real or just a quirk of personality?

"Are you happy?" he managed to ask her one day, ensuring that his mother was not within hearing distance. It was the shortest question he could think of.

"I am not sad," she replied, somewhat amused, which only further added to his confusion.

At the same time, his job was an unsatisfactory medium of escape. The work was tedious, repetitive and felt trivial. He worked as a junior accounts manager for the local municipality, whose jurisdiction was limited to their small town. There was no real challenge, and worse than that, no real-time to engage in some other activity. Once at home, he was surrounded by his wife and mother, with the latter explicitly wanting him to spend his evenings with them. This drastic change in lifestyle as compared to his days at the university bitterly frustrated and angered him - emotions he couldn't even display openly. He was anguished by the fact that he was barely reading anymore, which he would have thought utterly unacceptable a few years back. He craved for his freedom, yearned for some time he could call his own, and often thought about the old librarian and how he would have been disappointed with him.

"This isn't right" reprimanded his mother. "You can't treat her this way."

"I am not doing anything."

"You are alienating her. She is your wife."

"I don't know what to do."

"Talk to her. Spend some meaningful time with her," she added, visibly irritated. "You hardly react to anything. Do you think it's fair?"

"It isn't fair to me."

"Is that all you can think about? What about her? She is home the entire day, bored and listless. And when you came back, it's almost worse. I feel that she should get a job, the poor thing."

Vinod looked up at his mother with surprise. "Wasn't she supposed to be a nurse?"

"I don't know. Why don't you ask her? She is your wife. You probably never thought about it."

It was true. He hadn't. All this while, while he sat in the office, working and mulling over the depressing nature of his daily life, Shashi was at home, probably doing the same, without even the work to distract her. For a moment, he envied the amount of time she had for herself without being encumbered by his presence. But this thought was soon replaced by the feeling of guilt.

"You worked...or were going to...as a nurse?" he asked her that very day. "I remember you had said that."

"I had started for a while," she replied, surprised by the unexpected question.

"Don't you want to continue?"

"I would like that," she smiled and then added circumspectly, "If it isn't a problem."

"Of course it isn't," said Vinod quickly. He lowered his head and rubbed his palms slowly in front of him. "I am sorry. We...I never asked. I should have."

"It's okay."

"Why didn't you say something?"

"My mother told me not to."

Vinod shook his head and then looked straight at her. "There are only two small hospitals here. Let's find out something. I'll try."

"Thank you."

Vinod, overcome by guilt and shame, made the necessary inquiries. It wasn't too difficult to find a job for Shashi. Both the hospitals were always short of staff and thus Shashi simply picked the one nearer to their house. It was the first real instance of good news, the first celebratory moment that they all together were a part of. Vinod's mother was happy that her son had finally, actively and without much provocation, done something solely for the benefit of Shashi.

However, barely a few weeks after Shashi had started working, Vinod was told that he was being transferred to the nearby town of Konkur. For his mother, the news was quite unsettling. She had already spent three years alone without her son, and now, just under two years post his return, after he had gotten married, he was going to go away again, that too just at the point when she felt his relationship with Shashi was beginning to develop. For Vinod and Shashi, the thought of the transition was less troubling, even if it were a little intimidating. They were now going to have to live independently with only each other for company. Up until this point, their relation had hinged heavily on the presence of Vinod's mother. But now they would have to get used to the absence of that buffer.

"Promise me," she implored him. "You will be good to her."

"I will."

"I know you don't love her."

"Neither does she."

"But that shouldn't matter. You have to learn to live together; listen and compromise whenever possible."

"We'll try," he tried to reassure her, but it was evident that he was not succeeding.

"You *have* to," she cried, on the verge of tears. "Otherwise soon it will be too late to try. And then you shall just resent each other."

CHAPTER 13

The small house slowly rolled into view. Shashi, sitting in the rickshaw alongside Vinod, stared excitedly at their new home. The garden was the first thing to grab her attention. They both climbed down gingerly, tired from their long and uncomfortable bus ride. Their luggage was following them on two separate rickshaws, which arrived soon after them. Their belongings were unloaded right on the street before Vinod paid the three rickshaw pullers.

"It's nice," said Shashi, looking at Vinod who nodded in agreement. It was much better than he had thought it would be.

There was a small path cutting right through the garden that led to the main door. On its either side were two large windows, through one of which they could see a small bedroom with the help of sunlight that fell directly on it. This wasn't the case with the other window at that time of the day. The outer walls were pale yellow, the plaster breaking a bit at places after years of neglect.

"No one has lived here for many years," he said.

"You never mentioned that," she remarked, raising her eyebrows.

"Must have forgotten."

"It still looks fine though."

"They fixed it a little."

The roof appeared to be made from a metal frame, sloping gradually from right to left. It was covered with numerous broken leaves and twigs, which could easily be seen from where they were standing. Through that jungle of waste rose a small brick chimney. There was a narrow metal ladder fixed to the left wall of the house, given, they assumed, to climb onto the roof and clean it. It was an activity that would have to be undertaken frequently, thought Vinod.

The garden, though in shambles, was nevertheless green and robust. The grass was thick and overgrown but not to an extent that would have appeared congruous to years of disuse. Even some bushes at the front had been trimmed and a few patches of flowers grew at intermittent intervals. Evidently, the garden had been somewhat taken care of.

Slowly they carried their bags and put them just inside the main door. It took them a few trips to get everything. In front of them was a small living room with four chairs, two wooden and two plastic ones, with a central wooden table. On their right was the kitchen, which had a row of recessed panels built right inside the walls; they were empty. There were a few more shelves and drawers near the bottom, which Shashi opened one by one to verify that they too were completely bare. The kitchen's sole occupant was a rectangular stove with a cylinder of gas. They were kept right in the middle of the kitchen, waiting to be assembled.

Shashi walked towards a door that stood just between the living and the kitchen room wall. She opened it, peeped inside, and then nodded her head in apparent approval.

"It's the bathroom. It's bigger than ours."

Vinod walked away from the living room, towards his left were two more doors, placed nearby on adjacent walls, led to the two bedrooms. The one on the right was much bigger. It had a wooden dresser with a mirror and one steel cupboard just in front of the double bed, which currently had no mattress. On the wall right opposite to the door, a small window overlooked the trees outside that stood at the edge of the forest stretching behind them, rising gradually with the slope of the hill. Vinod stood inside the room for a while, tapping his feet slowly on the concrete floor, before leaving to see the other room.

This room was smaller and much more compact, had one cupboard and no dresser. However, it had a much bigger window, on account of the view it offered of the main street and the house opposite them. Vinod walked closer to the window and looked at the other house. He had barely noticed it when they had come. It looked almost the same as theirs. A similar size window was right opposite to this one, behind which he thought he saw a young child staring in his direction. He couldn't make out whether it was a girl or a boy. He turned around and walked back to the living room; it was empty. Through the open front door, he could see Shashi walking around in the garden.

He slumped down on one of the chairs and let his head fall back. He was tired and weary from the journey. His eyes drowsily gazed at the ceiling above, following the contours of the cracked and dull yellow plaster. There was a grim and serious look on his face, much apart from Shashi's who seemed quite a bit excited and curious about their new surroundings. He closed his eyes and tried to sleep, but despite the fatigue, his mind was restless and disturbed, unable to pinpoint the cause of the uneasiness. So he continued to stare out of the door, catching glimpses of Shashi who would walk by from time to time while continuously meandering around in the garden.

After a while, by which time his eyes had stopped focusing and were glistening with water, he noticed the presence of two people, a woman, and a small girl, presumably her daughter, who were approaching their house from across the road. They had to be the neighbours, he thought. The two greeted Shashi who at once waved in his direction, gesticulating the need for his presence. He grudgingly rose from the chair and walked outside.

"Hello," said the woman as she smiled at him. He nodded in response and gave her a quick look of appraisal. She was built rather heavily, the loose sari she wore not succeeding in hiding her bulk. She had a round face with such big eyes that they made her look even bulkier. The young girl who stood by her clutched nervously at her mother's sari, quite evidently intimidated by the sudden presence of two adult strangers. Shashi lowered her body, almost squatting on the floor, and smiled in the girl's direction.

"Hello!" she said to her, holding out her hand. "I am Shashi. What is your name?"

"Come on," encouraged her mother on seeing her daughter's reluctance. "Tell Aunty your name."

"Vidya," she managed eventually, not offering her hand in response, hiding further behind her mother.

"I am sorry," laughed the mother. "She is shy sometimes. I am Lata."

"It's okay. She's marvelous! I am Shashi and this is my husband Vinod. We have arrived today itself."

"Yes, I saw," she said, continuing to smile brightly. "Please come in for some tea. You must be tired."

Before Vinod could politely decline her offer, Shashi agreed with much enthusiasm. They walked across the road to her house. Once inside, Vinod noticed that it was identical to theirs, though just better maintained and furnished. They sat down and Lata went to the kitchen to make tea while Vidya made use of the opportunity to disappear inside her room.

"Is your husband at work?" asked Shashi.

"Yes," she beamed. "He comes back late in the evening. We own a garage in the Market Center. Perhaps you saw it while coming."

Vinod shook his head though Lata couldn't see him with her back towards the living room. Shashi rose all of a sudden and walked inside the kitchen.

"Let me help you."

"Oh, it is almost over. No need! Just pass those cups."

Vinod accepted his cup of tea and took a small sip while Lata and Shashi sat down with theirs. The current setting was vaguely reminding him of the time he had first visited Shashi's house. He could sense a similar air of uncomfortable formality, and thus, wishing to leave as soon as possible, was trying to catch Shashi's eye. She, however, was taking a much keener interest in their new neighbour.

"Was someone living in that house before we came?" she asked.

"At least not since I came here after marriage. So it has been many years."

"Oh."

"And when did you two get married?"

"It has been a year only."

"Where were you staying before?"

Vinod twirled his cup of tea impatiently in his hands; he was growing listless with irritation. He pretended to follow their conversation and nod from time to time but it was becoming more and more difficult every minute. His feet tapped noiselessly on the floor and his eyes darted around the apartment, not finding anything remotely interesting to rest upon.

"I have to leave," he said, standing and keeping the cup of tea on the table between them. "I am sorry. My head is a little heavy."

"Oh," remarked Lata. "Do you want some medicine? I can get.."

"No, it's okay. I just need some sleep."

"Are you sure?" asked Shashi.

"Yes yes. You carry on."

He quickly exited their house and walked across to theirs, wondering if his excuse had felt genuine or not. He entered the bigger bedroom and looked around aimlessly once again. His chest felt heavy, and he began to take in big gulps of air. He removed his shoes and laid down on the hard wooden bed. The heaviness in his chest refused to ebb away and slowly traveled to his eyes and surprised him by releasing itself in the form of sudden tears. The outpour lasted for a little while after which he wiped his face and slept soundly.

CHAPTER 14

Konkur was nothing like they had imagined it would be. They found it significantly smaller, consisting mostly of patches of forests and hillocks, between which and interspersed at random locations, lay the various man-made structures. Vinod and Shashi took their time to get accustomed to their new surroundings and their new lifestyle. The degree of isolation and seclusion that was on offer was in stark contrast to what they were generally used to. The silence as well; the almost complete absence of noise around their home ensured that they could, at all times, hear each other's footsteps in the house, and also those of others approaching it from outside. There would be moments when they were sitting next to each other and be able to hear the rhythmic sounds of their breaths.

They found the Market Center to be the only departure in this town's general style. This was the place of action and commerce. This was where the people of Konkur met and greeted each other, catching up and updating others on the multitudes of small stories that made up their lives. Among the citizens, there was an unsaid agreement, a tacit rule regarding the status of those who worked in the Market Center - they were placed in higher esteem than the farmers who toiled in the fields. These people, working in small offices or operating in narrow little shops, were considered to be part of the educated and ambitious lot, having broken away from the occupations of their fathers and grandfathers.

And so the first day Vinod joined the office of the Public Health Department of the local Municipal branch, a department consisting of not more than six people, he was immediately held in extremely high regard. He was the youngest among his colleagues, the only employee with a degree from a city college, the only one who was comfortable with English, the only one who read for pleasure, and the only one who had worked in a much bigger office that the rest of them. He was showered with such feelings of admiration and envy that he started to feel a bit uncomfortable. For him the experience was peculiar, and to a certain extent, unsettling. While he enjoyed, for a brief period, the extra attention being given to him, he soon grew weary of it, and the feeling of pride was quickly replaced by ennui with a hint of bitterness. He began to believe what his colleagues' behaviour seemed to implicitly state - he was better than them, more qualified and intellectually superior, a man not simply defined by his monotonous job but by his finer and more sophisticated interests. He began to believe in this fervently and it depressed him.

Vinod didn't make the same mistake as he had back home when they were staying with his mother and immediately prompted Shashi to inquire at the local hospital for a job. There was only one in Konkur, located near the Market Center, and it quite readily accepted Shashi as a member of its nursing staff. Once again, as had been the case with Vinod, Shashi found herself part of a setup that was much simpler and rudimentary to the one at home. The tasks involved required much less effort and were limited to just basic functions. Even though Shashi had never undertaken any formal education to qualify as a nurse, same as the rest of her colleagues in this hospital, her previous job had been comprehensive enough to act as a rigorous period of training. Here the nurses were supposed to act as mere aides for the doctors, without even having the power to conduct an overview and make elementary everyday decisions on their own. They were all mostly personal assistants rather than nurses. The ease and nonchalance with which Shashi performed her duties were immediately noticeable, as was her amicable and pleasant personality. As a result of being made to work at levels significantly easier than she was used to, Shashi exuded a sense of casual confidence that felt at once noteworthy and enviable. And thus just like Vinod, she was showered with words of praise and admiration, but unlike him, she felt completely natural while receiving them and reveled in the experience.

So this young couple, having recently moved to this strange town, and who until then had led fairly unremarkable lives bordering on anonymity, became instant celebrities in Konkur, by simply being different from its other inhabitants. They were the novelty circus act in an old entertainment routine; their tag of being strangers in a town where almost nothing had changed for years further added to the interest surrounding them. Their fame sprang from each of their workplaces and then traveled through the various households in the form of exaggerated remarks and anecdotes, until they reached their ears as well, at which point they could only nod and smile at the embellishments, giving them their tacit approval.

The Sehgals, on account of being their immediate and only neighbours, became their first close acquaintances. Every other evening, they found themselves at each other's home, spending an hour or two together before dinner. These gatherings were mostly unplanned, initiated largely by the Sehgals and always agreed upon wholeheartedly by Shashi who thoroughly enjoyed their company. Apart from Lata, with whom she began to share a great rapport, it was her new friend's daughter Vidya who held the greatest attraction for her. She loved the little girl immensely, a feeling that was reciprocated in equal parts by Vidya. Thus, she never let go of a chance to spend more time with her. For Vinod however, this increasing conviviality between the two couples was a nuisance. He didn't share his wife's enthusiasm for the Sehgals - neither for the parents and nor for the daughter.

"Lata is calling us," said Shashi, pointing through the window in the living room. "We should invite them more often. It doesn't look good that we go there mostly."

"Hmm. You go on. I will come later."

"You don't want to come?"

Vinod looked up from his cup of tea of which he had barely taken a few sips. It was almost seven in the evening and he had just returned from work. Shashi saw a mixture of tiredness and annoyance stretched across his face.

"Why do we have to meet every day!" he said, his face further twisting to showcase his displeasure. "It is too often."

"We don't have to, but .....I mean...don't you like them?"

"Not as much as you do. But that's not the point. Even if I did....it's too much. I am a little tired of it."

"Oh," she said and sat down next to him. "So what then? We don't go? She just called us."

"I don't know. You like it, so you go on."

"I can't go alone. That would look strange."

He leaned back on his chair and clenched his eyes shut for a brief instance.

"I would just like to have some time for myself."

"To do what?"

"I don't know," he snapped at her impatiently. "Anything. I used to read. Maybe that."

"Read? Read what? I have never really seen you reading anything," she said, exhaling in exasperation, clearly miffed at having been snapped at. "Maybe once more than a year ago."

"I know," he replied gruffly. "But I would like to do it again."

"So do it at night. Instead of listening to the radio."

"You don't understand," he said and got up brusquely, pushing the chair aside. He took his cup of tea and placed it within the sink, running some tap water over it. He wiped his hands and came back to the living room where Shashi was seated as before.

"Let's go. At least we can try to come back quickly."

"You'll be in this mood?"

"I'll be fine. I can hide it."

She stood up and stared at him for a while, biting her lower lip, before speaking in a much softer tone.

"They like us. And there is no one else around here. I don't want that to change."

"They like you. Everyone does. Don't worry, I won't adversely affect your popularity."

"That's not what I meant," she said, resorting to her earlier tone of voice. "There is no use. I'll tell Lata I am not feeling well."

"Forget it. Let's just go and get it over with."

"Why do you have to be like this?"

"Please," he said, rapidly moving towards the door. "Come on."

These evenings with the Sehgals were fairly usual and repetitive affairs. The moment they entered each other's house, Lata and Shashi would congregate in one corner, most of the time joined by Vidya who would spend the evening going around the two women in circles, listening attentively to what they were saying, and laughing each time they did, before getting tired and settling down in Shashi's lap.

Mahesh, on the other hand, would always take Vinod by the arm and suggestively ask for a drink, which Vinod often declined, much to Mahesh's amusement, who never let that stop himself.

"You have no idea what you are missing," he would say, wearing down that seemingly clever phrase after constant use.

Mahesh's drinking helped Vinod equally, turning the former into a much better conversationalist. Mahesh was a natural storyteller when inebriated, and as much as Vinod disliked spending time with him, it was infinitely easier when all he had to do was nod and laugh gently on occasion.

"And so this young guy, one of Suraj Bisht's sons, comes to the garage today, dragging his scooter beside him. "Well....well...you should have seen the state of it! I shall call you next time; come over. It looked as if someone had completely ripped one side of it. All of it would have to be replaced. The poor kid couldn't look at me because of shame. It was Suraj's scooter of course."

"An accident?"

"No!" he started laughing loudly, keeping his drink aside lest he dropped it, a few drops sloshing over. "That's the amazing part! According to the kid, he grazed along a bus while trying to speed past it. Almost took his foot apart. And more than that....the bus wasn't even moving. What an idiot!"

"Wow"

"Exactly! I can't wait to talk to his father when he comes to pay for it. It's going to take more than a week to set it right!"

Mahesh always had such anecdotes at his disposal, which came much more easily and fluently to him after a few drinks. And so the evening would progress in this fashion, two separate stories unfolding across the room from each other, until Shashi could sense the increasing displeasure of her husband and propose to postpone the fun to another time. It was usually rather late by when they got back home, leaving them enough time to just have a quick dinner and then fall asleep.

After they had been living in Konkur for almost a year, Vinod's mother came to stay with them for a few days. Before that, they had visited her once during Diwali and had gone to see Shashi's parents as well around that time. That had been a very short and hurried stay, dominated by the ongoing festival, and thus she hadn't gotten the opportunity to closely observe her son and daughter-in-law. But now the old woman had come with a specific task in mind and was determined to execute it, knowing fully well that she wasn't in the physical condition to make this trip one more time.

She was still working for that tailor, though her condition had forced her to reduce her hours of work, which had automatically reduced her pay as well. But she lived alone now and didn't have the same want of money as when she had first taken up this job. Although she was still fairly young, she hadn't aged well. Years of hard labour had weakened her, her frail body making it seem as if she suffered from malnutrition. The intense needlework had practically taken away her eyesight, for which she wore large round glasses that just about kept her from stumbling all the time. However, in her words one could still find the remnants of the strong and proud woman who had managed, despite her harrowing circumstances, to create a life for her son and herself.

"Now tell me," said Vinod as they sat down together. "Why did you insist on coming yourself? We could have taken some days off next month and come home."

"I wanted to see your house," she said with a smile. "Before I lose the energy to travel this distance."

"You know you can live with us."

"I don't want to. What would I do here? Do you even have any people living nearby?"

"We have our neighbours."

"No..no..this isn't for me," she shook her head vigorously and then inched closer to her son, clasping his hand. "Anyway. How are you two?"

"We are okay."

"Are you doing what I asked you to?"

"I am trying."

She sighed and held his hands tighter. "I know you are not telling the truth."

"It isn't easy."

"Do you think it was easy living with your father? It can't be tougher than that."

Vinod looked away, his brows furrowed and his teeth clenched together. "That's not fair. I cannot compete with your misery."

"Look, I understand. But you have to try."

"I am," he said getting up. "I think you should rest for a while. It's been a long journey."

She didn't speak to him about this subject for the next few days, and instead, silently observed their daily routine - how they were together, the way they talked between themselves and when among others - mostly their neighbours. She noticed the way they addressed one another, in inaudible tones, almost afraid to take each other's names; the way they could barely tolerate being alone in the same room, the uneasiness in the air when they all sat down to have a meal together, their customary greetings in the morning and at night. And thus she knew, without doubt, unlike others who were too blinded by what they saw on the surface, that all was still as it was back home more than a year ago. They were still two strangers living in the same house, oblivious to and unconcerned with each other's cares; neither seemed to have made any effort. She wondered how long this illusion was going to hold up before suddenly laying them bare before everyone. It wasn't going to take much provocation. It saddened her greatly, and thus further strengthened her resolve to do all she could in her power to fix their marriage.

So a day before she had to leave back home, she sat down with her son and took his hands again. She came as close to him as possible.

"Just listen to me this time," she implored, seeing the look on his face. "And then I won't ever say anything again."

"Okay," he relented with a sigh.

"You can continue to live in this manner and be miserable while pretending to be otherwise, or you can at least try to live happily together."

"We do try," he said in exasperation. "I told you that."

"Fine. You are trying. I don't know how but if you say you are then alright. But is it working?"

"Of course not."

"Then you must try harder or do something different."

"As should she."

"I am talking to you because you are my son! I cannot make the same demands to her."

"What do you want us to do?"

She looked around and could just about recognize Shashi in the garden through the window, tending to her plants and flowers.

"Her plants make her happy."

"You want us to buy more plants?"

"As does Vidya."

"Mother," he stiffened. "Please."

"Think for a moment," she said, imploring him. "It could work."

Vinod let go of her mother's hand and stood up with a wry smile on his face.

"Why do people always think that's a solution? It could be a horrible mistake."

"Don't talk like that," she said sternly. "I know better. I am your mother."

He sighed and sat down again. There were tears in her eyes.

"I am sorry...but I am not so sure about this."

"She loves children! You can see that."

"This isn't just about her."

"You will love your child, trust me. You just won't know it until you have one. It's different for men."

Vinod's face had shrunk with worry. Clear straight lines were visible on his forehead as he looked down towards his feet in deep deliberation. His mother let him be for a while, well aware of the fact that she was asking him to make a momentous decision. Shashi was still outside, oblivious to the conversation that was going to change her life irrevocably. A few minutes passed and the old woman got worried that Shashi might enter at any moment during this crucial juncture. She knew it would be greatly difficult to get such an opportunity again.

"Shouldn't we ask her as well?" he said finally.

His mother smiled, recognizing her victory and leaned across, whispering in his ear.

"Don't worry. I will talk to her."

Vinod looked up with fear and embarrassment in his eyes. He could feel his heart racing.

"Do you think it will help us?"

"I am sure of it."

CHAPTER 15

Raindrops slid silently down their windowpane, blurring the view of the trees outside. The wet leaves glistened and sparkled, despite the limited ingress of sunlight through the thick envelope of clouds. Vinod's gaze was fixed towards the window, his heavy eyes drooping from time to time but never allowing him to fall asleep. The pelting sound of rain on the earth was faintly audible; he hoped it wouldn't be loud enough to disturb Saurabh's sleep. He looked at the clock - it was six in the morning; another hour and he would have to get up for sure. Shashi lay beside him, her brow furrowed, highlighting the lines on her forehead as if she were having an unpleasant dream. Saurabh was between the two, tucked in warmly from both sides.

It was cold. Vinod pulled the quilt further up until it was almost over his eyes. He stretched his feet, and they slid a little beneath the quilt and hit the wooden edge of the bed; there was a loud thud. Saurabh woke instantly and started crying. Vinod put his palm over his son's head and tried to calm him even as strong spasms of pain shot up through his toe, worsened by the intense cold. But Saurabh's cries were much more troubling than the pain. He continued to slowly run his palm across Saurabh's small head until he eventually stopped feeling restless and fell asleep. He then looked towards Shashi who was as still as before, her unpleasant dreams seemingly continuing without interruption. Vinod sat up slowly and moved away from the bed. He knew he wouldn't be able to sleep anymore.

By the time he washed and got ready, Shashi was up and moving around the house in her usual hasty manner, making a pot of tea for them both while simultaneously warming some milk for Saurabh and packing some food from yesterday for Vinod's lunch. They sat down together and had their cup of tea in virtual silence, commenting on the weather, before she went back inside the room to nurse Saurabh. Shashi too had to leave soon for the hospital and thus there was a sense of rush in all her activities. The hour rapidly approached the time when Lata would be at their doorstep, ready to take Saurabh for the day. Vinod took some bread with his tea, and then, having nothing else to do, left early for work.

The Market Center was a little more than a kilometer away and he always enjoyed walking that distance. The rain had slowed down to a trickle by then, so he closed the umbrella he was carrying and let it hang limply on one side, his bag hanging from the other shoulder. The tiny water droplets felt as cold as ice as they slid down his face with the gentle wind blowing across them. Walking at a leisurely pace, he gazed at the surroundings passing by with a sense of comfort and satisfaction. The rain made everything more beautiful. He was quite disappointed when the road suddenly widened and he found himself entering the Market Center. The magic of his surroundings vanished almost instantly, and he then took the final few steps towards his office with a slight frown on his face.

It was empty as he walked in and took his seat. The peon sat up from his position in the corner and then slumped against the wall once again, after just a momentary glance at Vinod. Their office had a rather peculiar shape - squarish in the middle with an oval-shaped dome-like ends on either side. The peculiarity was almost impossible to miss, as it was further made conspicuous by how they all arranged themselves within the space. Four of them, including Vinod, sat in the middle section, clumped together in a dense pocket while the two senior members sat on either side of them, near the oval ends. The first day Vinod had walked into this office, it gave him the impression of a small boat, being steered at both ends, unsure of which direction to take.

Vinod opened the file he had been working on the day before; a spread of numbers handwritten on thin yellow sheets stared back at him. He switched on his computer, which slowly whirred to life, and then began entering the numbers on to a spreadsheet. The numbers corresponded to the quantities of Malathion used in the past month in their district, along with their associated costs. Vinod blocked everything else from his mind and steadfastly continued with the tedious process. Soon, as always happened and as he had expected, his shoulders and face muscles relaxed and he felt much more at ease.

The others trickled in one by one and the office was at full capacity within an hour. The peon too finally set to work, bringing tea to those who asked for it.

"Early, as usual, Vinod," remarked one of his neighbours. "And well into your work already. Always ahead of everyone."

Vinod smiled politely. "The weather was nice."

And so the boat embarked on its slow and predictable course, never straying away from the gentle waters, making its usual stops along the way, helmed at both ends by its two captains, for whom the sole aim was to ensure that it always stayed afloat. Both of them relied rather heavily on one of their stewards to guarantee the same.

"Vinod," called out one of them. "Just a moment."

Vinod stood up and walked across. "Yes, sir."

"Sit, sit," he said. "How's the baby?"

"Fine sir."

"What are you working on right now?"

"The Malathion report."

"Hmm. That isn't so urgent. Give it to Sanjay. I have to give a complete account of the vaccines we received last...ah..when was it?"

"Two weeks ago. On Wednesday."

"Yes....that. They have already been distributed right?"

"We dispatched them. That week itself."

"That's good. I was afraid we still had them. Anyway, that report has to be given by tomorrow morning. Start with that. Should be manageable I think."

"I'll begin," replied Vinod and got up to leave after taking the required files. His boss nodded and then looked down at his desk, his head darting from side to side, as if unsure of what he had been doing and what he had to do next.

Vinod left him to handle his particular predicament and returned to his seat. He immediately gave the file he was working on to Sanjay who sat just in front of him, his back towards the main door. Sanjay had been his immediate superior when he had joined. He was a forty-five year old man with graying hair and a thin frame who had been working in the office for the past twenty years. He raised his eyebrows in response to Vinod's outstretched hand.

"Sir said you have to complete it. I am going to do the vaccines report."

Sanjay sighed and shifted slowly in his seat, lifting the file marginally using his hand and casually glancing at it.

"Hmm. I'll see. You might have to help me with it though. You are much quicker."

Vinod ignored that response and started with his work. There was seldom any noise in their office. All work was a routine and fixed matter, carried out lethargically but in a methodical fashion; never hurried but then never incorrect. All six of them, except Vinod, were middle-aged and over, residents of Konkur ever since their birth, and then employees of the Municipal Corporation ever since employable. Their small number ensured that they all were individually occupied and responsible for their own work, rarely needing the intervention of one of their colleagues, unless an exigent situation demanded it, in which case Vinod, being the youngest and quickest, was always called upon. Hence they worked mostly in isolation, a situation that lent itself to peace, tranquility and a deep sense of boredom.

The one aberration among them all was Gaurav Verma - boisterous, uncouth and with a sense of slapstick humour that came second only to his monstrous belly. He was the only one who, each morning, greeted all of his colleagues separately and individually at their desks with the accompaniment of small talk and ill-conceived jokes. He was the oldest among them all and with the least degree of responsibility.

"And so our young genius is busy as ever," he said, rather loudly, slapping Vinod on the back. "How are things?"

"Good," smiled Vinod feebly.

"Did you get caught in the rain? I nearly slipped a few times. Ruined the shoes."

"It wasn't much."

"Rained all night! I could hardly sleep. That reminds me, how is the little baby?" he asked, laughing and then turning towards the others to see their expressions.

Vinod smiled once again and just nodded in reply. He then automatically turned towards his file, which seemed to be Grave's cue to move on.

"San jay! You look even slimmer today!"

Vinod tried to tune out the sound of Grave's voice and focus on the papers in hand. He stared at them for a long time, till the moment his eyes glazed over and he forgot what he was looking at, barely registering the blurry muddle of numbers. His trance was broken by the rain that once again began to fall rapidly, seemingly with a sense of determination. He welcomed the sound of the raindrops. They helped him to concentrate above the noise of Grave's intermittent exclamations. He looked at the clock and was surprised to notice that it had only been two to three hours since he had come. It was going to be a rather long day.

By lunch, he had merely completed twenty percent of the work. So he continued to scan through the files religiously and enter the details on his system while simultaneously having his food. All employees usually had food at their desks as there wasn't a separate section from them to go to, but working while eating was a different matter, rarely undertaken and thus always frowned upon.

"What's the rush?" asked San jay with a touch of irritation in his voice. "Let's have lunch in peace."

"Oh, I am okay. I just want to finish this."

His four colleagues clearly disapproved of his behaviour while the two bosses chose to ignore the matter. The rain ensured that none of them could leave the office for a little stroll or a cigarette as they were generally accustomed to. So they all quietly finished their food and sat in a small huddle, talking in whispers while stealing an occasional glance in Vinod's direction.

There was a lot of work to be done and thus Vinod continued to push through. He knew he was working inefficiently, without much heart, taking frequent breaks in between during which all he did was stare blankly at his screen. He was getting easily distracted by the slightest of stimuli - the sound of someone shuffling in their seat, a few words between colleagues, a sudden increase in rainfall etc..His fingers twiddled with the pencil in his hand and he hesitated to look at the clock. The peon who had barely moved from his place in the corner since morning, once again moved around the office, distributing tea, which Vinod refused as usual.

Gaurav was the first person to leave. The silent and quick nature of his exit was matched in intensity only by the noise he had made on arrival. San jay followed him and then soon did the others.

"How much is left?"

Vinod looked up towards his right shoulder and saw his boss peering down at his system. He was ready to leave.

"A few more hours."

"Go home. Do it tomorrow."

"I'll leave soon."

He nodded and walked out, leaving only Vinod and the peon behind.

"How much time will you take, sir?" asked the peon after a while.

"You go on. Leave the keys with me."

The peon thanked him and quickly departed. Vinod looked at his watch. It was 7 pm. Outside it was already dark, and he knew that Shashi would be home by now and that she would have already picked Saurabh from the Sehgals' house. They would be expecting him to come back home soon.

He closed his file and turned off the computer, stretching his arms and leaning back on his chair, his lips breaking into a yawn. Then he put his feet up on his desk and stared at the ceiling, lying in that position for a long time until he could feel the onset of sleep. The rain had stopped and a cool wet breeze wafted in through the cracks around the door and windows. He stood up, walked outside and stared at the surrounding darkness. The outlines of the surrounding shops, including Mahesh's garage, were only faintly visible. Only a few of the streetlights were working, creating an odd pattern of visibility around the Market Center. It was barely sufficient. He went back in, packed his bag and came out, locking the office behind him.

He started to walk slowly around the market, taking the circular path that led him from one shop to another. From time to time he would stop and close his eyes, allowing his body to feel the breeze leisurely. His tired mind welcomed this sudden flood of freshness, and thus he continued this perambulating journey until he had taken almost three complete rounds of the market. He knew it was getting late.

When he finally took the straight road towards home, it was already past 8 pm. However, the speed at which he walked wasn't affected by that. The line of trees around him rustled impatiently and a swarm of leaves flew in random directions. He neared the graveyard and passed it without a glance in its direction. It was exceedingly dark. He had nothing but muscle memory to rely on. He bent his neck and fixed his gaze on the road, feeling the mechanical motion of his legs. The rough tarmac was wet and little droplets of water seemed to jump each time his feet landed heavily on it.

The lights at both the houses were switched on when Vinod arrived. No one was outside. He approached the door and stood before it, his palm resting on the handle. Small noises emanated from inside and he could distinctly make out the crying voice of his son. The door was unlocked; he entered silently. From the direction of the noises, he could infer that they both were sitting inside the main bedroom. He put his bag away and approached the room slowly. The door was slightly ajar, and he pushed his head through it. Shashi was sitting on the bed with Saurabh lying beside her. She had placed a large newspaper sheet in front of her on which she was sifting through a heap of rice grains. Vinod stared at them both and stood in that position for a long time, waiting for them to notice his presence.

CHAPTER 16

Vinod's mother's attempt to give her son's marriage a much-needed boost proved to be ineffective. While Saurabh's birth, and the succeeding few years, definitely altered the dynamic of the relationship between the two parents, it would have been incorrect to say that it had changed for the better. It had evolved, taken a much more different and complex route than they had possibly imagined, and involved them living together and cooperating in ways that required much empathy and flexibility. They both learned things from it and changed in ways they couldn't have foreseen. But it didn't bring them closer.

They still managed to keep up appearances, a talent they had both developed over the years, necessitated by the high regard in which the people of Konkur continued to hold them. They still spoke to them and about them in awe, envious of the qualities they saw in them, which as ever was a combination of their relatively young age and seemingly better education, coupled with the fact that they were outsiders in a town that hadn't changed in decades. These tags, being as they were of a permanent nature, had stuck to them both. With time, they had learned to embrace them and to preserve the external facade of perfection that was attributed to the two. Their quasi-celebrity status was automatically passed down to Saurabh as well, his birth taking the form of a joyous event in Konkur, for a while becoming the talking point of every household.

Saurabh's birth had strikingly different effects on the two. For Shashi, the months of discomfort and anxiety evaporated almost instantly after his arrival. The feeling of love and attachment towards her newborn son came naturally and in waves of great intensity, deeply taking hold of her. The birth provided the invigorating boost that her domestic life was in want of. She felt much happier than before and reveled in the presence of her son. It further strengthened the dynamic of her relationship with Vidya, who, after overcoming her initial feelings of envy due to the attention Saurabh was garnering, became a perpetual presence in Saurabh's life, helping Shashi with all related tasks. The three of them, along with Lata, became almost inseparable, with Saurabh spending a majority of his time at the Sehgals' with Lata and Vidya after Shashi rejoined the hospital.

Vinod felt the impact of the birth of his son much more strongly. Unlike Shashi, who transitioned readily and happily into the role of a mother, Vinod felt overwhelmed by the situation his mother had contrived to put them in. More than the joy associated with becoming a father, which he did experience, albeit intermittently, there was the fear of having crossed a threshold into an unknown region about which he didn't know that well and from where he could never extricate himself. Initially, he thought, as his mother had told him, he would slowly learn to love his child as he became a part of his growing process, that the feelings of confusion and bewilderment he felt each day were natural and would slowly ebb away with time. But they didn't. This was partly due to his hesitation and partly because Shashi never even thought to involve him in any activity related to Saurabh. He was a bystander in the life of his son, which was managed wholly by his wife, aided largely of course by Vidya and Lata. They seemed to have formed a separate group and entity from which he was tacitly excluded.

And so any new developments regarding Saurabh always reached him as they would to a distant relative - much later and without all the actual details. Thus he never really knew the exact moment when Saurabh started to crawl and then later walk, nor when he let out his first incomprehensible series of word-like-noises and then later slightly discernible ones. He didn't know what he ate and at what times or the vaccination shots Shashi got directly administered at the hospital. Sometimes he didn't even know whether he was at home or with the neighbours. This system of unconscious exclusion continued even when he was old enough to start school. What all he studied, his books, his lessons, his teachers, his friends - he neither knew nor inquired about any of them, depending on the things he overheard or was sometimes told.

Usually, when he came back from the office in the evening, he wouldn't find anyone at home. Shashi, having returned from the hospital before him, would be with Lata, and Saurabh would either be with them or Vidya. He would have the house to himself until they came back, and they all had dinner together, which was the only extended period they all spent with each other.

This sense of isolation, which he had somewhat always craved and hoped for, began to bother him. Yes, he was a father but he would have struggled to describe the feeling to anyone. For him, fatherhood became simply a psychological state of being inside of a continuous active experience. His daily schedule remained almost the same, hardly influenced by Saurabh's presence. At work, he always had to fend off questions related to the well-being of his son with small lies and made-up anecdotes. What was the alternative? He couldn't have possibly pleaded his ignorance and appeared foolish. Not him. Not the smartest guy in the office. And he just never could talk to Shashi about it; he couldn't cross that bridge. It was much easier to remain in seclusion and then lie about it.

Before Vinod could sense it, this feeling of discomfort and loneliness transitioned into a habit and then sheer indifference. It happened gradually and automatically, subconsciously and without his consent, until one day he suddenly realized that it didn't bother him anymore. Shashi was completely oblivious to the internal turmoil her inadvertent behaviour had put her husband in. For her, Vinod's lack of involvement was a result of his reticence, something which he had always held so dearly. It would have seemed immensely strange to her that he needed her intervention to be able to spend more time with his son.

In this manner, their relationship evolved and took unexpected turns. Instead of uniting them in the task of raising their son together, Saurabh's birth created a much bigger division than had existed before. This division, however, wasn't acrimonious or bitter in nature. It was further indicative of how different their personalities were and how difficult it was for them to establish an emotional connection. They didn't like or dislike one another, but simply ignored each other's existence to the extent to which it was possible. They had been and still were strangers sharing a common home. This wasn't even close to what Vinod's mother had been hoping for.

Vinod returned home from work one day and was surprised to see Shashi sitting alone in the living room. Her reaction on seeing him enter the house seemed to suggest that she had been waiting for him, a fact that he found rather unusual. He instinctively kept his bag down on the table and took the seat in front of her. She appeared distressed and a little frazzled. Vinod waited for her to speak but she couldn't seem to begin.

"What happened?" he asked, eventually.

"Saurabh had a fight," she replied. "In school. He broke a child's nose."

"Oh," he straightened his back in surprise. "That's strange.....isn't it?"

"Of course!" she said, giving him a puzzled look. "He is so harmless."

Vinod nodded. "What did he say?"

"Nothing," she said, her palms falling in front of her, her face betraying her distress. "He has been suspended for two weeks! He isn't talking at all. I am getting really worried."

"Hmm. Maybe he needs a little time. He must be upset."

"Would you talk to him? Try once."

Vinod looked at her keenly, as if making sure that he had understood her correctly.

"Are you sure? But what would I say?"

"Just talk! Make him speak."

She rose from her chair and turned sideways away from Vinod, as if making space for him to directly go towards Saurabh's room. She tapped her fingers impatiently on the table, clearly waiting for him to do what she had asked him to. Vinod got up hesitantly.

"He probably needs some time," he tried again, but she shook her head and looked at him pleadingly.

"At least try."

Knowing he couldn't avoid it any longer, he walked past her and entered Saurabh's room. He was lying on his stomach, his face turned away from the door. For a moment Vinod thought that he was asleep and thus started to reverse his steps before he saw his son's hand move towards his hair, accompanied by a small whimper. He was crying. Vinod came closer and sat down by his side. He couldn't remember the last time he was alone with his son. Even at that moment, he wished he was somewhere else.

"Saurabh," he called out gently, thinking of placing his hand on his son's shoulder but then deciding against it. "Are you okay?"

Saurabh lay still and didn't respond. He was no longer crying.

Vinod shifted uncomfortably and sighed. He looked around the room distractedly, hoping Saurabh was going to speak up.

"Your mother is really worried," he added after a while. The words felt weird and unnatural coming out of his mouth. "What happened?"

The silence continued. Vinod knew that his half-hearted questions weren't going to break his son's resolve. He sat there for a little while longer before going back to the living room. Shashi got upon seeing him.

"Nothing," he said before she could ask. "As I told you, let him have some time."

A little later that night, the Sehgals came over to their house. After Saurabh's birth, their frequent social gatherings in the evenings had reduced to a certain degree; mostly because Lata, Vidya, Shashi, and Saurabh spent most of their time in each other's company anyway. But that day both Mahesh and Lata came to express their shock and surprise over what had happened and commiserate with their friends. Shashi was glad of their presence, while for Vinod, they made an already difficult evening much worse. They all sat in the living room while Saurabh remained inside. Words were thin in the air, more perfunctory than meaningful. Vinod was a little surprised at how seriously the matter was being treated; the level of concern being shown was, in his opinion, a little too exaggerated for an incident that wasn't too uncommon among young boys. But as was generally the case, he didn't offer his opinion on the matter. The Sehgals left soon, taking Vidya along with them, whom, quite surprisingly, they found outside in the Parashars' garden, talking with Saurabh.

Once they were alone, Shashi regressed to that forlorn look she had worn earlier. Vinod, who was about to retire for the night, stopped when he saw her sitting down dejectedly.

"It happens sometimes," he said to her, stifling a yawn. "Young boys fight over silly things."

Vinod went to bed early, the evening having drained him from the sort of mental activity he wasn't used to. He didn't sleep that well though, not out of worry and concern for his son, but for the role he had been made to play that day, even though he knew it was an aberration, a momentary departure from his daily routine that generally never required any parenting. His lack of involvement in Saurabh's life had long ceased to bother him. Now, having grown habitual of it, he was averse to any situation that might increase that involvement. He knew that the ensuing weeks when Saurabh would be at home might demand something extra from him as well, but it would be temporary, and he was at least glad of that.

Saurabh's suspension wasn't hidden from the people of Konkur for long. The school wasn't discreet about it, and it would have been impossible to be so even if they had tried. For a while it became a topic of much discussion and comment, the parents' popularity being one of the major reasons for that. It was the first chink in the armor of the couple who could do no wrong, and thus, in a way, it was welcomed with a voyeuristic sense of pleasure. At work, Vinod and Shashi were constantly bombarded with questions and remarks about the incident, which they answered in their typical way - Vinod with slight nods and shrugs of indifference and Shashi with huge smiles that attempted to mask the seriousness of the issue.

"None of them mean well at all," she complained once to Vinod in the evening at home. It had only been a week since the suspension and thus the incident was still fresh in the peoples' minds. "You should hear the comments and suggestions I get to hear. It seems as if it is a great source of entertainment for them."

Vinod nodded. "It's the same thing at the office. Everyone's full of advice."

"One of the nurses said to me that he needs to drink more milk. That would help with the anger!"

Vinod laughed a bit and shook his head with a smile. "They'll soon get bored."

It had become a ritual for the two to share what all their colleagues had to say about Saurabh. They did this every evening. Vinod's assertion was correct to a certain degree. The interest around their son began to decline steadily once the suspension period was over and he started going back to school. Their daily conversations too were met with a similar rate of demise. The storm had passed, and they were once again free to sail over familiar routes, without being dependent on each other. It had been the first event since their son's birth that had brought them together to such an extent. While they had been glad of each other's presence, they were both equally relieved that they didn't require it anymore. Things were back to how they had always been.

Chapter 17

"This is now the fifth time that we are meeting under such circumstances," remarked the Principal, putting her arms on her desk, her slim chin resting on her knuckles. The desk was small and unevenly balanced on its four wooden legs, tilting slightly each time someone put their weight on it. It sat in the center of an equally small and modest room, overlooking the school's playground, which could be seen through a window. The room was replete with cabinets and cupboards, filled with various dossiers, some of which lay open and scattered at random locations.

The Principal was an old woman, well into her sixties, and had been at this post for over fifteen years. Her hair, mostly grey, interspersed with flecks of black in between, was tied together in a neat bun. The thin lines on her face were contorted with dismay and worry as she stared at the two parents from between her glasses, her eyes routinely shifting from one to the other. On her right sat a much younger teacher, wearing a slightly angrier and more annoyed countenance than the rest of them.

"How many chances do we give him? When will he learn?"

Shashi shifted uncomfortably in her seat, looking towards Vinod to see if he was going to respond. Vinod bent his head just enough to avoid eye contact with all of them. She frowned and returned her gaze to the Principal who was eying her keenly.

"We are really sorry," she pleaded, her anguish marked on her face. "I am trying...and..and so is he...he really is. I realize how difficult it must be for you. But please....," her voice trailed away at the end, reducing almost to an earnest squeak.

"Shashi," the Principal sighed with pity in her voice. "It is getting worse."

The teacher sitting behind her nodded in agreement, forcing Shashi to hang her head in shame and dismay. So it was finally going to happen, she thought, and once again turned automatically towards Vinod who was still making a conscious effort to not look directly at anyone.

"Vinod?" she called out softly, a mixture of anger and despair in her voice.

Vinod shook his head abruptly on hearing his name. He saw Shashi peering at him intently, struggling to mask her pain and fury. The Principal and the teacher too were now staring at him. Vinod leaned forward and put his palm on the desk, making it immediately tilt in his direction.

"What do you propose?"

"He needs to be home-schooled," she suggested gently. "Perhaps some time alone, without the presence of other children, would do him some good."

"No..." said Shashi instinctively and almost lurched forward in protest.

"Isn't that too harsh?" asked Vinod, ignoring Shashi's reaction. "It might hurt him more."

"We don't know that. And we have to think about the safety of the rest of the students as well," she replied.

"But you have a responsibility towards Saurabh too. We know he has to change, but if the school gives up on him...."

"The school has stood behind your son for quite a while now," she interrupted him, noticeably annoyed. "We could have expelled him a long time ago. The other parents have already complained multiple times."

Vinod sighed and sank back in his chair. He looked outside the window towards the playground where groups of children, of different ages, were playing, creating a small cloud of dust all around them. Shashi's hands and feet were trembling as she rapidly kept moving her eyes from Vinod to the Principal and back.

"Two weeks of suspension......" began Vinod.

"We have tried that before..."

".....for the final time," he insisted and looked straight at her. "And then we won't say anything. You may do as you please. We can put this on paper if required."

Now it was the old woman's turn to sigh and lean back. She contemplated the proposal, regarding the two parents. She had been quite keen on carrying through with the expulsion before they had met, but now she found herself thinking about the alternative once again. Her resolve began to waver. She turned towards Saurabh's teacher, looking for some sign of confirmation, but was met simply with an impassive face.

"I don't know why I am agreeing with you," she said finally. "I shouldn't but I am. He has one last chance."

"Thank you so much," said Shashi, reaching for her hand. Vinod nodded.

The two left the room quietly and walked through the small playground towards the exit. Young boys and girls stared at the two adults as they walked by, stopping and pointing in their direction. Vinod ignored them and moved ahead while Shashi couldn't help but catch their eyes. Perhaps, she thought, they are wondering whether they will see Saurabh again or not.

A rickshaw approached them as soon as they came out of the gate. Shashi got in first and shifted to make space for Vinod but he didn't climb in.

"I have to go to the office," he told her and gave the rickshaw man 10 rupees.

"Are you sure?" she asked. "Saurabh would be at home and.."

"I'll see you both in the evening."

She nodded and turned away from him as the rickshaw began to pull away. Vinod stood there until his wife was out of sight and then made his way to the office.

All five of his colleagues, as well as the office peon, looked up as he entered inside. Vinod could feel their eyes on him as he greeted them casually and then took his seat.

"And so?" began Gaurav, asking the question to which everyone was itching to get the reply. "What happened?"

"Two weeks suspension."

"Oh nice!" he exclaimed dramatically, slapping him on the back. "Your boy has a knack to somehow get out of trouble. That's the best thing you could have hoped for."

"The school has been very generous with him," said Sanjay, staring at Vinod from across the desk. "This is the fifth or sixth time right?"

Vinod nodded and switched on his computer. He was hoping his show of indifference would help to cut short the conversation. He opened one of the files kept on his desk and blindly flipped through it.

"Well you just straighten him out," declared Gaurav, as if pronouncing the solution to the problem.

It was still only 11:30 in the morning when Vinod began his work, grateful for the distraction it provided. This was why he had decided to come to the office instead of accompanying Shashi back home. The rest of his colleagues, including the two bosses, didn't mention Saurabh for the rest of the day, which allowed him to go about his work in his usual methodical manner, following the same regular patterns as always, finding a sense of solace and peace in its monotony.

By evening, as was the norm, the others started to slowly trickle away while Vinod stayed back for a while. On this day, however, he wasn't alone as Gaurav stayed put on his desk until it was just the two of them who remained behind. It was quite unusual for the old man to be in the office at that hour and thus Vinod suspected that it had something to do with him. He was correct.

"Well, Vinod," he began after the peon left the keys with them and went home. He put his hands behind his back and stretched them while simultaneously letting out a huge yawn. "What will you do about your son, huh?"

Vinod raised his eyebrows and looked up at his much older colleague. He was unsure whether Gaurav was being serious or not, and as to what exactly he meant by that question. In any case, he switched off his computer and prepared to leave. His time at the office was now clearly outliving its usefulness.

"Don't worry about it," he said and got up. "I'll take care of it."

"Now, now, sit down," he said and came over to his seat. "What's the rush. I know why you go home late every time."

Vinod's face turned red and a huge frown appeared on it. "Whatever your assumptions are, they are wrong," he said firmly and started to walk away.

"Look, don't get angry," he said in a serious tone, making Vinod stop at the door. "I didn't mean to offend you. But sometimes one needs to take control and be firm." Gaurav was now himself preparing to leave, as he saw that Vinod wasn't going to give him any time. He picked up his bag and came near him. "The years behind me haven't been all for nothing. I know this. A boy needs his father's strong hands."

Much to Gaurav's surprise, Vinod turned away from him and left without responding. His steps were quick as he made his way home, without slowing down for even an instant. He was breathing heavily and his hands were trembling, which he curled into two tight fists to calm himself.

He entered the house, expecting Shashi to be sitting in the living room, but she wasn't there. He called out her name but didn't receive a response. The door to Saurabh's room was slightly ajar, and he moved towards it with the same speed he had when walking outside. The speed felt rather unnatural inside the house and thus he slowed down. Saurabh was sitting on his bed with a notebook. He looked surprised to see his father.

"Where's your mother?" he asked him.

"Next door."

He nodded and went back to the living room to look through the window. He stood there for a few minutes, contemplating whether to go over or not, and then retired to his room. He continued to pace around for a while, the energy that had built up inside him taking its time to taper off. He was walking inside his room with such intensity that soon beads of sweat developed around his forehead; his feet started to burn with exhaustion, yet he didn't take off his shoes, nor did he settle down.

He didn't know for how long he had been compulsively walking in this manner when Shashi arrived. She was surprised to see him in such an agitated state but simply moved towards her side of the bed without saying anything. Vinod stood beside her, tired and transfixed, the sudden cessation of motion making him aware of his level of fatigue. He took in great gulps of air while finally sitting down and removing his shoes.

"So you told them everything?" he asked in a tense voice. His level of frenzy seemed to be diffusing rapidly and he couldn't remember what it was that had put him in such a state of mind. Yet, some remnants of it remained and manifested in his tone of voice.

"Yes of course."

"They are probably laughing at us."

"They are our friends. Why would they do that? And is that your only concern?"

Neither of them was looking at each other as they spoke, preferring instead to glance around in the room in an arbitrary fashion. Without waiting for a response from his side, Shashi got up and moved towards the door.

"Where are you going?"

"To get dinner ready."

"I am not hungry."

"There are other people in this house."

Vinod lifted his head, looking straight at her for the first time. The vehemence in her words didn't correspond with the expressions on her face. It was the same tired and resigned look that had started to become synonymous with her. But Vinod didn't see any of that.

"That was unnecessary," he said. "I was only speaking for myself."

"I know. Do you ever think about us?"

"What's wrong?"

"Why did you go away?"

"I don't understand."

"You left right after we came out of school."

"I had work to do," he replied, stressing deliberately on each word.

Shashi shook her head in annoyance and kept standing near the door, her hands folded near her chest. Her feet tapped impatiently on the floor as she thought over the right words to say. But now Vinod had stood up again and was standing much closer to her, as if ready for a confrontation.

"This is a difficult time," she said after a while. "And you....just don't seem to care."

"I don't care! I am the one who managed to avoid getting him expelled!"

"That's not the same thing."

"Then what do you want? Tell me. I haven't created this mess."

"Is that so?" smiled Shashi. "What are you trying to say? Am I to blame for everything?"

"You are doing it again. Don't take my words to mean more than they are meant to."

"Well, what do they mean then? Why don't you speak clearly? Say what you want."

Their voices had turned loud and acquired a hint of menace. They were now unabashedly staring fiercely at each other, almost taunting the other person to continue and push this conversation as far as possible. Unlike during their other quarrels, none of them was willing to relent, and they both could sense that resolve in each other.

"I just think...." he began a bit softly, hesitated for a second, and then continued, "I think it would have helped if I had played a bigger part when he was growing up."

Shashi broke into a laugh, almost backing away from its force.

"You never cared about him!" she cried. "You have never cared about any of this. So you think I made him this way? That I, his mother, is responsible for this problem."

"I am not saying that!" he said, his voice rising again. "All I know is that he spent all his time with you and Vidya. Perhaps he needed me more. Maybe"

"Oh what conceit!" she laughed at him hysterically. "Just because you are a man and he was always around women? Is that your point? What would have you done? Tell me! Perhaps it is just as well you never involved yourself. It would only have made matters worse!"

"Don't be ridiculous!"

"You are the one being ridiculous!" she screamed, moving away from the door and into the living room. Her eyes were wide with shock and amazement, her fingers fiercely entwined with each other. Vinod followed her, equally enraged.

"How dare you blame me!" she kept yelling. "With what right?"

"Do not yell!" he replied, as loud as her. "What I said wasn't wrong. He did and continues to spend most of his time with you and Vidya. Maybe that needed to change."

"Well, why didn't you ever change it then! What stopped you? What's stopping you now? Go ahead! Involve yourself! Do it now. Can you? I think you should try it. Just go.."

Shashi had edged near Saurabh's room and was pointing her finger toward his door when she suddenly saw him standing outside it. Almost instantly her face shrank with horror and she lost her voice; one could hear the sound of her panting breath. Saurabh was staring at them both, alternating his gaze from one to another. She shuddered to think how long he had been standing there for and what all he had heard. It was only at that moment that she realized how loud they had been. Her mind quickly raced through all the things they had said to each other; she trembled with anger and disgust.

Vinod, thinking along similar lines, stood with his head bent down, his eyes fixed on his palms, which he mindlessly rubbed against each other. Even though it was a rather cold evening, sweat dripped from his temple. He wasn't sure if he was angry or tired or embarrassed. He didn't dare to look at his son or his wife, knowing that he wouldn't respond well to the expression on their faces. What could they be possibly thinking? For just a moment, he felt a tinge of pity developing within himself towards his son. He shouldn't have heard what he most probably had. That was too harsh for a young boy...wasn't it? But the feeling disappeared as quickly as it had come and was replaced by an overwhelming sense of self-pity.

None of them said a word. After a while, they had even stopped looking at each other. They all appeared as part of an image - an image of a small living room, consisting of three people, all standing in separate postures, their eyes turned away from each other, their mouths firmly shut as if afraid that words would escape from them. There were slight movements once in a while, grazing of arms against clothes, the shuffling of feet, but still, no one reacted or took the initiative. It was soon approaching the point where their situation was looking like a ridiculous farce.

'It was Shashi who broke first and took a step towards her son. "Saurabh," she called out gently, holding out her hand. She appeared calmer than before and much more under control of herself, having benefited from the small period of silence. "We are so sorry," she added, inching closer.

Saurabh glanced at his mother's outstretched hand and then immediately turned around and went back to his room, closing the door behind him. Shashi's hand and head fell with dismay as she felt the tears rising within her. They came swiftly and poured out, and she, rapidly wiping her hands across her face, hastened back inside their room.

Vinod sighed with relief and sat down on a chair. He had neither the inclination nor the energy to further discuss with Shashi. He was just glad that it was over for at least a while. The table in front stared at him invitingly and he lowered his head onto it. He closed his eyes and let his thoughts wander randomly, bumping into old ideas and situations until they automatically came to rest on his deceased mother. He thought of the last discussion he had had with her in this house just a day before she had to go back. A wry smile appeared on his lips and he fought the urge to laugh out audibly, instead, he buried his head in his arms.

Chapter 18

Shashi lay still in bed with her eyes closed as she felt Vinod get up and walk to the washroom. After she heard him close the door, she opened her eyes and turned over slowly, stretching her limbs under the quilt, feeling her joints crackle. Saliva had dripped over her lower lip and onto her chin, which she wiped away nonchalantly with her palm. As had been the case for quite a while now, Shashi felt tired and fatigued after a long night's sleep. The longer she slept, the more drained she felt the next morning. Her eyelids drooped but didn't fall completely. The gentle rays of the sun that just about streamed through their window were strong enough to cause her discomfort. Yet she didn't turn away and lay extremely still.

A little while later, she could once again sense Vinod's movements as the washroom door opened and closed. He entered their room, moving towards the opposite side where the cupboards were. She heard the sound of clothes being shuffled through and then and worn. Soon the mattress on which she lay lurched as Vinod sat down heavily in one corner. He must be tying his shoelaces, she thought. The minutes rolled by as she continued to guess her husband's actions by sensing the sounds and movements around her - the water running in the kitchen, the creak of the living room chair, the strap of the office bag being pulled across his shoulder, and finally a string of footsteps followed by the gentle thud of the main door.

She sat up and looked at the clock, even though she knew it would be around half-past eight; that was the hour Vinod left home each morning. There was still some time before Saurabh would wake up and thus she fell back on the bed, not with the desire to sleep some more but the lack of it to do anything else. She lay there waiting for the clock to run down, paying great attention to every breath of hers, sensing the rise and fall of her chest; she wondered how it was that one generally remained unaware of this continuous bodily activity that, on close inspection, seemed rather deliberate and conscious.

Finally, when enough time had elapsed, she raised herself and moved barefoot to the kitchen. She warmed some milk, poured it into a steel glass, and carried it to Saurabh's room. The door was closed, so she nudged it and entered inside. Her movement was enough to wake up Saurabh, who lay sprawled on his back. Shashi handed him the glass of milk, which he drained within a matter of seconds and then fell in the same position as before. Shashi let him be and took the glass away.

The curtains were drawn in the living room, blocking the morning sunlight. She discreetly peeped from behind one of the curtains, checking to see whether Lata had stepped out of the house yet or not. Sometimes, in the morning, she would find her hanging out clothes to dry in the garden or watering the plants. But unlike today, Shashi herself would be too busy preparing to leave for the hospital to take much notice of that. At that moment, however, she wished Lata was outside so that she too could step out under some pretext and spend as much time with her as possible. But there was no one to be seen. Vidya had already left for school by then. Shashi fully pushed aside the curtains and sat on the chair opposite the window, in full view from the street outside. She was hungry but felt too lazy to make something for herself.

Being idle made her head droop with sleep once again so she stood up and grabbed an apple from the kitchen, munching her way back to her room. Instinctively her gaze moved towards the clock on entering. It was almost 10 am. By this time, she thought, she would have already completed her first round of the ward at the hospital, stopping and chatting with her long time patients. The doctor would have arrived and been in the middle of examining some admitted patients while many more would fill the small waiting area they had at the entrance. Shashi would then proceed to the make-shift pantry they had in one obscure corner of the ward. She would put a large pot of water on the stove and set it to boil. Some of that boiled water would be used for sterilizing tools and the rest for making tea. Shashi, who was in charge of the tools, would collect all the used ones from the previous day's work and dip them in the pot one after another using a tong. The water for the tea would have already been separated by then.

Shashi finished her apple and then looked around aimlessly. Her eyes fell on the lot of dirty clothes that had been lazily piled in one corner of the room. She picked them up and carried them to the washroom where she nearly slipped on entering. There was water all over the floor. She shook her head and exhaled loudly in annoyance. Carefully, maintaining her balance, she filled a bucket with water and immersed the clothes inside, simultaneously adding some detergent. Her hands were still deep inside the bucket when the doorbell rang. She left a trail of soapy water all over the living room floor as she went to open the main door and let Lata in. She was carrying a small pot in her hand.

"I made some tea," she smiled.

"Careful!" Shashi told her, pointing to her feet. "The floor is a little wet. And thanks."

"What were you doing?" she asked as she entered and set the pot down on the living room table.

"Was about to wash clothes," she replied and wiped her hands in the kitchen before handing two cups to Lata.

They both sat down and started to slowly sip their cups of tea.

"This is really nice of you," Shashi said, smiling a little. "But don't spoil me. I shall feel very bad."

"Oh, it's nothing! I just thought....being your first day away from the hospital....you might like some."

"I do."

"Think of the positives! We can spend more time; have tea together each morning!"

Shashi smiled and nodded.

"Geeta and Harish sir would be coming today?"

"Yes. In the afternoon."

Lata extended her arm and placed it on top of Shashi's. "It will be fine," she said. "I am sure it will work."

Shashi nodded and slowly slid her arm away.

"And....is Saurabh not awake yet? It's almost 11."

"Maybe. I haven't checked."

Lata left after a while, leaving Shashi sitting alone at the table. They had drunk two cups of tea each and thus she felt rather awake and invigorated at that moment. She got up and opened Saurabh's door.

"Are you awake?"

"Yes."

"When you go to take a bath, just put aside the bucket of clothes."

"Okay."

"Do you want anything to eat?"

"No."

"Okay. Tell me whenever you are hungry. And have a bath soon."

She turned back and stared at the empty living room, at the slightly askew chairs and the empty cups of tea on the table. On her left, her bedroom door lay open, the tousled sheets in plain view. She took a pause and just stood there, blinking at the surrounding stillness. What was she supposed to do now? she asked herself. At the hospital, the tasks came swiftly one after another. There was never any need or the time to think about the work at hand. It was all automatic and easy; a succession of busy moments that flowed along smoothly until the day was at an end and it was time to go home. But here, now, at 11 am on a weekday in her own house, she felt like a stranger unsure of her next step. Should she finish washing the clothes or tidy up her room? Should she clean the house or tend to her garden? Then there was lunch to be made as well. She could do all or just some of it. Should she set herself some priorities? Did she know what they were? Was there something she had missed? She slowly moved to the table and picked up one of the teacups. Perhaps, before all, she should wash the cups. And so she did.

Later, in the afternoon, Shashi and Saurabh sat down together for lunch that lasted some rather awkward 20 minutes, during which time both of them appeared quite distracted and ill at ease. Shashi racked her brains to come up with something to say, something to reassure her son and herself that it was all going to be alright; but she couldn't and just waited for the time to pass. Afterward, she rummaged through her kitchen drawers and retrieved the large garden scissors that she hadn't used for a very long time. Her garden had always held such importance for her before but had been then almost completely sidelined after Saurabh's birth. She filled a small bucket with water and carried both her tools outside. The sun shone through beautifully, providing some necessary warmth from the cold weather. She set down the bucket on the grass and gave a long appraising look all around the garden. She was struck by how similar it looked to when she had first seen the garden on the day of their arrival in Konkur. The thick and haphazardly growing bushes, the spurts of intermittent flowering, the tall and unkempt grass - it was all in shambles. Shashi knew that she had been neglecting its maintenance for quite a few years now, but she hadn't imagined, and neither had she noticed in between, that the garden would be in such a bad state.

Unsure of how and where to begin, she walked leisurely around the garden, snipping randomly at plants and bushes; the scissors were so heavy that they required both of her hands to lift them. She was enjoying being out in the sun, especially with the gentle and cool breeze that blew across the street. From time to time, she looked expectantly down the road, into that tunnel of trees, from where she knew Vidya would emerge at any moment. She had barely met her ever since Saurabh's expulsion, and she felt this sudden urge to see her and to talk to her.

As she had expected, she soon saw Vidya approaching from far down the road, walking at a steady pace. She noticed the look of surprise on Vidya's face on seeing her in the garden. Shashi tried her best to give her a confident and welcoming smile.

"Hello Vidya," she greeted her.

"Hello."

"It's a really nice day today, isn't it?" she added. Her each word and movement felt rather conspicuous, as if she was feeling extremely conscious of herself. "You and Saurabh should be out today in the evening. It's been so long. He is very bored being inside the house all the time. Aren't you?"

"A little," she replied. "I'll come and take him later."

"That's great."

It took only a moment's pause for Vidya to turn around and continue on her way home. Shashi stared at her retreating back and then once again focused her attention on the scissors in her hand. She cut and snipped for a little while longer, with much more intensity than before but without any real purpose. She soon lost interest and, abandoning her tools in the garden itself, went back inside. She entered Saurabh's room.

"Geeta ma'am would be here soon," she said. "Get ready."

"Can I go outside for a little while?"

"You can go in the evening after classes. Vidya will come."

There was nothing in particular for Shashi to do but wait for Geeta, who arrived at the appointed hour. While Saurabh and Geeta sat down at the small study table in Saurabh's room, Shashi went and lied down on Saurabh's bed, keeping an eye on the two. This was to be her position for the next few hours until both Geeta and Harish had come, taught and left for the day. Shashi took the day's newspaper with her, which she had been saving for this very period. She began to read through it diligently.

Geeta left after an hour and was almost immediately replaced by Harish. By then, Shashi had gone over the newspaper almost twice. She kept it aside and offered to make Harish a cup of tea, which he politely declined. So she once again sat by the bed, staring outside through the window, painfully aware of the slow passage of time. She stifled a few yawns and shifted down further along the bed, making herself as comfortable as possible.

She felt a firm tug on her shoulder and woke with a frightened gasp. Vinod was standing over her, calling out her name. A little dazed, she propped herself up and opened her eyes fully. The sun no longer shone through the window; it was evening. The study table in front of her was empty. In a state of panic, her eyes hurriedly searched for the clock - she had been sleeping for more than three hours. She got up from the bed and nearly slipped, grasping Vinod for support.

"Relax," he said, surprised. "It's okay."

"Where's Saurabh?" she asked, barely registering what he said. "I can't believe I slept for so long." She tried to steady herself and leave but Vinod held on to her.

"He is in the living room. I found him there just now when I arrived. He had been out with Vidya."

Still not completely reassured, she freed herself from his grasp and walked quickly towards the living room. Just as Vinod had said, Saurabh was sitting there on the chair by himself. Seeing that his mother had woken up, he stood and walked past her inside his room.

"Did Vidya come to take you?" she asked him.

"Yes."

"Where did you go?"

"To the graveyard."

Shashi nodded. Bit by bit, she started to feel at ease. Vinod looked questioningly in her direction as if to ask whether she was okay; she gave him a quick smile.

That night, a few hours after they had finished their dinner, Shashi and Vinod lay together in bed. While Vinod was curled up on one side, almost ready to fall asleep, Shashi was staring at the ceiling, wide awake and fully alert. She turned towards Vinod, whose back was against her.

"I can't do this every day," she said softly.

"Hmm.."

"Are you listening?"

"Now...yes," he said and turned over. "What happened?"

"I cannot do this every day."

"I know it's difficult.....but today was the first time. It will get easier."

"There is *nothing* to do at home," she persisted.

"You could do your gardening again," he suggested. "You used to enjoy that; spend more time with Lata."

"You don't understand," she continued, shaking her head. "There is just too much time. And then I have to just sit in his room while he is studying! What can I do then?"

Vinod sighed and looked directly at her. He shook his head on seeing the expression on her face.

"We knew this. We talked about it. You know there is no other way. We have to give it a try. At least for a little while."

Shashi clicked her tongue in annoyance and didn't reply. A part of her knew that Vinod was right, and as much as she wanted this system to work well for Saurabh, she was dreading the part she would have to play in it each day. Vinod could sense how annoyed and uncomfortable she was; it saddened and irritated him in equal measure. He felt a little guilty over the fact that Shashi was the one who had to leave the hospital and be at home all day with Saurabh, while his life continued to be minimally affected by it all. The tacit assumption that it was going to be her who would have to make this sacrifice further added to that guilt, compounded by the fact that he had gone along with that assumption. Shashi's overtly begrudging display reminded him of that guilt, making him impatient.

"Do you have any other solution?" he asked.

She shook her head slowly. "Not right now."

"Well then, let's give it a try. You might feel better. Maybe Saurabh gets better and goes back to school again. Who knows?"

"Okay."

Vinod turned away once again, determined to fall asleep this time. He closed his eyes and started to breathe softly. When he was just on the verge of sleeping, he felt the bed shake, followed by the sound of Shashi's footsteps.

"What's the matter?" he asked sharply, frowning into his pillow, without bothering to look up.

"Nothing. I just forgot to wash the clothes."

Shashi's answer was surprising enough for him to will himself up and lift his head. Shashi opened their bedroom door and walked out, leaving it a bit ajar. The light from the washroom flooded the living area and slipped inside their bedroom. He could hear her drag the small stool and then sit on it. Soon, the sound of clothes being dipped and taken out of water reached his ears. He was about to say something but then he looked at the clock, sighed, and attempted once more to fall asleep.

CHAPTER 19

Shashi felt a strong push against her abdomen and her body lurched backward. Her feet moved rapidly in a desperate attempt to restore her balance, but the distance between her and the bed was too less, and thus her thighs rammed forcefully against its edge. Her feet left the floor, and she fell violently on the bed before the momentum carried her over the edge and she landed on her right arm.

The next minute comprised of a whirlwind of sensations. A surge of pain shot through her arm and back, making her cry out sharply; she heard quick footsteps and then felt someone's arms around her shoulder as she was held and propped against the bed. Her eyes stung because of the sharp ingress of sunlight through the window. She closed them and shook her head slowly from side to side, trying to relieve herself of the pain.

"Shashi!"

On hearing the voice, she opened her eyes once again, just in time to catch the sight of her son outside, running across the street and disappearing from view.

"Shashi!" repeated Harish and knelt in front of her with difficulty.

"Are you okay? Just....just don't move. I'll get Vinod....and some water."

The old man got up slowly and left the room. Shashi continued to stare outside the window, beads of sweat forming around her face. Her right arm was throbbing with pain and her lower back felt numb from the sudden shock; a dull ache erupted from time to time. She didn't try to stand up or even move a little, neither was she waiting for someone to come and pick her up. A great sense of inertia seemed to be upon her. She felt she could have easily sat in that position for a long time, with her eyes fixed to the window, not feeling the urge to move, speak or think.

Vinod hurriedly entered the room with Harish behind him. Shashi's rigid frame struck him immediately; he felt afraid to go near and touch her.

"Shashi," he said softly from the back.

She didn't respond and he thus tiptoed his way in front of her and sat down. Her pallid face seemed to not register his presence; her eyes looked right through him.

"Shashi," he said once again, this time placing his hand on her shoulder.

His touch broke her trance, and the moment she met his eyes, she burst into violent tears. He came closer and held her gently, feeling the reverberations of her head against his chest. He looked sideways at the study table where two books lay sprawled open, their pages flapping lightly. The chair was on the floor, next to which lay a pen, its deep blue ink dripping constantly. He then turned towards Harish.

"Where is Saurabh?"

The old man shuffled his feet and shook his head from side to side in dismay. "He ran out. I couldn't stop him. I didn't think of it."

Vinod nodded and turned his attention back to Shashi, who was still crying but with slightly reduced intensity.

"Let's get up from the floor," he whispered to her. "Lean on me. Can you?"

She tried to put her hands around his neck, but the moment her right arm had to bear some weight, she screamed in agony, clutching at it.

"Oh...okay...okay... wait," said Vinod, setting her down again. "Harish sir, you will have to help me a bit. Once again now, just give me your left arm."

Harish came to Vinod's aid and they gently raised her from the floor, placing her on the bed. Vinod took a close look at her right arm, lifting it gingerly, until the point she winced.

"It's probably just a sprain," he said. "Does it hurt anywhere else?"

"My back," she said, sniffing and wiping away her tears. "More than the arm."

"Don't move. I'll just come."

Vinod walked out of the room and gestured Harish to follow him. He went to the kitchen and took some ice out of the fridge.

"What happened?" he asked, as he put the cubes of ice on a piece of cloth.

"Oh I don't know," he replied, removing his glasses and rubbing his eyes. "I need to sit down."

Harish took a chair and rested his head on his palms. He could feel his legs trembling as he took some deep breaths to recover from the shock.

"I am sorry," he said, looking at Vinod. "I couldn't do anything. Ah.....Saurabh...well, he wasn't really concentrating. She entered and I told her that.....as a joke....harmless really..."

"So he hit her?"

"Not immediately, no. When I told her, she smiled and just asked him to focus....not harshly....but I don't know. It just happened. He pushed her."

"And then ran out."

"Yes," he said and then got up suddenly, exclaiming, "Oh God! We should look for him."

"Don't bother," said Vinod, tying a knot over the cloth and walking towards Saurabh's bedroom. "He'll be fine. Where can he go?"

"But.."

"There is no need," he smiled grimly. "And please, don't trouble yourself. Go home and rest. I'll take care of this."

"Okay. I'll go in a while. Let my legs settle a bit."

Vinod nodded and then entered the room. On seeing him, Shashi tried to sit up straighter.

"No no. I'll put some ice on your back."

"Saurabh," she began as he slipped his arms beneath her and slowly turned her over. "You have to look for him."

"Not right now," he said and started to apply the ice.

She winced a few times as the ice touched her skin, leaving behind a few droplets of water. Her head felt heavy and she closed her eyes. Her mind automatically started going over the entire sequence of events. She wondered if she had been too stern with her remark, trying to gauge the tone she had used but she couldn't place it anymore. The push had been so sudden, accompanied by the crash of the chair as Saurabh got up. It all seemed to have happened in a single moment. And then she had tripped, and as she visualized her fall, once again she became conscious of the pain in her arm and back, as if they were being reminded of the wound they had suffered. But it wasn't the fall that troubled her the most. Instead, it was the image of her son running across the street as she lay propped against the bed. That image stayed with her for a long time.

"What are we going to do?" she asked as the tears overwhelmed her once again. "God...what can we do?"

Vinod stopped rubbing and put the damp cloth on the side table. He held her gently by the waist and made her lie on her back. Their eyes met for an instant and then quickly shied away from each other.

He got up and left the room with the cloth, returning a few minutes later with white gauze. He took Shashi's right arm and was about to bandage it when she stopped him.

"This won't do. I'll need a proper crepe bandage. I'll get it done at the hospital."

"Is it a sprain?"

"Seems so. Should be fine in a few days."

He nodded and put the gauze aside, sitting awkwardly next to her on the bed. He kept his eyes towards the floor.

"I don't know," he said, not lifting his head. "I can't think of anything right now."

"It's okay. We'll talk about it later."

"Hmm. Well, you should rest now," he said and got up. "Do you... ah..do you want to come to our room? Lie there."

"No. I am fine."

"Okay," he said and stared for a few moments at the bed before leaving.

Vinod entered their bedroom and switched off the radio he had been listening to. The Sunday paper lay sprawled on the bed, which he then folded and kept aside. He had left the door open in case Shashi called for him or Saurabh returned. He stood between the door and the bed, looking around the room without registering anything. He seemed dazed and lost, unsure of what to do. He approached the window and looked at the trees outside. His head drooped, and he ran his finger along the window sill, brushing away the layers of dirt. Turning around with a jerk, he thought of lying on the bed, before moving away from it and then out of the room towards the kitchen. He poured himself a glass of water. The idleness of the moment was tormenting him. Wasn't there something that was ought to be done in the present circumstance? Surely the events of the past hour merited an active response. But what should that be? What could he do?

His eyes fell on the open door to Saurabh's room. He inched closer to it, trying his best to not make his presence felt. He peeked inside and saw Shashi sitting on the bed with her legs crossed. Her hands were folded in her lap and she was looking out of the window, possibly waiting for Saurabh to come back. Her eyes were red; her cheeks stained with tears, which continued to flow noiselessly. There was a look of complete dejection on her face; a mark of abject defeat.

Vinod carefully walked across the door and returned to their room.

A few hours later, Shashi was still sitting in the same position Vinod had found her in. She had nodded off for a while in between, but now her gaze was once again fixed towards the window. Her throat was uncomfortably dry but she wouldn't dare to move from her position lest Saurabh arrived during that time and she missed him. She didn't know what it was that she would accomplish by being present at the very instant of his arrival, but she was adamant about it. So she waited, with rapt attention, ignoring all of her body's signs of hunger and thirst.

Saurabh, in direct contrast to how he had run away, came back strolling at a languid pace. Shashi's tired eyes grew wider as she saw him approach the main door. Automatically, and intuitively, she followed his footsteps from behind the solid wall separating them, until he stood in front of her just at the foot of the bedroom door. They both stared at each other for a while.

"I am sorry," he said finally, lowering his head.

Shashi tried her best to not cry in front of her son. She got up, ignoring the pain in her back, and gave him a light hug which he didn't return.

"It's okay," she said. "You should lie down."

She left him in his room and found Vinod lying idly in theirs, staring at the ceiling.

"Saurabh is back," she told him. "Do you want anything to eat?"

Vinod looked up at her with a jerk, her sudden presence catching him off-guard. He barely registered what she had said. "What?"

"Saurabh is back."

"Oh...when?....I mean...how is he?" he asked, standing up.

"He seems fine."

He took a few steps towards the door and then stopped, looking around at Shashi.

"Did you talk to him? Should I? And you should lie down."

She shook her head. "What will you say?"

"I don't know. What did you tell him?"

"Nothing."

He came back and sat on the bed, facing Shashi. Despite the acerbic nature of her tone, she looked at him earnestly, as if expecting him to say something that would instantly bring some measure of relief, a modicum of respite, and just lift her away from the swarm of clouds in her mind in which she seemed to be drowning. But he looked equally lost and bewildered.

"What are we going to do?" she cried.

Vinod raised his shoulders, looking away from her. He felt extremely uncomfortable in the situation he found himself; here she was, his wife, having just been hit by their son, clearly distraught and in need of some help and care, which their relationship mandated that it come from him, while they tried to talk and discuss the future of their son whom they both couldn't understand. There seemed to be no good path in front of him.

"We have to be strong," he said, perfunctorily. "And....I'll discuss this tomorrow with Harish sir."

"What's left now?" she said loudly, almost hitting the bed in her hands in frustration. "Where are we finally going to end?"

"I don't know," he said. "I can't think of anything."

"I think I know," she said frantically, holding her head in her palms. Despite the pain, she was walking at a rapid pace inside their room. "I hate this. But there is no other way."

"What?"

She looked up at him with her red bulging eyes.

"He needs to go," she blurted out.

"Go? Where?"

"We have to send him away," she said, coming closer to him. "Someplace where they will ensure he can't hurt anyone."

"You need to calm down a bit. Let's think about this...I will..."

"No..no," she said, breathing heavily now. She had stopped crying but her eyes were still red and swollen, a hint of delirium in them. "He hit me! His own mother! Who do you think is safe?"

Vinod shook his head slightly but didn't reply. Shashi kept staring at him for a while, expecting a response, but then she slid away and lay down on her side of the bed.

"Let's talk about this tomorrow," he said. "You should take some rest. Should I get you something to eat?"

"No."

He looked at the clock. It was late in the evening. He wasn't inclined to leave the room lest he encountered Saurabh. Shashi was lying very still now, facing away from him. He too lied down, and both of them remained in bed the entire night, their backs to each other, drifting in and out of sleep.

The next day, Vinod left for work at the usual hour, and on his way to the office, visited Saurabh's school and told Geeta, his only other teacher, to not come home for the next few days, making some excuse about Saurabh's health. He met Harish as well and requested him to keep the truth to himself.

Shashi, who had been staying at home ever since Saurabh's

expulsion, spent the day with Lata. During that time, amid frequent fits of tears, she told her friend about the incident. She didn't see Saurabh except for when she had to give him food to eat. Saurabh too stayed in his room the whole time; he had been firmly, but cautiously, asked to do so by Shashi.

In the evening, the four adults assembled at the Sehgals'. This time, instead of dividing themselves into the two customary groups, all of them sat together and engaged in serious deliberations about a subject that was now evidently much beyond their capabilities. Vidya, now almost an adult, too sat with them but didn't offer any opinion. Her face remained impassive throughout; none of them could discern what was on her mind. It didn't take Shashi much time to bring up the matter of completely isolating Saurabh from everyone.

"I am sorry Vidya," said Shashi. She was in tears throughout. "I don't think you should meet him for some time. How can I let something happen to you? It's unimaginable."

Lata nodded discreetly and looked towards her daughter who still wore the same expression on her face. Evidently, she had made up her mind to not speak at all.

"You know.....," said Mahesh, "young boys sometimes have to just let go of some steam...I mean, of course, it's terrible....but you really think isolation is the way to go?"

"I don't know if there is an answer," said Shashi, pacing around the room. She was the only one among them who was continuously on her feet. "But how can we take that risk?"

"So what will you do?" asked Lata. "He still needs to finish school. And please do sit down, you will tire yourself."

Shashi stopped and looked at Vinod, as if checking to see whether he was going to support her with what she was going to say next. He caught her gaze and nodded slightly.

"We think we need to send him away."

"Maybe a boarding school," mentioned Vinod, but didn't say

anything further.

"Oh...well..they are pretty strict there...I have heard," remarked Mahesh.

"Wouldn't that be good for him?" asked Shashi, sitting down now and looking directly at Mahesh, hoping for confirmation.

"I can't say," he said, uncomfortable at being questioned with such earnestness. "If he misbehaves, they are going to handle it much better. They will be tough on him though."

Lata came closer to Shashi and put her arms around her. It seemed as if she was stuck in a cycle of frenzy and depression, switching from one to another intermittently, and right now it was evident that she was going to break down again.

"It will be fine," she said, holding her tightly. "It is a phase. It will go away as he grows older and matures. You need to have hope."

They declined the Sehgals' offer to have dinner and left after a little while. They found Saurabh in his room and gave him his food before retiring for the night.

"Why don't you go to the hospital tomorrow?" asked Vinod when they were both lying in bed with the lights switched off.

"Huh?"

"It might be good for you."

"How can I? Saurabh would be at home."

"He'll be fine. Lata can check on him from time to time."

"I can't ask her to do that."

"It's up to you."

They both fell silent and rolled on their backs. Vinod closed his eyes and tried to sleep, while Shashi kept staring blindly in the dark, her mind churning ceaselessly, going over the random details associated not just with yesterday's incident, but with all the others that had taken place over the years. They were all like little pieces of an incoherent jigsaw puzzle. She just couldn't add it all together to make some sense out of it.

"Are you awake?" she asked Vinod.

"Yes."

"Should we do it?"

"The boarding school?"

"Yes. What do you think?"

"We'll never know whether it will work without trying it."

"I just hope the other children don't make it worse."

"They could. It's a gamble."

"So should we take it? Tell me please!"

"I suppose so."

"Yes!" she said with a certain fervor. "Yes, we have to!"

CHAPTER 20

Lata wept softly and noiselessly, continuing to wipe away her tears using her palm. Shashi was sitting next to her, holding her friend by the shoulder, looking at her with concern and dismay. Her own eyes, red at the edges with dark shadows beneath them, were reflective of the kind of pain her friend was currently experiencing. They were in Lata's house; it was a little while after Vidya had left for school.

"Do you want me to talk to her?" asked Shashi but Lata shook her head.

"I know her. You know her. She is extremely adamant. She won't listen to anyone."

Shashi nodded and looked away. She was well aware of that.

"What about Mahesh?" she asked. "She won't even listen to him?"

Lata gave a short laugh but then started to cry once more.

"His words mean nothing to her," she said softly, as if embarrassed of what she was saying. "She is not scared of him."

Shashi held her closely as a fresh torrent of tears ran down Lata's face. "She'll be fine," she tried to reassure her, feeling a lump in her throat. "She is so strong."

Lata nodded and shook her head rapidly in order to compose herself. Shashi gave her a glass of water, which she gulped down in one go.

"When does she want to leave?"

"After Saurabh goes away. Her school term is almost over."

"Did she say why?"

"Not exactly....but I know...so do you," she said hesitatingly. "It hasn't been easy for her."

Shashi looked away again. "Yes, I know."

"Can you help her?"

"How?"

"She still wants to be a nurse; like you. Do you know someplace close by?"

"I don't. But I can ask at the hospital," she replied. "She won't like to work here before?"

"Not anymore. I have said that so many times. But nothing seems to convince her."

"I'll ask then. Don't worry. I am sure someone will know something. When....ah..when did she tell you this?"

"Last night. While we were having dinner. Mahesh...he yelled so much, I was afraid you might hear him across the road."

They both sat together quietly for a while, looking away from each other, not willing to further talk about what was on both of their minds. They were scared and sad, unsure of what the future held for them and their children. Their hands lay loosely entwined, secure in each other's presence. Shashi wasn't used to providing a comforting hand to her friend; it had always been she who had needed Lata's reassurances, which she had inevitably received. And now, for the first time, it was Lata who lay broken and distraught, helpless in the situation her daughter had placed her. Shashi's eyes filled with tears of shame as she realized that even now, it was she who had placed this large burden on her friend; her son who was in a way responsible for driving Vidya away from them all. Vidya - that girl whom she loved as her own daughter, whom, much like her son, she had seen growing in front of her own eyes - was now a stranger to her, as well as her mother. She disliked them all; rage and disappointment shone through her eyes whenever she was in their presence. Shashi couldn't help but think that it was all her fault, borne out of her home, and thus she let the tears of guilt roll down without restraint.

"I am sorry," she said to Lata, placing her head on her friend's shoulder.

Lata too couldn't help but cry on seeing Shashi in such a state.

"No," she said feebly. "What have you done? Nothing....absolutely nothing."

"How...how did we get here?" she asked, struggling to speak through her tears.

Lata shrugged and didn't answer.

"Tell me...tell me honestly," she continued. "What did I do wrong?"

Lata just shook her head again and smiled while wiping her face.

"Don't ask that question," she replied, looking straight at Shashi. "I don't know. I just feel as if I don't know anything right now"

Shashi nodded. "Neither do I."

On the day of Saurabh's departure, he and Vinod left early in the morning towards the Market Center. From there, they would catch the bus to drop Saurabh at the boarding school to which they had managed to get him admitted. While they were going through their last-minute preparations at home, Shashi cried at regular intervals, giving Saurabh one long hug just before the two set off. Lata and Mahesh stood nearby with solemn looks on their faces. As soon as the rickshaw pulled away, Lata came closer to Shashi and held her firmly, while the latter buried her face in her friend's arms. Vidya slept through it all.

Vinod was gone for a total of four days, during which time Lata stayed permanently with Shashi in her house. She didn't ask and Shashi didn't protest. Lata took charge of her friend's well-being, for whom the shock of seeing her son going away had been too overwhelming. Shashi barely said or did anything, spending most of her time lying in bed or out sprawled on a chair in her garden.

"You can go back and work at the hospital once again," suggested Lata one day, hoping that the proposal would bring some cheer to her friend.

But Shashi simply shrugged and dismissed the notion. It had been almost two years since she had worked last. While the loss of her job had affected her strongly at first, the feeling had dulled over time, to the point now that she hardly even thought about it. That job just didn't matter to her anymore, and thus the prospect of returning to it wasn't one that gave her any semblance of pleasure.

When Vinod returned, he was immediately thronged by Lata and Shashi, who asked him endless questions about the boarding school. Where was it exactly? What was it like? Did he meet the Principal? How was the hostel? Were there other students there? How was Saurabh? Despite his fatigue from the long journey, he answered all of their questions as patiently and in as much detail as he could.

"He seemed okay when I left," he replied. "It'll be fine. I've told them to call us immediately if anything goes wrong."

"Look," he added, seeing the lack of conviction on Shashi's face. "We did what we thought was best. Now let's wait and see."

Vidya, on the other hand, was conspicuously keeping to herself the entire time. She was no longer interested to be part of any conversation that the four adults engaged in. She hadn't asked a single question regarding Saurabh, neither to Shashi nor to her mother. Shashi had managed to get her a job at a hospital in Ketupur, a town around 500 kilometers away from Konkur. Her day of departure too was now fairly near, and she couldn't wish for it to come sooner. Her final year in school had officially ended a few weeks before and now she was simply sitting at home, idling away her time, counting down to the days to when she could leave.

Lata was dreading the moment when she would be placed in the same situation as Shashi had been; her friend's deteriorating state of mind after she had seen her son go away felt like a forewarning of sorts. But she knew it wasn't the same. Vidya had made the choice by herself. She didn't want to stay with them any longer and instead wished to build a life somewhere far away, free of their presence. It was this fact that differentiated the two situations, that swirled constantly in her mind, hurting and embarrassing her at every instance of recollection.

As had been the case with Saurabh, Vidya was accompanied to the bus stop one morning by her father; it was a little over a month after Saurabh had left Konkur. There were no elaborate goodbyes - just brief hugs and wishes of good luck, as the four adults once again took leave of one of their children. Lata managed to somehow restrain her emotions, having already shed countless tears in private. Yet Shashi stood next to her and held her in her grasp, as Lata had done for her. Much more than Lata, it was Shashi who seemed to be having a harder time. Vidya's going away reminded her of that of her son. She offered to stay with Lata until the time that Mahesh came back.

"Thanks but it's okay," smiled Lata and shook her head. They were still standing outside on the street. It had only been five minutes since Vidya and Mahesh had disappeared from view. Vinod had already returned inside. "I'll be fine."

"Are you sure?" she asked, still holding her by the shoulder. "Let me."

Lata looked into Shashi's eyes for a brief moment and then nodded. The two hugged each other tightly and succumbed to their emotions. They stayed in that embrace for a long time, all alone on the street, feeling abandoned and betrayed by those they loved and left behind with those they didn't. This was the irrevocable bond they shared - of having raised their children together, only to be robbed of them. They walked slowly to one edge of the street and sat on the dirty pavement; there was nothing they could think of doing.

Mahesh returned some days later and was subjected to the same number of questions that Vinod had been and gave similar taciturn responses. Yes, the hospital there looked small but decent. Yes, he had found her a room with a neighbouring family. Yes, they had fought a bit once. Yes, they had both yelled at each other. No, there was no need to worry.

Vidya's and Saurabh's departure caused a ripple among the rest of the residents of Konkur. Children moving away from their parents wasn't something that happened in this town; generations after generations were born and then died in the homes of their respective fathers, spending their lives in the vicinity of people they had always known. Aberrations were rare, almost non-existent.

As Shashi and Lata only occasionally ventured to the Market Center, they weren't exposed to the remarks and questions that their husbands faced daily. The feeling among the people was more or less the same - shock as regards to Vidya and solemn inevitability for Saurabh.

"You did the right thing," said Gaurav to Vinod. "A hostel would set him right."

"Let's see."

"I just know it!" he exclaimed in his garrulous manner. Vinod simply nodded and smiled.

"And what's this I hear about that young girl? The Garage owner's daughter? She left?"

"Yes. She is working for a hospital in Ketupur."

"Why not here?" he asked, raising his eyebrows, his eyes wide with surprise. "We have a hospital."

"She didn't want to."

"God! I would never let my daughter go away alone to some strange city. What was he thinking?"

"I don't know."

For Vinod, such conversations occurred fairly regularly in his office, with Gaurav being responsible for almost all of them. Vinod responded as tersely as possible, tired of constantly fending off similar remarks. Some of them, disguised in the form of questions, felt akin to verbal attacks that were constantly trying to breach his defense, to get him to admit that theirs was a situation beyond repair, that he had made a mistake in sending his son away to a place where he would have no control over his day-to-day behaviour, where he would fall into bad circles that would further aggravate his condition, that he had let his son be influenced by that girl who now herself had ran away, that maybe she was the cause of all his troubles, that he had treated his son too nicely and should have been tough with him in order to instill some discipline, that he had been an extremely ineffective father, and in fact that he had never really been a father at all. He didn't know how many of these remarks had such veiled intentions and how many he was imagining by himself.

But the questions and discussions didn't die once he left office. They followed him and continued at home.

It had been more than two months since Saurabh had left but Shashi had still not rejoined the hospital, despite Vinod having suggested the same many times. Had two years of being confined to their home made her habitual of the confinement? Was she embarrassed about facing her friends at work? Was she angry? Was she depressed? These were the questions Vinod asked himself but dared not to ask her. All he knew that she was not okay and that she was slowly losing her health and her mind. Each evening when he returned home, he was met with the same blank stares and silent pleas to which he didn't know how to respond. She was always so quiet, seemingly in a state of deep thought. And when they were in bed, she always asked him the same questions, irrespective of the fact whether he answered them or not. It was a while before he realized that she was putting those questions to herself.

"Would he be happy in that place alone? What if he fights with someone? Do they properly know about his problem? They wouldn't be too hard on him, would they? We did the right thing.....the more I think the more I believe it was right...I hope the hostel is nice...I wonder if he eats properly.....And Vidya?......I don't understand her anymore... She was such a sweet child.......Lata is distraught......I too would be......I hope it's working."

And so such an endless chain would encircle Vinod every other night. At first, he had responded diligently, albeit with a hint of annoyance, to everything his wife said or asked, but slowly he understood that his responses didn't matter. He could simply lie there and let her talk while making small noises from time to time to just let her know he was awake. And then suddenly she would fall asleep, sometimes in the middle of a sentence, and it would take Vinod a little while to realize that she wasn't speaking anymore, at which point he too would finally manage to sleep.

Thus one day, when he had just returned from office, Vinod was surprised to see Shashi somewhat alert and sharp or at least trying to be. She was dressed well and was moving around the house with a certain energy and purpose. She even smiled feebly on seeing him enter.

"I was waiting for you," she said. "Lata and Mahesh have invited us for dinner. It's been such a long time. Should be good."

Vinod nodded. It definitely had been quite a while since the four of them had congregated together in the manner they used to so frequently before. Though Vinod had always dreaded those evenings, even he felt that it might just be the distraction they were all looking for; if only for one evening.

"Get ready quickly," she urged him.

Fifteen minutes later, they were both standing outside the Sehgals' doorstep, waiting to be let in. Lata opened the door and welcomed them with a beaming smile. She too had taken the necessary pains to dress well for the occasion. Mahesh stood behind her, looking equally pleased to see them. The entire scene felt from more than a decade ago. The only conspicuous absence, of course, was that of Vidya.

As before, Mahesh led Vinod by the hand in one corner, offering him a drink that he had already begun to pour. Vinod accepted, which further brought a smile to Mahesh's face.

"Good!" he said, giving him a glass, "you are learning."

By habit, Vinod turned to look at the women, who were in the kitchen, preparing tea for themselves. He would have much preferred to have some tea, he thought. They both looked happy for a change, with huge grins on their faces, talking endlessly about random things, even though there wasn't the small prancing figure of Vidya around the two.

"You wouldn't believe who came today in the garage," began Mahesh boisterously. Vinod pretended to hear what he was saying. "Harish...."

Vinod's ears pricked on hearing his son's teacher's name, but he refrained from making a comment and tried to focus on the drink in his hand. He wasn't a drinker by any means, having never developed or derived any sense of pleasure from it. The bitterness made him gulp it down quicker than he should have, hoping to quickly get rid of the unpleasant taste. But that only resulted in Mahesh refilling his glass, along with his own.

Harish's name had triggered his mind to go down a specific path of memories - the day the old teacher had hurried inside his room, a look of fear and anguish on his face; the image of Shashi sitting on the floor against Saurabh's bed, staring outside the window, almost in a comatose state; Gaurav's insinuation that he had let Saurabh slip away from his hands and let him be controlled by the women; the fight he had had with Shashi in the living room, with Saurabh standing in one corner; the last time he saw Saurabh before returning home; the sound of Shashi washing clothes in the middle of the night.

He slipped the empty glass clumsily on the counter next to him and stood up. He started to move hurriedly towards the main door.

"Hey," called out Mahesh, following him. "Where are you going? What happened?"

Vinod stopped and turned around. All six eyes were on him, a mixture of confused and sad glances.

"I just feel like going home," he said, looking down on the floor. He was feeling extremely unsure of himself at that moment.

"Just sit down," said Mahesh, laughing and coming closer. "The drink has hit you a bit. It will be fine."

Vinod felt Mahesh's arm coming across his shoulder, but he pushed it away with a sudden surge of violence.

"No!" he shouted, making Lata and Shashi stand up in alarm. "What are we doing here?" he added, not looking at anyone. "It's all useless. It's all so useless."

With that, he quickly left and marched on to the street. The other three were too stunned to follow him. Shashi began to weep.

Outside, Vinod stopped for an instant in the middle of the street, taking in the view of the hills rising behind their house. He looked on either side of the road, his eyes stretched wide, trying to gaze as far into the darkness as he could.

Part 3

Only that day dawns to which we are awake

Henry David Thoreau
(Walden & Civil Disobedience)

CHAPTER 21

A cool breeze was blowing across the Market Center. It was around 7 in the evening, and thus most shops had already closed down for the day, while others were in the process of doing so. It was dark but some street lights were functioning, giving a strange appearance to the area.

The other passengers of the bus soon dispersed in random locations - some on rickshaws, others on foot. A few among them recognized Vidya but didn't approach her. Vidya waited until most of them were out of sight. She stretched her arms and legs, feeling the pain in her limbs. She then slowly took the familiar and lonely road that headed straight from the Market Center and into the darkness.

She was in no hurry. The journey, as it always did, had left her extremely fatigued. Her back was stiff and in immense pain from having to sit uncomfortably in a cramped and rickety bus for almost 12 hours at a stretch. She was struggling to carry her bag, which she shifted from one shoulder to another at frequent intervals. She now regretted saying no the rickshaw puller and wondered why she had refused him so outrightly.

There was a torch in her bag that she generally kept for this stretch of the road but she was too tired to even stop and take it out. Her eyes slowly adjusted to the darkness, and she began to see the outlines of trees and bushes on either side, yet she stumbled a few times on the rocks that lay about on the road. She looked up at the sky; slowly a few stars made themselves visible and she could see the profile of the moon behind a thin cloud. Their light never reached this path, always failing to penetrate through the towering trees.

A little while later, her head automatically turned towards her left as the entrance to the graveyard approached. She hadn't been there since the night before Saurabh had left; that was four years ago. Since then, she had walked past it on quite a few occasions, but had never ventured inside. Today, knowing that Saurabh was home and that she would soon be seeing him, she stopped and moved towards the gate. It was still held together by that old rusty lock. She felt a sudden urge to climb over it but her fatigue intervened once again. She simply stared through the iron bars, the small white headstones just about visible.

She walked on, now with more pace and intensity, and then eventually slowed down once again as the two houses came into view. They were both lit. Vidya's gaze fell on Saurabh's window; it was dark inside. Could he be asleep at this hour, she thought. Her feet tapped nervously on the road as she wondered whether she ought to go and see Shashi first. However, she quickly realized that she wasn't in the mental or physical condition to meet Shashi and Saurabh at that moment. She turned towards her own house and rang the bell. Lata opened the door and almost shrieked with surprise. She immediately came forward to tightly hug her daughter.

"Why didn't you say you were coming?" she chastised her affectionately, cupping Vidya's cheeks in her palms. By now Mahesh had come out too, having heard Lata's scream. Vidya gave him a quick hug as well.

"I didn't remember," she replied. She had indeed completely forgotten that she had rather vehemently said no to coming back home but had then later changed her mind without informing her mother.

Lata, however, wasn't in the mood to complain, and so she didn't question her further. Instead, she made Vidya sit down beside her, holding her hand.

"You must be tired and hungry. Should I get you something to eat?

Vidya nodded. The only thing she wanted to do right then was to quickly eat something and then sleep. "I am really tired," she added.

"Of course," exclaimed Lata. "I'll just come. We will talk in detail tomorrow."

Vidya had a small meal before retiring to her room. She threw her bag in one corner and fell on the bed, not bothering to change out of her clothes. In that instant, her eyes caught a faint flicker of light coming from across the street; it was too dark to miss it. She stood up straight and looked through the window. The light in Saurabh's room was now on, but she couldn't see anything inside because the curtains had been drawn; not even a shadow was visible. She slumped down on her bed once again, almost instantly entering into a deep sleep.

The next morning, she woke up with the sunlight flooding inside her room. Small lines appeared on her forehead as she turned her face towards the dark. Her watch was still on her wrist, but her water-filled eyes took a while to focus and discern the hour; it was 10 am. She turned away from the watch and stretched herself lazily on the bed; she had been asleep for over 12 hours.

The door to her room was open. She assumed, with a slight frown on her face, that her mother had been in and out of her room, probably waiting for her to get up. Let her come once again, she thought. Continuing to lie on the bed, she thought of the things she would do that day. Nothing appealed to her greatly.

Vidya had barely been with Saurabh for the last four years - not after that night in the graveyard, the day before Saurabh had left for the hostel. It wasn't as if the opportunities hadn't presented themselves. Saurabh was officially permitted, as per the rules of his school, to go home thrice a year - 1 month during the summer, 15 days during the winter and 1 week during Diwali; and he was always home during those periods. Vidya tried to arrange her visits to not coincide with those of Saurabh. Even when that wasn't possible - on a few instances during Diwali - she maintained a strictly perfunctory relationship with him, engaging only in as little conversation as possible. If Saurabh was in any way surprised by her behaviour, he didn't show it. He simply kept it to himself, as he always had.

Vidya's reluctance to be around Saurabh surprised her as much as it did Lata and Shashi. She discovered this reluctance by chance when she came home during Diwali for the first time after having left Konkur. Her mind and body naturally tried to escape from Saurabh's presence; perhaps they recognized in it the source of many tumults, instances of mental agony, long periods of restlessness of the years gone by, and thus attempted to avoid it altogether. Or perhaps just the thought of sitting and talking with her friend once again about the same old things appeared as an exhausting proposition. Whatever the case might be, Vidya found herself automatically staying away from the one person she had tried to cling onto till the very end, despite the families' intervention. And hence her behaviour, while inexplicable to others, was a cause of great distress for her, as well as a piercing sense of guilt.

Tired of waiting for her mother, she got up from the bed and went to the living room. Lata, who had been chopping some vegetables, smiled and rose on seeing her. Her good mood from the night before had lasted well into the morning.

"Did you sleep well? Want some tea?"

Vidya said yes to both and sat down. She automatically picked up the knife and started to chop a few vegetables herself.

"I am almost done," shouted Lata from the kitchen. "Let it be."

Vidya dropped the knife and sat idly, waiting for her cup of tea. "How is Shashi Aunty?" she asked.

Lata didn't reply immediately. She finished making the cup of tea and brought it over. After they had both taken a few sips, she put her cup down and looked at Vidya.

"She has worsened. You know she hasn't been well for a long time now. It wasn't getting better....and now....since she found out about Saurabh's expulsion...." Lata finished the sentence with a few shakes of her head, as if unable to describe the grave nature of the situation.

"How long has Saurabh been home?"

"Only a few days. I called you just a day after he returned. I wasn't really expecting you to come," she said and smiled. Vidya could easily sense that her mother was pleased with her. She got up and took her empty cup to the kitchen, rinsing it in the sink.

"I'll go and see them both soon," added Lata. "In an hour or two."

"Okay. I'll come with you."

Vidya went back to her room and started to unpack her bag, which she had casually thrown in one corner the night before. She had brought clothes only for a few days, not reflecting in her haste as to how long she was going to stay. In any case, she put them in her old cupboard, which still contained some of her old clothes. About an hour later, she was ready to leave. They both walked across the road and gently knocked on the door. It was around noon by then, and though the sun shone bright and high up in the sky, there was a distinct chill in the air.

The door was opened by Saurabh; Vidya hadn't expected that. But then, she realized that Vinod would be at work and Shashi was unwell. Saurabh stared at the two women without any remarkable expression on his face.

"Hello," he said, letting them in.

Vidya nodded awkwardly and stepped inside while Lata exchanged a few pleasantries with Saurabh, which Vidya was too distracted to register. She stood right in the center of the living room, near the main table, her hands clasping the chair in front of her. She felt at a complete loss of what to say or do; she almost jumped when her mother gently tapped her on the shoulder.

"I'll first go and be with Shashi for a while. You two be together."

Vidya nodded and sat down and was soon joined by Saurabh.

She could hear her mother's voice as she entered Shashi's room. For a while, she focused only on the sounds coming from that bedroom, even though she couldn't make out the words. She then turned around and looked towards Saurabh; they hadn't said a single word to each other this entire time.

"So," she tried to begin. "When did you come?"

"A few days ago?"

"And what happened this time?"

"I got into a fight. The usual."

For a moment, Vidya felt as if she detected a tiny hint of a smile on Saurabh's face as he said that; but if so, then it had quickly disappeared. She thought of asking him some more questions about his hostel, but then remembered that he had just been expelled; she avoided it. She barely knew anything about his hostel life - what he studied, the friends he had, the troubles he had gotten into - which was in stark contrast to when they had both been in Konkur. She had known everything then. Now, she thought, it was too late to start making any inquiries.

"How is your hospital work?" Saurabh asked her suddenly, breaking her chain of thought.

"Uh..oh..it is normal. There is a lot of work."

"We have a small clinic at the hostel as well."

"Is there a doctor there?"

"A doctor, a nurse and another lady who sits at the front. Not permanently; they all come and go."

His voice had changed, she thought, and her glance automatically fell on Saurabh's face, as if expecting to see any visible representation of this new tone of voice; it was much fuller and deeper than she remembered. Her gaze fell on the small scar just at the corner of his right temple, which ran all the way down to his right ear. She then involuntarily appraised him from head to toe, trying to spot other scars or scratches that he might have collected over these years, but they were none that were easily visible. She had known that his incidents had continued to occur periodically at the hostel; she had heard about a few of them from her mother.

Slowly a familiar feeling started to build up within her. There was anxiety and concern, mixed with confusion and anger. She felt as if she was once again sitting next to Saurabh at the pond, asking him those questions that burned inside her, wondering why he never seemed to have any answers, unsure of whom to blame for a problem that none understood. Those same old questions, that for a while had remained buried in obscurity, started to appear an inch closer to her heart. She looked down and clenched her fists tightly.

"You still don't know, do you?" she finally asked, unable to control herself. Her voice broke as she uttered the words. Saurabh was looking at her impassively.

"I don't. I never have."

Vidya nodded, looking away and blinking rapidly. The answer disappointed but didn't surprise her. It had been the same all along. Perhaps this was why she had unconsciously stayed away from him these last few years. She was angry at herself for having asked the question, knowing well that it never had and probably never would help either of them. She turned towards Shashi's bedroom door, fervently hoping that her mother would return soon.

"When are you going back?" he asked her.

Vidya looked at him and attempted to study his face for an instance. There seemed to be no sign of discomfort or pain, two characteristics that she was sure were quite visible on hers. How could he look so calm and at ease while she could barely find words to say to him? But then her face broke into a little smile - a smile of dismay - and she shrugged away her thoughts. That's how it had always been, she again said to herself. Her time away from Konkur seemed to have made her forget these simple things that she had always known and was now encountering once again. Nothing has changed, she thought, a realization that reassured and saddened her in equal measure.

"I don't know yet. In a few days. And you?"

"Where do I have to go?" he shrugged.

"And your studies? Don't you have to complete school?"

"I almost have. Just a year to go. What could I miss? What have I learnt?"

The lines on Vidya's forehead deepened as her eyebrows slanted towards the top of her nose.

"What will you do then? You won't find work like this!" she said, with more impetus in her voice. "How can you stay here?"

"You found work. And they don't teach you how to be a nurse in school. I'll do something here."

"Here! In *this* town!"

Saurabh got up from his chair and moved away. The expression on his face hadn't changed but his body showed clear signs of agitation. Vidya, unafraid, slowly gaining confidence and regressing to the time when she as a young girl used to take care of Saurabh, pressed him once again.

"You must do something Saurabh," she implored him. "Here... there is nothing for you. They won't let you live in peace. No one will work with you. You have to go away. You must learn how to live by yourself."

Saurabh wasn't looking at her. His gaze was fixed towards the window by the main door. Outside, some clouds had gathered, alternatively hiding and revealing the sun. The street continuously switched between being bathed in sunlight or being under shade. A shaft of light broke through the window and ended up near Saurabh's feet, appearing and disappearing at will. His eyes automatically fell to observe the phenomenon.

"How did you learn?"

"Sorry?"

"To live by yourself. How did you learn?"

"It....just happened....," she said. "And it will happen for you too. But not here."

Saurabh continued to stare at his feet for a little while longer before coming back and sitting down in front of Vidya once again. He was about to say something when Shashi's door opened and Lata emerged from inside. She immediately turned towards the two, her somber face breaking into an uneasy smile.

"Vidya," she said. "Come."

Vidya didn't leave her seat. The prospect of confronting Shashi, especially now when she was in the middle of this conversation with Saurabh, didn't appeal to her at all. In addition to that, she could discern by the look on her mother's face that Shashi was rather unwell. It had been so long since she had last spent some time with her; she wondered what she would say or how she would act in front of her. She looked pleadingly at her mother.

"In a little while," she said, though she knew Lata wouldn't accept that. "I am talking with Saurabh."

"It's great that you two are talking," said Lata firmly, "but you can always do that later. You have a lot of time."

Vidya briefly thought about retorting but then gave up the idea. She didn't have the energy for it. She reluctantly got up and moved towards her mother. At that point, Saurabh too got up, but instead of following Vidya, he walked away and went outside to stand in the garden. Lata immediately turned towards Vidya.

"What's wrong?"

"Nothing," she said impatiently. "I just didn't feel like seeing her."

"She is asking for you! And she is not well. You know how she has always been so fond of you. And you liked her too!"

Vidya didn't reply and nodded gently, looking away from her mother.

"Come on."

Vidya glanced outside to where Saurabh was standing. She wanted to know what he was going to say before her mother came. She sighed and looked away.

"Okay."

CHAPTER 22

Vidya stood outside Shashi's room, scared to go in. She felt a prod on her shoulder and looked behind; Lata's imploring eyes were locked on her as she nudged her daughter forward. Saurabh was still outside, but now Vidya couldn't see him across the window. She finally took a deep breath and entered inside.

The first thing that struck her immediately was the smell. It had a familiar tinge to it. The room was hot and damp, and it felt as if a layer of stale air had permanently settled inside it. The windows were all closed with the curtains drawn across them. Her body recoiled and it took her a moment to stabilize herself.

Shashi was lying in one corner of the bed. Her head was propped against a pillow, and despite the heat, the rest of her body was covered with a plain sheet. She lay straight, barely moving an inch. But her eyes were open and alert, and at that moment, hooked on Vidya.

"You have come," she said. Her voice sounded weak and tired. Vidya could barely understand what she was saying. She came closer and stood beside her. Shashi's face was pale and shrunken, with deep wrinkles all over. Vidya hadn't expected her to be in such a bad state. She knew that Shashi's health had been progressively worsening over time; she had been a witness to that. However, when she had last seen her over 6 months ago, she had looked considerably better than today. Vidya felt like taking her hand and reading her pulse but then checked herself.

"You don't look good Aunty," she said.

"Why would I," replied Shashi, giving a meek smile. There was no strength in her voice. "Sit down. How are you?"

Vidya sat on the edge of the bed uncomfortably and simply nodded in response to the question. She looked at her bedside table and saw a small box of tablets kept on it. It was close enough that she could read the label.

"Do you take them every day?" she asked, pointing towards the bottle.

"Just one. I can't sleep without them. But don't worry, I am careful."

"Why don't you go to the hospital?"

Shashi shook her head with as much vigour as she could muster. "I can't go back there. I cannot be among those people. I cannot hear the same things again and again."

"It will not be that bad. You need to go."

"I won't."

Vidya got up and moved towards the window. She was finding it hard to breathe.

"Can you even breathe here! I am opening the windows."

Shashi winced as some light fell on her face. Vidya had drawn the curtains away and fully opened the windows. She took some deep breaths and began to feel better. Once again, she sat down beside Shashi.

"Have you spoken with Saurabh?"

"Yes. We were sitting outside."

Shashi's eyes began to brim with tears; she turned her face away but couldn't control herself and thus began to cry quietly. Vidya sat there, transfixed, uncomfortable, not knowing what to say.

"What do we do with him Vidya?" she asked, her voice utterly broken. Vidya didn't respond and just continued to sit there in silence, her head down and her fingers tightly entwined within each other.

Shashi, somewhat embarrassed, slowly lifted herself until her back was completely straight against the wall. She removed the sheet from above her and brought her legs closer to her body, wiping away her tears.

"I am sorry. I am fine," she said, trying to sound more alert. "You tell me. How is the hospital."

"It's the same."

"And Madam Sinha? She still troubles everyone?"

"That's her habit. But she means well. I am directly below her now, so she treats me a little better."

Shashi nodded and looked away, seemingly deep in thought.

"You have done good Vidya," she said after a while and smiled at her. "When you left, we didn't know what would happen. But you did well."

"It wasn't all that difficult. I was lucky."

"I don't know," she said, her voice starting to break once again. "Maybe it wasn't, but you did it and it was all good. Lata must be so proud of you. I am proud of you."

With that, she started to cry once again, and this time didn't let the shame of doing so stop her. Vidya, trying hard to not follow her, dug her fists firmly into the mattress. She looked hard at Shashi, her eyes flared and her eyebrows raised.

"I had your help. I had the opportunity. Maybe that's all that Saurabh needs."

Shashi looked up with surprise, not understanding what Vidya was trying to say. Her tears were flowing freely but she couldn't be bothered to wipe them away.

"What do you mean? We didn't help him?"

Vidya got up from the bed, her body trembling.

"Well...He.....he was never given a chance," she said, her voice rising automatically. "I mean....after the first few times...it was just always him....it was always his fault."

"You were there! You know what he did," replied Shashi, biting her lower lip to ease the flow of tears. She looked quite aghast at what Vidya was saying.

"I know....but..." Vidya was shaking her head as she paced around the room. She wasn't in control of what she was saying or what she further was going to. There just seemed to be a chaotic mass of thoughts swirling inside her head that threatened to breakthrough.

"He couldn't have been wrong every time," she said finally, walking faster and faster. "But he was blamed for everything, even things he could never have done. No one helped him. No one understood."

Shashi practically stood up, her knees burying into the bed as she steadied herself.

"What are you talking about!" she retorted, her voice now matching Vidya's intensity. She looked visibly hurt. "We tried to help him every time. How can you blame us? Do you even know how many times Vinod and I had to plead before the school to let him stay? He would have been expelled years before if not for that!"

"That's because no one was patient enough! No one tried to understand the problem. No one.....," Vidya stopped and ran her fingers all over her face as she tried to control her frustration that was now clearly rising above her. There was a part of her that knew that what Shashi was saying was correct, but she just couldn't bring herself to agree with that. There had to be a mistake. There just did. She slowed down and stood in one corner. "I am just saying that....no one...no one tried or did the right thing."

Shashi got off the bed to confront Vidya. She stood right next to her.

"I love my son more than anyone," she said with bitterness. "And I know what I am talking about. He hit his friends, his teachers; he hit me! So don't you tell me that I didn't try! I tried long enough and I am still trying."

Shashi was looking straight at Vidya as she said this. But Vidya didn't retract and held her ground.

"You sent him away! You sent him to a hostel where you knew he would be surrounded by so many other strangers who would make it even more miserable for him. And they did. And now he is back. What was the point! No...you didn't try."

Shashi and Vidya were practically glaring at each other when Lata entered the room on hearing their raised voices. She saw the two of them standing near the window, with hostility and anger on their faces.

"Vidya....," began Lata softly. "What's happening?"

"Your daughter," said Shashi, not waiting for Vidya to respond, "is accusing me of being a bad mother."

"I didn't say that."

"That's exactly what you meant."

Lata seemed too afraid to speak and just kept looking at each of their faces, one after another. For a while none of them said anything. Shashi began to calm down, and as she felt her heartbeat stabilize, she remembered the frail nature of her condition and thus moved towards the bed. She didn't lie down though, merely sitting in one corner. Vidya continued to stand beside the window, mulling over the things that had been said.

"Maybe you are," said Vidya all of a sudden, turning towards Shashi who looked at her with surprise.

"What?"

"A bad mother."

"Vidya!" exclaimed Lata jolted out of her silence. "Are you mad!"

Vidya ignored her mother and continued to speak to Shashi, who was staring at her without moving a muscle.

"With each passing year, you became more and more estranged from him," she said, her voice firm as she inched closer towards Shashi. "Every incident only further plunged you into sadness and despair. How could have you helped him when you couldn't even help yourself? And so finally you just sent him away, getting rid of a problem you couldn't solve. You shirked from your responsibilities."

Shashi's lower lip trembled and shivers ran through her body.

"Vidya!" Lata winced, aghast at what her daughter was saying. "Stop! And apologize right now!"

Vidya finally turned towards her mother and saw the look of horror on her face. She shook her head. She wasn't going to apologize. Whether what she said was completely accurate or not, appropriate or not, she neither knew nor cared at that point. It had all just been an amalgamation, an incomplete and ill-structured amalgamation, of what she had wanted to say for all these years, and she had finally said it.

"I won't," she replied.

The three women remained silent and static in their positions, the once irreplaceable bond between them stretching until precariously taut, being forced apart by a mixture of stubbornness, guilt, shame, and hate.

Lata made the first move. She went and sat by Shashi, wrapping her arms around her friend who continued to cry quietly. From time to time, Lata would look up at Vidya, as if imploring her to say something and somehow redeem herself and this situation, but her daughter avoided her gaze, holding firm.

"I have asked Saurabh to leave town," she broke the silence. "This place is not for him."

"What!" exclaimed Lata, holding Shashi even tighter, whose tears seemed to have frozen instantly on hearing that statement. After she composed herself, Shashi finally lifted her head and looked at Vidya with burning fury in her eyes. She freed herself from Lata's grasp and stood once more.

"How dare you!" she said, seething in anger, her teeth chattering. "Who are you to say that to him!"

"I didn't say anything wrong."

"Wrong? It..it doesn't even matter whether it was right or wrong. You have no right to meddle with him."

Vidya almost laughed with disdain. "I have no right? I have been as much a part of his life as you were! I was always there!"

Shashi was about to retort but then stopped herself, an abstract but potent thought having just drifted inside her head. She played with it in her mind, her eyes growing wider by the moment.

"Yes," she said in a very soft voice. "You were there. Always. From the beginning. Maybe that was the problem."

"What?"

"You were right when you said I wasn't a good mother," she continued. "That's because I never saw this before. It was you all along. It's your presence and influence that has made my son this way. I should have stopped it all those years ago."

Vidya's face turned white.

"That's not fair," she muttered.

"Why?" asked Shashi, still brimming with anger. "You said it yourself. You were always there. All these years, he never could get better because you were there!"

Lata had never felt as scared before as she observed the two hurl one verbal attack after another on each other. Neither of them seemed even remotely dissuaded to continue.

"Shashi," she tried, gently prodding her friend on her shoulder. "Forgive her. She didn't mean it. She is a child."

There was no response. Her words escaped unheard. Shashi was determined to further probe Vidya, who, for the first time now, appeared to crumble.

"I only wanted to help him," said Vidya softly.

"Then where were you?" Shashi challenged her. "Where were you during these last four years? You barely spoke with him! Ran away from his presence. Four years! And now you somehow have the audacity to tell me what you think is best for him."

Vidya was determined not to cry and thus appear defeated. Her hands and feet were trembling, and layers of tears had completely covered her eyes.

The outburst had exhausted Shashi, who once again held Lata for support.

"You don't know anything Vidya," she said as Lata helped her lay on the bed. "You understand nothing."

Lata gently placed Shashi's feet on top and covered her with a sheet.

"Please close the windows."

Lata dutifully nodded and closed both windows before drawing the curtains across; the room fell into darkness.

"You should rest now," said Lata to Shashi, and placed her arm across her forehead to see how warm she was. "You will fall sick. Try to sleep."

Shashi nodded and closed her eyes.

Lata then motioned towards Vidya, who had been standing quite still, waiting for some external force to jolt her out of her thoughts. She expected her mother to scold her profusely, or at the very least, act in a very cold and stern manner; instead, Lata approached her and placed her hand on her shoulder rather indifferently, and with perhaps just a hint of pity.

"Let's go," she said softly. "She needs rest."

Vidya quietly obeyed her mother and they both exited the room. Vidya's eyes sought Saurabh through the window, but he was now once again sitting in the living room. He stood up as the two of them came in. Vidya wondered how long he had been sitting inside and whether he had overheard any of their conversations; they had been loud enough. And then she remembered that Saurabh had been about to say something to her before Lata had taken her away to meet Shashi.

"Saurabh..." she began but Shashi's words stormed back in her mind; she hesitated. Lata firmly took hold of Vidya's arm.

"Please Vidya," she said and then looked amicably at Saurabh who didn't return her smile. "We'll go home."

Vidya's head dropped in acquiescence. She let herself be dragged away by her mother - out of the door, onto the street and back to her room, where she lay silently for a long time, replaying her entire conversation with Shashi again and again in her mind.

CHAPTER 23

Vidya stayed at home the entire next week; she barely even left her room and was relieved when Lata chose not to interfere and just let her be. She slept a lot, more than twelve hours each day. The rest of the time too was spent idling away, occasionally helping her mother with the household chores. As worried as Lata was about her for a few days, her fear of saying something that might upset Vidya and thus disturb this brief period of calm, ensured that she remained silent.

"You send food over each day?" asked Vidya, the second time she saw Lata packing dinner and taking it across to Saurabh's house.

"Shashi cannot cook anymore," she explained, carefully balancing the tray of food. "At least not regularly. She hardly eats anything either. Hold the door for me."

At times Vidya would sit and stare out of her window for hours, as long as the lack of activity didn't make her fall asleep. There was nothing to see and yet she sat there, sometimes well into the evening, when it was almost too dark to make out anything except the slow-moving figure of Vinod coming back home, walking with extremely measured footsteps. She saw Saurabh too a few times, leaving the house and walking away to someplace; she wondered whether it was the graveyard. The urge to speak with him was still there, but she could barely strengthen her will by the time he was out of her sight. Once she even saw him looking in her direction, but he then quickly turned away and moved on.

Then one day, finally forced into action by boredom, she decided to walk to the Market Center to call Palak. There was only one shop in the town that had access to outstation calls. It was run by an old woman who smiled as Vidya entered and pointed towards the phone.

"Come in," she said enthusiastically. "I am seeing you after such a long time! Your mother would come here every Sunday to call you. Very particular that woman."

Vidya smiled politely in reply and dialed the number of her landlord in Ketupur. It was quite late in the evening and thus Vidya was sure that Palak would be at home at that time.

"Hello!" Palak's vibrant voice filtered through after she had been handed the receiver. "I was wondering when you would call! How are you?"

"I am fine," replied Vidya and found herself involuntarily smiling. She was almost surprised to hear that Palak had been expecting a call from her side. It was only by chance that she was calling today. "How is the hospital?"

"Oh, it is the same! Why would it ever change! But stop....first tell me how could you leave so early in the morning without even waking me up! I was so shocked!"

"I am sorry Palak. I just wasn't feeling too good."

"Anyway...let it be. Is everything okay at home....you know...with Saurabh? And when are you coming back?

"I don't know. Things are fine, just a little complicated. I am not sure when I'll be back...in another week perhaps."

"Hmm. Madam Sinha is missing you so much!" she said in an exaggerated tone and then burst into laughter, which made Vidya laugh as well.

"Has she said anything?"

"Anything! She talks about you almost every day! She is so confident that you are never going to come back. She is just using that as a way to yell more at us."

"That's not surprising," laughed Vidya.

"Once, she was shouting around as usual and she mentioned your absence while taking her round....and....," paused Palak as she was overcome by a fit of laughter... "and...that lady in Bed 6....the one who coughs.....she said..."I miss her too"...."

Vidya had to lean against the counter to avoid falling due to laughter. Her stomach ached as she imagined the look on Madam Sinha's face.

"How is that lady though?"

"Oh...as bad as ever."

They continued to talk for a little while longer until Vidya noticed the wide grin on the old lady's face and remembered that she was on a very expensive call. Soon she paid her bill and was on her way back home. On reaching, she found her mother once again arranging food on a tray to be taken across to Shashi's place.

"I'll take it over today," she offered.

"Are you sure?" Lata asked.

"Yes."

"Alright. But don't linger."

Vidya didn't pay much heed to her mother's suggestive comment. She picked up the tray - it was much heavier than she had imagined - and slowly carried it across. The door was opened by Vinod. Both of them looked equally surprised at seeing each other.

"Hello Vidya," Vinod said after a few seconds and took the tray of food from her. "Come in."

Vidya hadn't properly met or spoken with Vinod ever since she had come. She gingerly stepped inside and followed Vinod towards the living room table. He asked her to sit down.

She had never felt comfortable in his presence, never felt at ease before his serious and somber demeanor. Even as a child, she had been afraid to be near him lest Shashi was around. But at that moment, as uncomfortable as she still felt, she knew that she would rather be with Vinod rather than face Shashi again, especially since their fight.

"Your mother has been very generous," he began. "I would say no to her but I am embarrassed to admit that I can't."

Vidya nodded and saw, with a glance, the slightly ajar door of Saurabh's room.

"How is Shashi Aunty?" she asked.

"Not good. She is not getting any better."

"Shouldn't she see a doctor?"

"She won't. She is very stubborn about that."

Vinod shifted in his chair, his hands clasped tightly in front of him. He seemed restless and fidgety.

"Shashi told me about your fight," he said finally.

Vidya felt her face grow hot. She hadn't expected him to bring that up.

"I...I'm sorry," she said meekly. There seemed to be nothing else she could say.

"No...you shouldn't say that. Yes, it was hard on her...and on you too I presume. But what I mean is....perhaps you weren't completely wrong."

Once again Vinod appeared restless and ill at ease. There were clearly certain thoughts swirling in his mind that he wished to let through, but was struggling to decide whether he ought to or not. Vidya remained silent, not inclined to reply until he said something more. She was quite surprised by what he had already admitted.

"You have spent much more time with Saurabh than I have," he began. "It's true. You and Shashi both.....and I suppose that's why it has affected you two the most."

"I don't know."

"That...well," he continued, unsure of his words. "That wasn't the point anyway. I mean....maybe you were right when you said that we didn't try....or that we didn't try enough. But....it felt enough at the time....do you understand?"

Vidya nodded, though she wasn't sure whether she had. She still couldn't believe that Vinod was speaking with her about all of this. And why her...she wondered. Perhaps Vinod too realized the same for he suddenly fell silent, his head hanging low, an unblinking stare directed towards his hands. For a moment, Vidya considered making a motion to rise to signal her intention to leave and thus not further embarrass Vinod, while also extricating herself from this rather uncomfortable situation.

But Vinod wasn't done yet. He looked up, alert once again, ready to follow through with this conversation, which was being forced out of him by a whirling mass of inner turmoil that simply refused to subside by itself.

"You said that Shashi was a bad mother," he began, making Vidya go red again; he quickly waved aside her attempt to apologize. "I don't know about that.....at least I don't think she was. She was always with him....you both were....apart from at the very last stages before he went away. Those were the hardest years."

"They were. That's where we all failed...as did I."

"Maybe. But that was the difference between us. I mean....between me and you two. I never even tried. Shashi wasn't a bad mother. I never..."

Vinod stopped as he saw Saurabh standing outside his room. He hesitated, unsure of what to do. From the corner of his eye, he saw that Vidya was about to get up."

"No...no. Saurabh, come here. Sit down."

Vidya's heartbeat started to race as Saurabh nonchalantly walked across and sat next to her. Her earlier state of discomfort had now morphed into panic. What was he trying to do here? What was he hoping to accomplish?

Vinod steadied himself once again and looked directly at both of them.

"When you were young, I was never present. Not enough anyway. Sometimes.....sometimes I felt I wasn't given the chance to. You... Vidya...you and Shashi were always there....were always...I thought.... enough. So I just let it be."

"I didn't know that," replied Vidya.

"Of course you didn't. Why would you? You were a child. In fact," he leaned back and shook his head slightly, his lower jaw trembling a bit, "you are still very young. I shouldn't even be troubling you with all this. But....just know it wasn't your fault. Not at all. Neither was it Shashi's. I just used that as an excuse to not try...because...because I never really wanted to."

He was breathing quite heavily now and small beads of sweat had appeared on his forehead. Vidya glanced towards Saurabh who sat as impassively as ever. Part of what Vinod was saying, Vidya had always known subconsciously. Even so, hearing him say it was a frightening experience, and she couldn't even imagine what Saurabh was thinking at the moment.

"And so," he added, "all that you said....to Shashi....it was true...but not for her; it was for me. She wasn't a bad mother. You two did what you could. I never did anything. Maybe that was the difference."

At this point, Vinod, unable to control himself any longer, felt tears slowly trickling down his cheeks. It was an odd sight for Vidya, seeing this self-assured and reserved man lose all sense of inhibition and crumble before them, especially in front of his son. Saurabh was looking away, probably to save his father from any further embarrassment. Vinod coughed a few times and sniffed loudly, wiping his face that was still very clearly streaked with tears.

"I am sorry," he said, his voice a bit hoarse, and then turned his attention directly to Saurabh. "Do you remember your grandmother?"

Saurabh shook his head.

"You were too young," he conceded. "She was so happy when you were born. The happiest among all of us. And of course, you are here because of her."

He paused, as if waiting for some response, and then hesitated for an instant. But, as before, he quickly overcame that moment of hesitation and continued.

"Your mother and I....we haven't been perfect for each other; never were. We were so different....and still are...that it has always been difficult. I think you know that."

Saurabh nodded quietly. For the first time, he too was starting to show visible signs of discomfort.

"I had never thought about having children...I don't know about your mother...but I never did. And...your grandmother..she thought it was...would be a good idea. That it would help us...your mother and I...through you..to be better with each other. And so..."

Vinod had started to tear up again, finding it difficult to get words out of himself. His whole body seemed to be shaking, his feet tapping rapidly on the floor. He couldn't sit still; a mixture of sweat and tears lined his face. Vidya had closed her eyes. This had gone on for far too long now, she thought, but she knew there was no way she could stop it. Vinod seemed determined to let everything out, no matter what the consequence. She feared for Saurabh. With all that he had been through, did he deserve to sit and listen to what Vinod was saying?

"And so...," Vinod tried, "sometimes I wonder....with all that has happened....in all the ways that we tried and failed...with all the problems you and your mother had to bear....was it really fair? Was it fair to her and to you? To me? Was it fair that in our attempt to salvage something so broken, we created something equally broken? Should I have listened to your grandmother? Should I have....?"

The doorbell rang at that instant and Vidya saw through the window that it was her mother. It was as if a spell had been broken. Saurabh immediately got up and went to his room. Vinod, as shocked and tearful as he was, too got up and steadied himself. He looked at Vidya with embarrassment and remorse.

"I am sorry," he said and walked away, leaving Vidya behind who was still trying to gather all that she had just heard. The bell rang once more and she quickly got up and opened the door.

"Vidya!" Lata exclaimed. "What is taking so long! I told you not to linger!"

Vidya's mind was too preoccupied to respond. She shook her head and walked past her mother, who closed the door behind them, glancing at the untouched tray of food.

CHAPTER 24

Shashi refused to get better. The process of decline and degeneration, that had started long before Saurabh had been sent away, accelerated at an alarming pace. The changes were subtle at first, slowly becoming more and more evident. The constant presence of pain, guilt, anguish, and despair weighed heavily on her, chipping away at the walls of hope and fortitude. She started to speak more softly, smile less often, keep mostly to herself at the hospital......all things that further intensified the day Saurabh's expulsion forced her to stay at home permanently.

But it was only after Saurabh left Konkur that this process manifested itself physically. A debilitating sense of lethargy settled within her, making her question the value of every movement and action. She never rejoined the hospital, started to sleep for much longer hours, and stayed within the confines of her own house, if not her own room, for long periods. Sometimes Lata would urge Shashi to walk with her in the evenings, which she would rarely agree to; and even on the days she did, she would get tired very quickly and they would return home. Her garden, on which she had spent years to make it nourish and develop, was left once again to slowly plunge into disarray. Vinod saw and noticed all of this, but chose to remain silent, waiting for the course of depression to naturally complete its cycle before the healing process could commence; and the more it seemed to take its time, the more he seemed willing to wait.

Sometimes it appeared that Shashi had decided to run faster than time, to go past it and then turn around, waiting for the rest of them to catch up. She seemed to have willed the process of aging to accelerate, voluntarily seeking its embrace, finding within it not the soothing hand of grace and solace that she so desired, but instead the suffocating clutch of deep regret and sorrow, that only further drowned her in its midst.

As news of Saurabh's subsequent incidents at his hostel regularly filtered through, she kept descending further and further until she was completely entrenched within this condition of frailty and gloom that she herself had created. Around the time that Saurabh's second expulsion loomed heavily above them, she took to the bed as an invalid, refusing to leave it except for the most basic of tasks. Vinod stopped waiting and accepted the inevitable eventuality for which Shashi was readying herself.

Vidya too caught glimpses of this decline during her short visits. It had now been almost a month since she had been home. Despite her original intention to go back within a few weeks, she had stayed on, though she wasn't sure why she had done so. Maybe it had something to do with Shashi's condition, or the result of Vinod's unexpected outburst, or the fact that she couldn't leave until she was sure of what Saurabh was going to do next. Whatever the case might be, she had stayed behind, much to her mother's surprise and delight, who nonetheless was a little concerned.

"Are you sure you will get your job back?" she asked.

"I will. They are always short of people."

"But shouldn't you at least inform them?"

Vidya nodded silently; she knew that it was true. She hadn't bothered to call the clinic and tell Madam Sinha that.....but what would she have told her anyway; that she would be back but she didn't know when?

That wasn't the sort of statement that she could give to Madam Sinha.

So she avoided that call and stayed on. After the first few weeks, she had visited Shashi again; both of them tacitly agreed to not mention the fight they had had. Vidya decided to nurse her, spending more and more time in their house, forcing and cajoling Shashi to take the right medicines and to have more food. She even convinced her to get up from the bed and start talking short walks inside the room. Shashi tried her best to give in to Vidya's earnest demands. Somewhere within both of them lay the guilt of having said all those things they had to each other, and thus each tried to do the best they could in that situation. And so Shashi tried, rallying herself to infuse a modicum of energy within her. She smiled a little more often, ate what was given to her, and stood up on her feet to walk once again, even allowing Vidya to keep the windows open.

It lasted for a week. The old ache, the far-reaching debilitating pain, that had somehow been overshadowed for a little while, akin to the sun momentarily seeking refuge behind the clouds, shone through once more, throwing her back into that chasm of depression and sorrow. Vidya once again channeled her reserves and pushed Shashi as much as she could, but was often greeted by her patient's tired eyes that spoke only of defeat and despair.

When she wasn't next to Shashi's bed, Vidya spent her time with Saurabh. They would take walks outside on the street or sit in the garden. They even went to the graveyard a few times, sitting idly in front of the headstones, the way they used to all those years ago. Once they walked to the small pond, whose landscape was the same as ever, and sat and talked about nothing in particular - a few shared memories, her work at the hospital, his time at his hostel....nothing that would cause any major discomfort. As keen as Vidya was to talk about his future, she avoided it completely, unsure of how that conversation would pan out, and thus not willing to take that risk, when, after a long time, they were able to comfortably be with each other.

It was around 10 in the morning when Vidya stepped outside her house and rang the Parashars' bell.

"Is she awake yet?" she asked Saurabh, who shook his head and let her in.

"She was still asleep some minutes ago."

Vidya frowned in disapproval. Shashi's daily hours of sleep were inching towards 16, even after Vidya had started to strictly regulate her intake of those pills. She quickly entered insider her room; Shashi was lying still as ever, with the windows firmly shut, and that familiar smell of stale air, which had become synonymous with his room, hanging inside.

She came closer and hovered over Shashi, placing her fingers across her neck, trying to feel her pulse. She ran her fingers beneath her rose and then finally lowered her head and rested it on Shashi's chest. Her hands trembled as she picked up the bottle of pills kept on the side table; it was empty.

Vidya took a step back, breathing heavily, too shocked to think clearly at that moment. For what felt like ages to her, her muddled mind reeled until she managed to set that aside and let her instincts as a nurse kick in. She rushed outside.

"Saurabh," she yelled, entering his room. "Quickly go and get a rickshaw. Right now!"

Her tone was serious enough to make Saurabh run outside without asking her any questions. Vidya went back to Shashi and stood next to her once again, staring at her. She then removed the sheet on top of her and started pushing on her chest, breathing inside her mouth the way she had been taught; though this was the first time she had had to do it.

"Wake up!" she yelled at Shashi's seemingly lifeless body, slapping her face a few times. She moved away and opened the windows, tapping her feet impatiently on the floor and looking rapidly all across the room. There was only so much she could do right then and she knew that. She waited, for what seemed like an interminable amount of time for Saurabh to get back. He might have to run all the way to the Market Center, she thought.

He came back eventually, sweating profusely. He barely had any time to react to seeing his mother this way before he and Shashi carried her outside and placed her in the rickshaw. Vidya sat beside Shashi as the rickshaw raced as quickly as possible towards the hospital. Saurabh, once again, came running behind.

Throughout that bumpy ride, Vidya held Shashi firmly lest she fell. She kept staring at her limp body, fervently wishing for her to wake up, her hopes diminishing with every passing second. When they arrived in the market area, their presence caused quite a stir among the people the minute they saw Shashi's condition. Once inside the hospital, Shashi was taken away from Vidya's hands and wheeled to one side where a doctor was soon on her.

"She took sleeping pills," was all Vidya said before she was asked to wait in the corner; a group of nurses quickly blocked her view. She could do nothing but sit idly where she was soon joined by Saurabh, sweating and panting as before. He gave her an inquiring look, but she simply shook her head.

"You should call your father," she said to him.

Saurabh nodded, took a few seconds to catch his breath, and then left once again. Vidya sat anxiously in her chair, jumping at the sight of every nurse who passed her by, waiting for some information. It took a few minutes for her mind to settle down so that she could reflect over the incidents of that morning. She pictured herself standing inside Shashi's room, the empty bottle of pills beside her. She shook her head; she shouldn't have allowed her to have them by her at all times. But she hadn't known or thought that it was that bad. Yes, Shashi was depressed, and exceedingly getting more and more so, but it had simply never occurred to Vidya how deep she had fallen.

She closed her eyes and took a deep breath. There is no need to overreact, she told herself. They were just sleeping pills. She didn't remember how many were left in that bottle, but even if she had taken them all, it shouldn't kill her. No, she thought, it shouldn't. It might take a while, but she'll be alright.

She stood up as a nurse approached but she quickly walked past Vidya without even giving her a look. Vidya moved towards the open door, trying to get a glimpse of Saurabh, but he wasn't to be seen. She realized that neither of them had told Lata anything in their hurry to get Shashi to the hospital. She was most probably still at home, oblivious to the situation.

"Hello?" a voice called her from behind and she turned around. "Please follow me."

Vidya had barely turned around before the nurse set off. She hurried behind her, entering inside the ward where the doctor, surrounded by two or more nurses, was standing next to Shashi, who lay still on the bed. She looked exactly as Vidya had seen her in the morning. The doctor looked up as she came in.

"I am sorry," he said softly, in the trained voice of a doctor used to giving bad news. "She is in a coma."

One of the older nurses who stood near Vidya burst into tears. Vidya ignored her.

"Please," said the doctor to Vidya, pointing behind her. He led her to his cabin. "Please sit down."

"I know it is difficult right now," he began, "but I need to ask you some questions."

"But how could this be?" asked Vidya. "They were just sleeping pills."

The doctor nodded gravely. "Her body is very weak. How many did she take?"

"I don't know."

"Well...hopefully she will be able to fight it. But, you must realize that I have to inform the police."

Vidya nodded, staring past the doctor, lost in her thoughts.

"You are Lata's daughter, right? Does Vinod know?"

"He is coming."

"We'll wait then," he said and got up. "You can wait in my office. There's water on that table. I'll just come."

Vidya didn't move as the doctor walked away, leaving her alone in the office. Her hands and feet were trembling and she was finding it a little difficult to breathe. She gingerly got up and poured a glass of water for herself, but spilled most of it on the floor. She kept the glass back without drinking and left the cabin, walking out of the hospital. Her eyes nervously scanned the market place, waiting for Saurabh to return.

The attempted suicide was a major scandal, one that had never occurred before in Konkur's living memory. It was further intensified by the arrival of the police, who took statements from Vidya, Saurabh, Vinod, and the doctor, before assigning a female officer permanently at the hospital lest Shashi woke up and tried to kill herself once again.

"I didn't know suicide was illegal," said Saurabh to Vidya, who cringed on hearing the word and didn't respond. "How does that help anyone?"

The fact that it had only been a little over a month since Saurabh had returned was very quickly linked with the situation; it had to be, of course. Saurabh, the perennial wrongdoer, the incorrigible trouble maker, had struck once again, forcing his own mother down the lonely road of depression and misery, until she had suffered enough to try to end it all. It was not so surprising, they said and argued; that's what he is capable of. Hadn't he even hit her mother once? Yes...yes...it was inevitable, especially after all the pain that boy had brought upon those two wonderful people.

However, unlike before, such remarks and assertions weren't subtly exchanged behind the Parashars' backs. Shashi's coma appeared to have given everyone a license to discuss everything openly and without restraint. The whispers were seemingly endless and repetitive, mostly borne by Vinod each day when he went to his office and then to the hospital before returning home, where he further had to contend with Shashi's parents who had immediately come over on hearing about their daughter's condition. And so after a few days, the weight of those remarks, the words of pity, the innuendos....they all grew so heavy on his shoulders that he stopped going to work, only taking out time twice a day to go and see the doctor at the hospital, who had the same report to give him every time.

"Nothing yet. We can only hope. There is no way to tell."

Even if Vinod agreed with the assertion that Saurabh was somewhat to blame for Shashi's present condition, he felt no anger or hatred towards his son. That's because he placed himself in the same boat as Saurabh; in his mind, they were both equally to blame. He had to admit that the fact that Shashi might never fully recover or even die wasn't one that caused him great distress, but he did feel guilty that he would be one of the causes for that. It was how it had always been. Both of them had led such extremely detached lives, brought together only by Saurabh's recurring mishaps, that even the prospect of death wasn't going to do much to bring them closer. He was concerned for her, that was sure, but perhaps not a lot more than he would have been for any other acquaintance of his.

Lata, on the other hand, was extremely distraught and in complete disbelief. She sat by Shashi's bed each day for hours and hours, holding her friend's hand tightly, willing some life from within her to flow through. The presence of the policewoman annoyed and irritated her, as she felt that her being there was a mark of great disrespect to her friend who was so precariously battling between life and death.

"Why can't that woman go away?" she complained to the doctor. "We are not criminals!"

Vidya too accompanied her mother many times, watching from over a distance; it wasn't a pleasant sight. Shashi's frail body, already severely weakened over time, continued to lose all essence of life. Her cheeks sank inward with deep crevices appearing across them.

Her hair, disheveled, combed sporadically by the nurses, lay in great swathes around her head, that appeared lost in its midst. Her thin arms rested lifelessly beside her, the outline of her veins clearly visible. The rest of her body was always covered with white sheets, but the space it occupied always seemed too less, almost insignificant, as if she was slowly disappearing from within. And thus Vidya stared from that distance, lost in her tumultuous thoughts that occupied her mind more than ever. Every once in a while, she and her mother would lock eyes, as if the same incisive and destructive idea had taken hold of them. But they were careful not to mention it to each other, afraid as to where it might lead them.

All this while, Saurabh remained at home, having been specifically asked to do so by both Vinod and Vidya, who were well aware of the sort of behaviour he would be subjected to if he went out in public. Saurabh, having had a virtual curfew imposed on him several times in the past, wasn't overly perturbed by that. Moreover, Vidya was with him most of the time during the day and in the evening, keeping him up to date regarding Shashi's condition, which itself never really changed.

And so they all waited - Mahesh in his garage, Lata and the policewoman by Shashi's side, Vinod and Saurabh at home, and Vidya alternating in between - until two weeks later, their agonizing wait came to an end and Shashi breathed her last.

CHAPTER 25

The nearest cremation ground was over 50 kilometers away in the surrounding village. The general practice among the people of Konkur was to hire a van to transport the body while the family members and friends would follow on a local bus. So common was this arrangement that the hospital itself would book the van on behalf of the family of the deceased. Hence, it was quite a surprise for everyone when Vinod refused this offer.

"Where will you do the cremation?" asked the doctor.

He thought over it for a while and then said, "Near the pond. That should be fine."

Lata was evidently displeased when she found about his decision, considering it rather sacrilegious. The same view was held by many other people of Konkur, as well as Shashi's parents. But they all abstained from saying anything to Vinod, content to simply mutter among themselves as to how strange and bizarre things were.

With Shashi's death, the scandal had come full circle. A wave of sympathy, initially buried under layers of shock, swept over the town, washing over Lata, Vinod, Vidya, and somewhat over Saurabh as well. One shouldn't lose one's mother at such a young age, they said, even if one were responsible for it. And poor Vinod....a widower in his youth...a single father...that too with Saurabh.

Vidya was both surprised and pleased to hear that the cremation would happen next to the pond. One of her strongest memories with Shashi, before Saurabh was born, was when the two of them, and her mother, would go to the pond almost every other day to swing from that old tree. She couldn't understand why Vinod chose that place but she didn't bother to ask.

The arrangements, handled by Mahesh, were all made rather quickly. The morning after her death, they all set out on foot towards the pond, dressed all in white, with Shashi's body being held aloft by a group of four men Mahesh had hired for that very purpose. Vidya and Saurabh walked together on one side, slightly distancing themselves from the crowd. Vidya looked around this familiar street on which she had walked countless times, and she couldn't help but remark that she had never seen so many people on it.

The march was slow and measured, deliberately lethargic, warranted so by the situation. All faces pointed towards the street, silent in their contemplations, apart from the four pallbearers who were chanting slowly under their breath. The wooden structure they held had been crafted by them that very morning. On top, Shashi's body lay wrapped in white sheets.

The point arrived at which they had to take the left turn off the road and into the woods. At times, it was difficult to find enough space to easily go through but the four men somehow managed to do it, stopping and shifting occasionally, once even tilting the wooden structure at an angle. They all came through and arrived at the clearing. A group of people was already present, and they stiffened the moment they saw Shashi's body being carried in, their voices quickly dying away.

The pallbearers took no notice of them and went directly towards the edge of the pond where the local Pandit was waiting. Shashi was set down and the four men moved away. The Pandit called Vinod and other family members to come closer. Shashi's parents, Saurabh and Vinod approached the body and stood by, awaiting instructions. Once more, the murmurs in the crowd began to escalate, and Vidya could see groups of them starting at Saurabh rather conspicuously. It had been quite some time since he had been out in the open, in the presence of so many people, and it was clearly a matter of interest for them all.

The Pandit asked Vinod to remove the white sheets just enough so that Shashi's face would be visible. As he did so, the crowd seemed to move in a little closer, trying to get a final glance. From where Vidya was standing, just a little behind Saurabh, she could see Shashi. Her face had been drawn in by death, as if having collapsed on itself. She turned her gaze away.

The Pandit had a small metal box in his hand, in which there was some kind of paste that he dipped his fingers into and rubbed gently on Shashi's forehead. He then asked Vinod to do the same. Vidya noticed that Saurabh's legs were trembling just a bit as his father bent over Shashi to apply the paste.

"And now the son to anoint the deceased."

Vidya keenly watched Saurabh who seemed not to have registered what the Pandit had said. As soon as Vinod placed the box of paste in his hands, he looked at it questioningly, quite unaware of what he was supposed to do. All eyes were on him and the whispers were becoming louder and louder.

"Go on," urged the Pandit, a little firmly.

Saurabh set the box down by his feet and started to walk away. Nobody called out or tried to stop him. All heads turned in his direction, watching him walk out of the clearing and disappearing among the trees.

Vidya saw him leave, her eyes too followed him till the last possible moment. She watched Vinod pick the box up from the ground and return it to the Pandit; the ceremony continued. Vidya turned towards her mother, who seemed to have noticed her restlessness and was thus staring quite sternly at her. But this didn't stop Vidya. She slipped away from the crowd, drawing further looks and murmurs of surprise, and didn't look back even once. She felt much better once she was ensconced among the trees. She walked slowly but with purpose, following the trail she imagined Saurabh would have taken. It didn't matter though. She knew where he was headed.

The street appeared and she crossed it, walking along the other side until the graveyard appeared on her left. She jumped over the gate and moved a few steps inside. Saurabh was sitting on the ground, his fingers playing with the dirt.

"Why did you come away?" she asked, though she knew the answer. She came nearer and sat down beside him.

"I wasn't feeling good."

In front of them lay a headstone, covered with dust to such a degree that the buried person's name was no longer visible. They both knew how it looked though, having often sat in this same position. Vidya looked around lazily at the surrounding trees and bushes, at the rows of white headstones arranged symmetrically, at the hills in the distance, and then at Saurabh, who was still playing with the dirt, his head bent down. Vidya could see the 8-year-old boy once again, his little feet surrounding a little patch of earth.....a small stick in his hand.

"Do you remember the kitten?"

Saurabh looked up at her, his eyebrows drooping inward. "What kitten?"

"Never mind."

She let it be, leaning backward and supporting her weight on her palms, while Saurabh continued to sit hunched forward, focusing on the dirt. There was a nice cool breeze blowing across the graveyard. Here, sitting next to Saurabh, amid the isolation provided by the old and forgotten headstones, she felt so much more at ease than among the thick throng of people near the pond, constantly staring, whispering and pointing. She looked upwards; it was still quite early in the morning. The sun had barely ascended even a quarter of the distance, hiding behind the thin white clouds, which gave it a translucent appearance.

This picturesque view was suddenly encroached upon by a slow-moving column of light grey smoke, making its way across the skyline. Vidya turned her head towards the left, following the source of the trail, which led her to a point just behind the tall trees that blocked her view. There, the smoke was much denser and grey, before it slowly disintegrated into thin wisps.

"When are you going back?" asked Saurabh suddenly.

Vidya turned towards him and saw that his eyes too were fixed on the column of smoke.

"Soon now," she replied. "I never meant to stay here for so long."

"Do you like it here?"

Vidya leaned forward, surprised at the question, more so that it was Saurabh who had asked her that.

"Not really. I am not sure. I got used to it. Less so now."

He nodded and smiled. There was something about the expression on his face that puzzled Vidya. There was something there, apart from the usual impassiveness - a hint of content, perhaps? But not the sort that comes as an aftermath of some achievement. There seemed to be a touch of serendipity to it, a moment of assuredness, an accidental brush with happiness.

"What now?" she asked him.

"You were right," he replied almost instantly, as if he had been waiting for her to ask that question. "I can't live here. Not among these people. I will go away."

"Where?"

"I don't know yet. Somewhere."

"And your father?"

"He won't mind."

Vidya nodded. He probably wouldn't. Her thoughts drifted to the day when the three of them had been sitting around the living room table. Vinod's broken and teary figure appeared before her eyes. Those tears though, she thought, were for him alone. All of that inadvertently made her think of Shashi, and the accusations they had hurled at each other the day after she had arrived.

"Why don't you come with me?" she asked.

Saurabh looked at her quizzically. "With you? To Ketupur?"

"Well....it might be easier," she said, hesitatingly, without much conviction in her voice. "I could get you a job. I know someone who delivers medicines around the town. Maybe that."

Saurabh said nothing, looking straight at Vidya, as if mulling over the idea in his head. Vidya wasn't sure whether she wanted him to accept her proposition or not. He finally looked away.

"I think I should be alone."

Saurabh got up and walked towards the headstone in front of them. He used his bare hands to brush away the dirt and the leaves that had accumulated on its front. When he was done, those familiar lines and patterns were visible once again, as they had been so many years ago. He came back and sat down, satisfied with himself, and once again his fingers started to scrape at the dry earth. A sudden murmur drew their attention towards the street outside the graveyard's locked gate, where small groups of people had started to appear. They looked away and ignored the presence of the mourners, continuing to sit in front of that headstone, long after the last person had disappeared out of sight.

Acknowledgements

The idea for this novel came to me when I was reading Henry David Thoreau's book Walden - a chronicle of his experiences and musings when he decided to live alone in the woods for over two years. There was something about the geography of the town near which he lived that then somewhat developed into the basis for a novel. The fictional town of "Konkur" derives both its name and geography from Thoreau's "Concord". This novel wouldn't have existed if I hadn't read that book.

The journey from that initial basis to this story was a long one, to the point that the finished product barely resembles the ideas that helped develop it. During the process, and especially after I had finished the first draft, I relied on the feedback and impressions of my friends and family, to whom I would send a chapter to review every week. I am very thankful to them all for having persisted with me during that rather long 25-week period.

A special thanks to Keshava Guha for his kind words and encouragement.

About the Author

Vidit Uppal was born in Mumbai and currently lives in Gurgaon. An engineering consultant during the day, he writes short stories and poetry during his spare time, which can be read on his website: www.atruesentence.com. *A Stick in the Dirt* is his first novel.